Praise for the bestselling novels of

IRIS JOHANSEN

No One to Trust

"Gritty, powerful and fast-paced, *No One to Trust* starts off with a bang and never lets up. . . . This is one thriller that will keep you on the edge of your seat."
—*Romantic Times*

"With its taut plot and complex characters, *No One to Trust* is vintage, fan-pleasing Johansen."
—*Booklist*

"Fast-moving plot . . . another zippy read from mega-selling Johansen." —*Kirkus Reviews*

"Not a word is wasted in this fast-moving thriller . . . highly recommended." —*Mystery News*

"Johansen simply knows how to write a good, entertaining story." —*Charleston Post & Courier*

"Ms. Johansen's fast pace and deft plots usually land her books on the bestseller list and keep her fans loyal."
—*Richmond Times-Dispatch*

"Johansen once again gives her legions of fans an edge-of-the-seat thriller with heart-stopping action from start to finish." —*Abilene Reporter-News*

Final Target

"A winning page-turner that will please old and new fans alike." —*Booklist*

"A compelling tale."
—*The Atlanta Journal-Constitution*

"Thrilling . . . will have fans of the author ecstatic and bring Ms. Johansen new readers." —*Bookbrowser*

The Search

"Thoroughly gripping and with a number of shocking plot twists . . . [Johansen] has packed all the right elements into this latest work: intriguing characters; a creepy, crazy villain; a variety of exotic locations."
—*New York Post*

"Johansen's thrillers ooze enough testosterone to suggest she also descends from the house of Robert Ludlum. Johansen pushes the gender boundary in popular fiction, offering up that rarity: a woman's novel for men."
—*Publishers Weekly*

"Fans of Iris Johansen will pounce on *The Search*. And they'll be rewarded." —*USA Today*

"A spine-tingler." —*The Miami Herald*

"Sabotage, dangerous secrets, and lots of dark action characterize Johansen's enthralling thriller."
—*Abilene Reporter-News*

The Killing Game

"Johansen is at the top of her game . . . an enthralling cat-and-mouse game . . . perfect pacing . . . The suspense holds until the very end." —*Publishers Weekly*

"Most satisfying." —*Daily News,* New York

"Fast-paced, clever suspense novel that kept me intrigued to the end. In fact, I read it in one sitting." —*The Roanoke Times*

"An intense whodunit that will have you gasping for breath." —*The Tennessean*

"For a well-plotted thrill-a-minute read, you can't go wrong with this one." —*The Pilot,* Southern Pines, NC

The Face of Deception

"One of her best . . . a fast-paced, nonstop, clever plot in which Johansen mixes political intrigue, murder, and suspense." —*USA Today*

"The book's twists and turns manage to hold the reader hostage until the denouement, a sure crowd pleaser." —*Publishers Weekly*

"Johansen keeps her story moving at breakneck speed." —*The Daily Sun,* Chicago

"This is a great mystery with exciting twists and turns." —*Baton Rouge Advocate Magazine*

And Then You Die

"Iris Johansen keeps the reader intrigued with complex characters and plenty of plot twists. The story moves so fast, you'll be reading the epilogue before you notice." —*People*

"Fans of Mary Higgins Clark will enjoy Iris Johansen's latest, a supercharged thriller. There's peril, romance, and suspense aplenty as the good guys race the clock to stop the villains."
—*Alfred Hitchcock Mystery Magazine*

"A well-crafted romance thriller." —*Kirkus Reviews*

"From the first page, the reader is pulled in to a realm of danger, intrigue, and suspense with a touch of romance and enough twists and turns to gladden the hearts of all of her readers." —*Library Journal*

Long After Midnight

"Iris Johansen is incomparable."
—Tami Hoag, *New York Times* bestselling author of *Dark Horse*

"One of the most thrilling books I have curled up with in a long time." —Michael Palmer, *New York Times* bestselling author of *Silent Treatment* and *Critical Judgment*

"You'll be racing through to the last page."
—Catherine Coulter, *New York Times* bestselling author of *The Maze*

IRIS JOHANSEN

No One to Trust

BANTAM BOOKS

NO ONE TO TRUST
A Bantam Book

PUBLISHING HISTORY
Bantam hardcover edition published October 2002
Bantam mass market edition / September 2003

Published by
Bantam Dell
A Division of Random House, Inc.
New York, New York

Library of Congress Catalog Card Number: 2002018396

ISBN 0-553-58437-5

Manufactured in the United States of America
Published simultaneously in Canada

OPM   10 9 8 7 6 5 4 3 2 1

No One to Trust

Chapter One

A COCKROACH WAS CRAWLING UP HER ARM.

Elena Kyler shuddered as she brushed it off. God, how she hated cockroaches. This cell was teeming with them, but at least they weren't as bad as the rats. . . .

Close it out. Life was not this cell. Go away from here. Think of something beautiful. Father Dominic had always told her that was the only way to endure the unbearable. But this situation was not truly unbearable. The unbearable would be to give in and let that bastard win. So she wouldn't think of anything beautiful. She didn't want to bring anything she valued into this filthy cell.

She drew the blanket closer around her. So cold. It was warm during the day, but as soon as the sun set it became chilly. The cell was damper than the huts they'd kept her in on the way here, and the blanket she'd been issued was thin and worn. She hadn't slept all night.

Stop feeling sorry for yourself.

There might be more opportunity here. These guards seemed more complacent and they didn't know her. Just get ready. The time would come.

She threw aside the blanket and started doing the warm-up that preceded her routine. She'd exercised four hours every day since they'd captured her and she was even stronger now. Without weapons, she had to be. She'd eaten every scrap of the meager rations they'd given her to maintain that strength and spent the rest of her waking time planning her escape.

She'd be ready.

SAN FRANCISCO

"Is he here?" Ben Forbes demanded as soon as he entered John Logan's office. "Did you get hold of Galen?"

"He's here. Or rather he'll be here in a few minutes." Logan leaned back in the leather executive chair. "But he told me to warn you that he has no intention of taking the job. He said he's had enough of all that bull happening in Colombia."

"Haven't we all," Forbes said wearily. "But it goes on and someone has to do something about it."

"Tell that to Galen. He lost two men on the last extraction job he did down there. He doesn't like losing men. And he doesn't like working with the DEA either. He wouldn't even be coming to this meeting if you guys didn't go way back."

"Not as long as the two of you," countered Forbes. "Can't you use your influence?"

Logan shook his head. "Galen goes his own way, and you don't stay his friend by trying to change his mind."

No one knew better than Forbes that Sean Galen walked to the beat of a different drummer. He had been everything from a mercenary to a smuggler, with a multitude of other shadowy careers in between. But, different or not, he was unquestionably the best at what he did. "I *need* him, Logan."

"He got paid over a million dollars for the extraction of that executive he did for Folger's coffee. Can you match that?"

"Nah," Galen said, appearing at the doorway. "Not unless he's suddenly gone on the take. And that's not likely." He strolled into the room. "How are you doing, Ben?"

"I've been better." He shook Galen's hand. "But things could look up for me if you'd cooperate."

"I just came off a tough job. I'm on vacation." He sat down in the visitor's chair. "Logan and I are going deep-sea fishing."

"You'll be bored," Forbes said. "I have something more interesting for you."

"I could use a little boredom right now." Galen grinned. "And my mum always said I didn't play well with others. Particularly the feds. They always want to run the show."

"Shall I leave?" Logan asked.

"Why should we run you out of your own office?" Galen asked. "This won't take long."

Logan leaned back in his chair. "Okay. Pretend I'm not here."

That would be difficult to do, Forbes thought. John Logan was a powerhouse and not the least bit self-effacing. But then, that's what it took to reach his position in the business world. It was strange looking at Galen and Logan together. They were as different as stone and quicksilver, and yet the closeness between them was almost visible. Forbes had heard the rumors about Logan's involvement in some of Galen's extremely dubious enterprises before Logan became a successful tycoon. Those experiences had clearly forged a bond with Galen that had stood the test of time. Could he use it? "Feel free to jump in, John. I know you contribute heavily to that drug rehab center in Los Angeles."

Logan shook his head. "You're on your own."

Forbes sighed and turned back to Galen. "You wouldn't have to worry about dealing with the U.S. government. No DEA intervention."

Galen's brows raised. "You're DEA."

"I'm working on my own on this one."

"Uncle Sam won't like that."

"Tough. It's part of the deal. It's the first chance I've had to get Chavez in the last ten years."

Galen's expression didn't change, but Forbes could hear a new tone in his voice. "Chavez?"

"Rico Chavez. The Chavez cartel. I believe you've had some experience with him."

"Two years ago."

"That's when you lost your two men, isn't it?

You were trying to free William Katz, that coffee exec, from the band of rebels who were holding him for ransom, but Chavez turned loose his men to help them. You weren't expecting him to do that."

"Usually it's the rebels protecting the drug lords down there. So you're going after Chavez?"

"I've been after Chavez for years. I almost got him a few times. This go-round I may have a chance, if you'll help."

Galen's gaze narrowed. "You want me to kill him?"

"No, I want him here in the States, where we can prosecute him. I not only want him, I want to know who's doing his distributing in this country."

"Chavez won't come to the U.S. He'll stay where he's safe."

"Unless he has a good reason to come here."

Galen shook his head. "You're out of luck."

"Maybe not. I got a call two months ago from a woman named Elena Kyler. She said she was with a band of rebels in southern Colombia and wanted me to help her get out and give her protection once she's in the U.S. She said she was in possession of evidence that Chavez would find compelling enough to draw him out of Colombia."

"What evidence?"

"She wouldn't tell me. She asked me to meet her at a house outside a small village near Tomaco and we'd discuss it."

"Trap. Chavez wants to take your scalp, Ben."

"I'm not stupid. I checked with my informants

among the rebels and there is an Elena Kyler. Her father was Frank Kyler, an American mercenary who went to Bogotá over thirty years ago. He married Maria Lopez, a left-wing freedom fighter with the Colombian National Liberation group. They had two children, Elena and Luis. Maria was murdered by government soldiers four years after Elena was born. Evidently, Elena and her brother were raised by their father, who was killed seven years ago. Both Elena and Luis were members of a rebel group in the hills." He paused. "The hills surrounding Chavez's coca fields. So there is a connection."

"You're reaching for straws."

"I'll find out when I see her. She wants me to meet her and be ready. It's all she asked. It's worth a shot."

"It's not worth *being* shot."

He smiled bitterly. "Maybe it is. If we take Chavez out, it will dry up one of the largest suppliers in Colombia. That could save a hell of a lot of kids. You don't like drug dealers any more than I do, Galen."

"But I'm more of a realist than you. This would be a finger in the dam. It's a losing battle."

"Not this time." He paused. "I've got a hunch. . . . I believe her."

"Good. Then go get her yourself."

"It may not be that easy. One of my informants told me that she was on the run from Chavez, that she's disappeared." He hesitated. "The word is that she's been captured and is being held in a prison in Belim."

"A prison?"

"It's a government jail, but Chavez bribes the warden to house his special prisoners."

"Then she'll be of no use to you. If she has any evidence, Chavez will have her tortured until she gives it up."

"Chavez is at an important meeting with the Delgado family in Mexico City. She may have a reprieve for a while. I've heard he likes to do his own dirty work."

He sighed. "Don't tell me. Not just a pickup. You want me to bust her out and deliver her to you?"

"It may be necessary."

"Forget it. Stage a DEA raid."

"And have the government yell bloody murder that we were overstepping our position as guests in their country?" He hesitated before adding reluctantly, "Besides, there may be informants in the agency."

"That hurt, didn't it?" Galen said. "Hell, yes, there are informants. When there's that much money floating around, corruption is a fact of life. You're the only DEA man I've ever met that I'd trust without question." He smiled. "You're a throwback to another age. An untouchable. The Eliot Ness of the drug world."

"I don't feel untouchable." Forbes grimaced. "I feel dirty. I've been at this game too long. I want to see something good happen for once. Do this for me, Galen."

"A prison?" Galen shook his head. "Too big a risk. I don't want to lose another man to that son of a bitch. I'm going fishing."

"Think about it. It would be an interesting challenge and a chance to thumb your nose at Chavez." Forbes turned to leave. "I'll call you in a few hours. There may not be much time. I don't know how long Chavez's meetings will last." He stopped at the door and looked back at Galen. His expression told him nothing. Well, he had done all he could. He had thrown everything at him, from saving kids from drug overdoses to revenge against an old antagonist. Was it enough? Galen was one of the toughest bastards he had ever run across and as volatile as a keg of explosives. He would just have to wait and see.

"What do you think?" Logan asked when the door had shut behind Forbes.

"What do I think?" Galen repeated roughly. "I think someone's setting him up. I think Chavez is probably tired of having a man as honest as Forbes after him and is going to stage an ambush."

"Forbes isn't dumb."

"But he's desperate. He wants this too much. He's been in drug enforcement for over twenty-five years and it's the most thankless job on the planet. After all these years Forbes needs to know he's made a difference." He crossed to the window and gazed out at the bay. "Crazy bastard."

"You like him." Logan smiled. "And I think you admire him. You've always had a thing about Don Quixote."

"That doesn't mean I'm going to help him tilt at his damn windmills."

"What's the situation in Colombia now?"

"No better than it's been for the last forty years. The leftist rebels fight the government, the paramilitary fight the rebels and protect villages *and* sometimes the drug traffickers. The drug lords sit on their thrones and pay off everyone and probably control the entire shooting match."

"And Chavez is head of the drug faction?"

"One of them. After the breakup of the Cali drug cartel, there was no longer a kingpin. The drug trade decentralized into several groups, which was just as profitable and safer. Keeping a low profile and using the Internet is the name of the game these days. Everything's under the table. The only clear fact is that there's hardly anyone in that entire country you can trust. Because almost everyone is on the take."

"It does sound a little suspect that this Elena Kyler would choose Forbes to ask for help."

"That's the only part of this story that makes sense to me. Forbes has turned down promotion after promotion because he doesn't want a desk job that would prevent him from personally tracking down drug suppliers. The DEA respects him and lets him run his own show, and his honesty is legendary among the guerrillas and paramilitary groups in the hills." He smiled crookedly. "Believe me, they know who's corruptible and who's not. He'd be the obvious choice for Elena Kyler—if she was for real."

"Which, of course, she's not." Logan stood up and followed Galen over to the window. "Water looks a little choppy. Maybe it's not a good week to go fishing."

"It looks fine to me. For God's sake, do you know how many extractions I've done in Colombia? The blasted place has more kidnappings than anywhere else in the world. This is not my business, Logan. Hell, Forbes can't even pay me."

"You've got enough money."

"Coming from a billionaire like you, that borders on the ridiculous."

Logan laughed. "It does, doesn't it? Well, I need it more than you do. I have a family to support." His smile faded. "The point is, you want to go."

"The hell I do." He scowled. "It's not my business. It's all a bunch of lies. It's too convenient that Chavez is in Mexico. That so-called evidence is probably bogus. The woman was more than likely bribed to lure Forbes."

"So Elena Kyler is not in that prison cell in Belim?"

"Is that supposed to bring up a pitiful picture and rouse my protective feelings? Bullshit." He stared directly into Logan's eyes. "She's probably shootingup in some luxury flat paid for by Chavez. There's no way Elena Kyler's in that cell in Belim."

BELIM

It's only my body, Elena told herself. And I am not my body. I am mind and heart and soul.

"Good." The guard plunged deep inside her, pressing her into the hard concrete cell floor. "Good little whore. You like it, don't you?"

"Yes." I am not my body. I can accept this defilement. It wasn't as bad as the time she was raped, because she'd chosen this. "I like it. You're a bull, Juan."

Block it out. Go to another place, as she had during the rape. No, she couldn't do that. She had to be ready.

I am not my body.

"Christ." He arched with a guttural cry as he released within her.

The moment of greatest weakness.

Now.

She lunged upward with a cry, her arms going around his neck. "Juan!"

He was panting. "I pleased you. I made you come, didn't I?"

Her arms tightened around his neck. "What a man you are. . . ." She pulled him back down. "Come here. . . ."

"You're holding me too tight." But there was smug satisfaction in his voice. "Give me a little time and I'll be ready ag—"

She gave a twist and broke his neck.

He went limp on top of her. Jesus, he was heavy. She pushed him off and jumped to her feet, then pulled him into the shadows across the cell and draped a blanket around him. No use putting on clothes. As soon as the other guard came, she'd have to lie down with Juan and find a way to lure the man into the cell. He should be here soon. They'd flipped a coin to see who would go first with her and he'd been very disappointed.

She huddled against the wall of the cell and tried to stop trembling. She felt hurt and bruised and violated. And dirty. Sweet Jesus, how dirty. She forced back the tears.

I am not my body.

I am not my body.

"Meet me at the airport in twenty minutes," Galen said curtly when Forbes picked up the phone.

"You'll do it?" Forbes said.

"Private hangar. We're taking Logan's private jet and pilot. I told him that he could damn well contribute more than lip service. We'll land the jet at an airport outside Medellín and there will be a jeep waiting for us to drive to Tomaco. You don't report in to your superiors. You don't talk to anyone unless I okay it. I run the show. The minute you call in the feds is the minute I step out of the picture. Understand?"

"We'll talk about it later."

Galen tried to hold on to his temper. "Listen to me, Forbes. I'm pissed. I have an idea I may get nailed because I'm idiot enough to go along with you. Therefore, it's not the time to fancy-dance with words around me. I know you like to run the show yourself and you may do a good job. But not this one. This one's mine or I don't get on that plane."

Forbes was silent a moment. "I made her a promise, Galen."

"My way."

"Okay." Forbes sighed. "Your show." He hung up.

Galen put his phone in his pocket and headed for the door. It was no small victory. Forbes was stubborn and had the confidence of his years in the field. Galen had a hunch that he also had a streak of old-fashioned gallantry and that could be why Chavez had chosen a woman to bait the trap.

If it was a trap. The scales were weighted against Elena Kyler's story being legitimate, but stranger things had happened in Galen's life than the scenario Forbes had described.

Galen would have to treat it like a trap: It was the only way to keep Forbes alive.

And his own skin intact.

"Repeat that very slowly, Gomez." Rico Chavez's hand tightened on the phone. "She escaped?"

"Last night. She killed two guards at the prison and escaped in one of their uniforms."

"You fool. You relied on prison guards instead of our own men?"

"Juarez, the warden, didn't like the idea of our men having the run of the prison. He said it wouldn't look good."

"He's paid well enough so that we shouldn't have to worry about what he likes and doesn't like. Why did you stow her at the prison instead of taking her to the compound?"

"We were close to Belim, and I thought a few days in that cell first might soften her up."

"Find her."

"We're already tracking her. A woman of her description was seen heading for the hills south of Belim. She won't get away. After all, she's only a woman."

"I wonder if that's what those two guards thought before she killed them," Chavez said silkily.

Gomez realized he'd blundered. "I won't take anything for granted. I'll report as soon as we've located her."

Idiot.

Chavez's knuckles were white as he hung up the phone. He forced himself to release the receiver. He had warned Gomez to be careful, but the man had no conception what Elena Kyler could do. He was the only match for Elena. If he hadn't decided it was essential to come to this meeting with the Delgados, this disaster would never have happened.

No matter. Two more days and the negotiations should be completed and he would be free to leave. He went to the mirror and straightened the lapels of his tuxedo. He found the Delgados' fondness for formal dress almost as tiresome as their lack of ambition. It would be another night of drinking and gambling and he would be expected to fuck the blonde they'd provided to entertain him. It was always a blonde, usually tall and curvy—and soft.

It was that softness he found most distasteful. A man was a hunter, a conqueror, and he couldn't enjoy his power if the woman was only a weak vessel. A woman should be strong and clever and have enough power of her own to provide amusement.

Like Elena Kyler.

He could hardly wait to leave here and get on the hunt.

"You've been on that phone since we've been airborne," Forbes said. "Am I allowed to ask whom you've been calling?"

"Jose Manero, for one."

"Manero?"

"He's one of the premier information gurus in the world. He's supplied me with info for any number of jobs in S.A. and the U.S. He has the best contacts in the business and has moles in practically every drug operation in Colombia."

Forbes frowned. "I've never heard of him."

"He likes it that way. You're DEA. And I'm trusting you to keep his name to yourself. I've also been getting a team together." Galen crossed out the last name on his list. "It will take twenty-four hours for all the members of the team to arrive in Colombia. That may still be okay. I called a contact in Mexico City and Chavez is still there. My man will let me know when he gets on the move." He looked down at his scrawled notes. "Belim Prison shouldn't be difficult. It's scarcely larger than a city jail, and the guards are as crooked as their warden. I'd rather put a bribe in place than have to use explosives. But explosives are quick and a bribe sometimes requires time and finesse. We'll have to see if—"

"I don't think you're going to have to worry about Belim."

Galen looked at him. "I thought that's what this was about."

"I've just called my own contact in Belim."

Galen's lips tightened. "I told you not to phone anyone unless you talked to me."

"It wasn't official and you were busy." Forbes hurried on. "There was a big stir at the prison two nights ago. Two guards killed. Elena Kyler escaped."

"I see."

"Your enthusiasm is overwhelming," Forbes said. "This will make it much easier for us. It's just a simple pickup now. We go to Tomaco and wait for her to come to us."

"Come to you, you mean. I'm out of it. I warned you, Forbes."

He stiffened. "I didn't do anything that would warrant—okay, I didn't follow your instructions. I won't do it again. No exceptions. Okay?"

Galen didn't answer.

"Please."

Galen gazed at him for a minute and then shrugged. "You may not need me now anyway."

Forbes suddenly grinned. "You're disappointed. You dug out all that information and made all those plans and now you're not going to get to use them. Too bad, Galen."

"I'll adjust." He threw his pen down. "And it may not be as simple as you might think. She may be captured before she gets to Tomaco. It's over seventy miles from Belim. Or maybe this is just another twist in Chavez's plans to zero in on you. Or it could be she'll be so scared that she'll take off and you'll never hear from her again."

"She won't run away." He shifted his gaze to the darkness outside the plane window. "You didn't talk to her. I've never heard anyone more determined. She's on her way, Galen. I can *feel* it."

The mud was in her mouth.

Elena spit it out and kept crawling. The rain last night had been bad and good. The wet earth left tracks, but it spoiled the scent for the dogs. If she wasn't stupid, she'd be able to avoid the trackers.

She wouldn't be stupid. She'd avoided them for two days and she'd keep on eluding them. She'd take her time and listen and move as her father had taught her. Keep to the ground. They couldn't see you if you were on the ground. The river was only a few miles over this hill, and that would drown her scent even more.

She stopped to listen. She had to wait a moment before she could hear anything but the sound of her own heart and labored breathing.

A dog yapping, far away. Good.

But Gomez might have sent men ahead to guard the river crossing. Everyone knew that this was the only place shallow enough to cross the river for another forty miles. She had to be prepared to go around them. No, she was so tired she wasn't thinking straight. Being prepared was only defensive. She had to attack. Her father had always told her that when hunted, the only thing to do was turn hunter and eliminate the threat entirely.

She closed her eyes. More death. More blood on her hands.

Stop whining. Chavez would agree perfectly with her father's philosophy. He would think nothing of killing her after he got what he wanted. Had Chavez come back and joined that pack behind her? How that bastard would enjoy the hunt. The thought sent a thrill of pure rage through her that banished any regret. If it had to be done, then do it. Start thinking about where they would be planning to ambush her.

Her eyes flicked open and she pulled out the gun she'd taken from the guard. She started to crawl forward again, her elbows digging into the mud. Her gaze searched the woods near the river. Are you there? Are you waiting for me?

Turn hunter. Eliminate the threat.

TOMACO

The house was a crumbling three-bedroom hacienda some five miles outside the town of Tomaco. After a preliminary search, Galen permitted Forbes to go inside.

"I'm not impressed. Not the greatest pad I've ever stayed at," Galen said as he ran his finger over a dust-covered table. "I'm disappointed in you, Forbes. You should have at least provided maid service for a man of my consequence. This is where she said she'd meet you?"

Forbes nodded. "She didn't want a chance of our arrival leaking to anyone in the village. She said no one has lived here for the past six years."

"How does she know? This is pretty far from the hills where the rebels hang out."

"I didn't ask. Which bedroom do you want?"

"None of them. Neither do you." He turned and headed for the door. "I told my guys to make sure to stash bedrolls in the jeep. We camp out in the forest and keep an eye on the house from there. My mum always told me that fresh air was good for me."

"And you don't trust Elena Kyler not to have lured me to this house as a trap."

"Did I say that?" He went outside and climbed into the jeep. "Hop in and we'll hide this fine vehicle in the brush before we unload and set up camp. As compensation for depriving you of a roof over your head, I'll fix you the finest al fresco meal you've ever eaten. I'm an extraordinary cook."

Forbes got into the passenger seat. "I suppose your mum told you that too."

Galen started the jeep. "How did you guess?"

It was after midnight when Forbes jerked wide awake.

Something was wrong.

A sound?

Galen's bedroll was empty.

Shit.

He tossed his blankets aside and jumped to his feet.

The house.

He ran through the woods. A branch slapped him in the face.

He could see the driveway of the house just ahead.

Two men struggling. Galen was on top. A gun was lying on the ground beside him.

Galen grunted, his head whipping back as the man's fist lashed out and caught him on the chin.

The man took advantage of the temporary weakness to lunge up and over, bringing Galen with him. Then he was breaking free, scrambling for the gun.

Forbes stepped forward and kicked the gun away.

Galen took advantage of his opponent's moment of distraction and chopped down on the side of his neck.

The man went limp.

Galen breathed a sigh of relief as he rose to his feet. "Fast." He picked up the gun. "And tough. She almost broke my jaw."

"She?" Forbes stiffened. "It's a woman? You're sure?"

"Believe me, even in extreme circumstances I can tell the difference."

Forbes gave a low whistle. "Elena Kyler?"

"Presumably."

Forbes took a step closer to get a better look. The woman was wearing black jeans, a dirty white shirt, and a leather jacket and was little more than a shadowy figure in the moonlight. She appeared to be of medium height with short dark hair.

"I felt something warm. . . . She's bleeding." Galen was kneeling, flipping open the leather jacket. The white shirt was stained with blood.

"For God's sake, Galen. Did you have to do that?"

"I didn't. It's a knife wound. It's been stitched, but it broke open. If we don't do anything, she could bleed to death." He glanced up at Forbes. "It's your call."

"What?"

"She was good. There's an excellent chance Chavez sent her to take you out. Don't ever let anyone tell you women can't be as deadly as males."

"You're crazy. It was probably Chavez who did this to her."

"Somebody stitched up that wound. Showing up here with a stab wound would make any story she told you much more believable. Hell, you want to believe her already. It's only her bad luck that she ran into me before she found you. So you tell me, do we stop the blood?"

"Of course we stop it."

"I thought that's what you'd say. I hope you won't regret it." He unbuttoned the shirt and applied pressure to the wound. "Go back to the camp. I have a first-aid kit in my duffel, and bring those two lanterns. I'll try to stop the bleeding. I don't think any major organs were hit. The blood flow seems to be lessening."

"Right." Forbes hurried back toward the woods.

"You're not out anymore. Open your eyes," Galen said. "Talk to me."

No response.

"Talk to me or I'll open that wound another two inches before Forbes comes back, and then we won't be able to save you. What a shame."

Her eyes opened. Huge dark eyes, staring up at him warily.

"Good. That's progress," Galen said. "Elena Kyler?"

"Yes."

"Where's Rico Chavez?"

"I don't know."

He lifted the compress. "Oh, my, it must have slipped. Look at all that blood."

"I tell you, I don't know." She glared at him. "I was at a prison in Belim. He may be near here. He may still be in Mexico City."

"You have the prison story right. That deserves a reward." He put the compress back. "Think about it. I'll give you a couple minutes. I'm sure you'll be able to pin his location down."

"Was that Ben Forbes who just left?"

"You could have seen who he was if you'd chosen not to play possum."

"No one was supposed to be here but him. It could have been a trap."

"My thought exactly."

"Who are you?"

"Sean Galen."

"DEA?"

"Not in my worst nightmares."

"I didn't think so. I've seen your kind before. I've fought side by side with mercenaries from all over the world. My father was one. You all have the same edge."

"Don't generalize. I'm unique. I'm also supposed to be your savior. Superman incarnate. Faster than a speeding—"

"Here's your first-aid kit. If you can call it that." Forbes dumped the large kit down beside Galen. "Good God, it's as complete as an EMT unit. And you have enough equipment in that jeep to withstand a siege. Talk about being prepared. What were you—oh, she's awake."

Galen nodded. "Wide awake. It is Elena Kyler."

Elena was looking at Forbes. "You're Ben Forbes? You were supposed to come alone."

"I needed a little help. It may be a difficult situation. I kept my promise. He's not a fed. Did you bring the evidence?"

"No, we'll have to go together and get it. It's nearby."

"Why don't you go and bring it to us?" Galen asked.

She ignored him. "I don't know how much time we have. Chavez will know I crossed the river ten miles from here. He may decide to call in more men and spread out over the countryside."

"And how does Chavez know that?" Galen asked.

"I had to kill two of his men to get across the river."

"My, my, that prison cell came very well equipped."

She ignored Galen and turned to Forbes. "I stole

some supplies from a pharmacy and some clothes in a village near the river. I don't have time for this inquisition. Just bandage me up and we'll get on the way."

"Unfortunately, if we do that you might bleed to death," Galen said. "I can stitch her up properly, Forbes. You can have a nice chat while I do it. It may distract her. Of course, it could hurt a bit."

She bit her lower lip. "Do it." She glanced at Forbes and then slowly held out her hand. "Will you stay with me until it's over? I don't want him to get too much pleasure out of this."

He smiled and his hand closed on hers. "I'll stay."

Elena's breath released in a relieved sigh. "Thank you." Her gaze shifted to Galen. "Get it over with."

Chapter Two

ELENA WITHSTOOD THE PAIN WITHOUT A WORD BUT slumped into a faint as Galen finished the stitching.

"Tough," Galen murmured as he started bandaging the wound. "Very tough."

"Is she going to be okay?" Forbes asked.

He shrugged. "Providing she doesn't get an infection. If it's any comfort to you, I think she did sew herself up. The stitches were pretty messy and uneven. We'd better get her back to camp before she wakes up." He lifted her and started for the woods. "Be sure and bring my kit."

"You're pretty good at this. And that first-aid kit—do you always lug that thing around?"

"Sure. When I need first aid, it's usually not for anything minor. Like the Boy Scouts, I'm always prepared."

"You're from Liverpool, aren't you? Did they have Boy Scouts there?"

"Of a sort. But my mum never liked me to mix with those rough-and-ready types." He looked down at Elena. "Like this one. She'd be turning over in her grave if she knew I was associating with such a piranha."

"I don't believe you have anything to worry about," Forbes said dryly. "A shark could gobble up a piranha."

"Really? Must hurt." They had reached the camp and Galen carefully laid Elena down on his blankets. "You know, she looks slight, but she's very strong. See her shoulders . . . ?"

"I think you're still brooding about that right hook."

"It's possible. How old do you think she is?"

"Mid-twenties maybe."

At the moment she looks younger, Galen thought. In sleep she had a childlike vulnerability. When Elena was awake, her expression had been so full of vitality and intensity that he had only been conscious of the character behind the face. Now he could see that the woman's olive skin was perfect, her cheekbones high and her mouth wide and well shaped. The lashes lying on her cheeks were very long and as dark as her hair. "She must have learned a lot in those years. Some of those moves could have killed me if I hadn't blocked them. She's been trained very well." He glanced at Forbes. "She could put you down in seconds."

"I can hold my own. I'm no amateur."

"You're a policeman. But violence isn't a way of

life for you. You told me she's been a guerrilla since she was a child. She's a pro."

He shrugged. "So are you. It's a question of choice."

"But she wouldn't be here if she hadn't made the choice before."

"Neither would you."

"You keep comparing us."

"Because you make me feel like an outsider. It's as if the two of you belong to a private club."

Galen smiled. "I'd never be so rude as to exclude you."

"The hell you wouldn't." He paused. "Give her a chance, Galen. She may be legitimate."

"And she may be drawing you into a trap. She's smart. She took one look at you and set out to appeal to every protective instinct in your body. I suddenly became the enemy, being cruel to a helpless woman."

"Would you really have hurt her?"

"I might have been a little clumsy. I need to know more. We can't afford to accept her at face value."

"I believe you've made that clear to her."

"Good. Then we may be—"

"We have to leave here." They both looked down at Elena and saw that her eyes were open. "How long was I out?"

"Ten, fifteen minutes."

"Not too bad." She struggled to a sitting position. "I hope. Let's go."

"Where?"

"It's not far. I'll show you."

"Where?" Galen repeated.

She glared at him. "You'll know when we get there. Do you think I'd trust you?"

"You trust Forbes."

"I had to trust him." She whirled on Forbes. "We made a deal. I'll give you what you want. Keep your part of it."

"Galen knows what he's doing."

"He could have been bought. Chavez buys everyone."

"He'll get you out of here, Elena."

Her hands clenched at her sides. "How?" she demanded, turning to Galen. "No village from here to Bogotá is going to be safe. Those who Chavez can't buy will be afraid of him. You can't trust the government, the paramilitaries, or the rebels."

"Not even your own group?"

"Particularly not my group," she said bitterly. "They've been funded by Chavez for years."

"Then it seems like a good idea to avoid them," agreed Galen.

"How?" she asked again.

"I have a team on standby in the area. When I call them, they'll helicopter in and pick us up. There's a jet waiting at an airport near Medellín."

She was silent a moment. "It sounds simple."

"It probably won't be."

"He's done it before, Elena," Forbes said. "He got Katz away from the splinter rebel group."

"Katz . . ." She frowned. "I heard about that. You blundered. Chavez caught you off guard."

"He won't this time."

"He'd better not." She started to get to her feet and then fell back down. She turned to Forbes. "Will you help me up?"

Forbes bent down and helped her to her feet. She swayed, holding tight to his arm to keep from falling.

"You've lost some blood," Forbes said. "We can wait a little while."

"No, we can't. I've not come this far to be stopped now." She took a deep breath. "Let's go."

"If you tell me where we're going, I'll be able to get us there if you pass out," Galen said.

"I won't pass out." She moved haltingly toward the jeep. "I've had wounds worse than this. I'll be fine."

"Whatever. Put her in the passenger seat, Forbes." Galen quickly folded up the bedrolls, tossed them in the back of the jeep, and climbed into the driver's seat. "The roads aren't great. It's going to be a rough ride for you."

"It's all been a rough ride. But it's almost over. . . ." She leaned her head back. "Go straight ahead. Turn right at the next fork in the road."

Blood.

Chavez squatted and touched the spattering of dark red on the floor of the pharmacy.

Elena's blood.

She was hurt and trying to heal herself. Like an animal on the run, she was seeking a place to hide.

No, if that had been the case, she would have hidden in the hills near Belim. There was a reason why she had pressed forward. She had a purpose, a goal.

And he knew what that goal was.

He stood up and turned to Gomez. "Spread out. Cover every town and village in the area. Someone must have seen her. She's hurt and she's moving too fast to be cautious. She may be trying to reach Dominic. If you can't locate her, try to find him." He smiled as he looked down at the blood on his fingertips. First blood, Elena. "No excuses. I want her found within the next twenty-four hours."

The headlights skewering the black road ahead were wavering, darkening, and blurring.

Don't faint, Elena told herself. Hold on. Only a little longer. After all these years, only a few miles more. The huge palm tree . . . "Turn left here."

"I thought you'd left us," Galen said as he made the turn. "You're sure you don't want—"

"Be quiet." She couldn't cope with him right now. From the moment she had opened her eyes and looked at Galen, she knew he was a man to be reckoned with. God, she wished Forbes hadn't brought him. She only hoped that he wasn't on the take. Forbes trusted him, but that didn't mean she could afford to. When she'd realized she had to leave, she waited months before choosing Forbes. She had investigated, asked questions, listened to every story about him. She now knew that he was a solid and honest man and suspected that he had his own thread of desperation. She knew about desperation. She had lived with it for years.

Galen was not a desperate man. He was hard and tough and glittered with a mirrorlike surface. He would be difficult to fathom and more difficult to handle.

Maybe she wouldn't have to do either, she thought wearily. Let him get them out and then she'd be through with him. "The next right."

"This place is hidden well enough," Forbes said. "But the road curves like a snake around the side of this mountain. Will we be able to get a helicopter in, Galen?"

"I'll take care of it."

The house.

Her heart leaped in her breast as the headlights gleamed on the glass of the windows. "Here. Stop here."

Galen stopped the jeep a hundred yards from the small adobe house.

"Wait here." She started to get out of the jeep. "I'll be right—"

"I don't think so." The muzzle of Galen's .45 pistol was suddenly pressed to her temple. "Let's wait and see if anything unpleasant happens."

"Nothing's going to happen." Her voice was shaking. "And you're going to have to shoot me to keep me from going into that house. I've waited too long—"

"Elena?" A man was standing in the doorway of

the house, his hand shading his eyes from the glare of the headlights. "I was worried. I expected you days ago."

"I had a few problems." She gave Galen a cold glance as she got out of the car and walked toward the man. "They're not over."

"You're here. We'll take care of the rest." He enfolded her in his arms and gave her a hug before looking beyond her to the jeep. "They're safe?"

She nodded. "DEA. They're going to get us out of here." She turned to Forbes. "You can get out of the jeep. No one is going to hurt you. This is Father Dominic."

"A priest?" Galen got out of the driver's seat.

"Yes."

"No," Dominic said at the same time.

"Among other things," Elena said. "He's also a teacher. He takes good care of the people in these hills."

"How do you do?" Dominic said to Galen and Forbes. "My name is Dominic Sanders."

"Is everything all right?" Elena asked him.

He smiled. "Fine." He turned and headed for the kitchen. "Introductions later. You all look like you could use some coffee."

She nodded. "Call your helicopter, Galen. Have him here at first light."

"I believe we have some business to transact first. You made a deal with Forbes."

"Oh, yes, his pound of flesh. Don't worry, it's here."

"Show me."

She looked at him for a moment and then deliberately turned to Forbes. "I'll show you. Come with me."

"Go on, Forbes." Galen followed them into the house. "You won't mind if I just trail along?"

"I do mind." She threw open a door down the short hall. "But you don't care about that, do you?" She lit the oil lamp beside the door. "Don't raise your voice or I'll cut your heart out." She moved toward the bed across the room. "It's okay, Barry. Don't be scared."

"Mama?" The little boy threw himself into her arms. "Dominic didn't tell me you were coming."

Her arms tightened around him. God, he felt so good. Warm and safe and wonderful. "He didn't know. How are you?"

"Fine. I'm learning to play Dominic's keyboard. He says I'm old enough now. I know one song. I'll play—" He pushed away from her and wrinkled his nose. "You don't smell good."

"I know." She gently brushed the dark curls back from his forehead. "That's why I tell you that you should take your bath every night. I haven't gotten a chance to do that lately. But you really shouldn't be so rude as to tell me about it."

"I didn't mean—" His brow furrowed. "I didn't make you sad, did I?"

"No. You never make me sad." She gave him a hug. "Go back to sleep, love."

"You'll be here in the morning?"

"Yes, and there may be a surprise for you."

"A present?"

"An adventure." She kissed him on the forehead. "A wonderful, splendid adventure like none you've ever dreamed of."

"Who are they?" Barry was looking beyond her at Forbes and Galen.

"Friends." She tucked him in and stood up. "You'll meet them tomorrow. Good night."

"G'night." His eyes were already closing. "G'night, Mama."

"Your child?" Forbes asked as she shut the bedroom door and led them outside the house. "How old is he?"

"Five."

"He's quite beautiful."

"Yes, he is." Her smile was radiant. "Inside and out."

"You probably did some damage to your stitches hugging him like that," Galen said.

"I didn't feel a thing."

"Oh, I think you were feeling all kinds of emotions in there," Galen said. "I suppose you want me to take him with us?"

"There's no question that he goes with us." She paused. "He's the prize. He's the magnet that you wanted, Forbes."

He frowned. "I don't understand."

"Barry is Rico Chavez's son."

"What?"

"You heard me. Any blood or DNA test would prove it."

"Wait a minute. You stole Chavez's son?"

"I stole nothing. He's *my* son. Chavez didn't even know he was alive until two months ago." Her lips tightened. "But that won't stop him from trying to take him away from me." She met Forbes's gaze. "Or from coming after him."

"I've heard he has a wife and children of his own," Galen said.

"He does. Three beautiful little girls. His mistress in Bogotá also has a little girl. He was tested by a specialist after she was born and told that there was something wrong. That he might not be able to father sons. He was furious. It damaged his self-image. He sees himself as a conqueror, and a conqueror has to have sons." She paused. "Then he found out he did have a son."

"How?"

"It doesn't matter. All that should concern you is that he'll follow him to the United States. I've got something that he can't get anywhere else."

"We only have your word for that," Galen said.

"What can you lose? You wouldn't be here if you hadn't intended to make a deal with me, Forbes. Take us to the United States, give us protection, and then wait and see. Chavez will come."

"Maybe."

"Wait." Forbes frowned thoughtfully. "It makes sense that Chavez would want a son and heir, and he has an extraordinarily macho reputation. There may be something in what she says. If it's the truth."

"He'll come," Elena repeated.

"And what do you want out of this?"

"Protection. United States citizenship and enough money to keep us comfortable until I learn a trade to support us."

"You could always join the Marines," Galen suggested. "Or teach at a karate school."

She ignored him. "I'm not asking much. If you handle it right, you could capture him. That's what you want, isn't it?"

Forbes nodded. "That's what I want."

"Then take us with you."

"I'll have to think about it," Forbes answered.

"Think fast. Chavez isn't going to give you much time."

"Elena." Dominic was standing in the doorway. "Come in and eat a sandwich and get a cup of coffee."

"Coming." She turned, then started back. "Before I have anything to eat, I have to go and wash up and change. As Barry said, I smell. Don't you upset Dominic. He's very sensitive to vibes and he's getting concerned about me."

"Misguided soul," Galen murmured as he followed her into the house. "And a little confused about his calling. Is he a priest or isn't he?"

"He says he's not. He doesn't want me to call him Father, but that's how I first knew him. I can't seem to think of him in any other way." She gave Galen a cold glance. "He's the kindest, gentlest man on this earth, and you will not hurt him in any way. Do you understand?"

Galen smiled. "Perfectly. I'll try to restrain my innate brutality. I'm sure you'll tell me if I offend."

"You can bet on it."

———

Dominic was a man in his late forties with graying hair and the brightest, most alert blue eyes Galen had ever seen. He was dressed in fatigues and army boots, and his conversation was as wide-ranging as it was witty. He was obviously well educated, and Galen could believe he was a teacher. However, he was like no priest Galen had ever met, he decided after being with Dominic for the next forty-five minutes.

"You're confused." Dominic smiled. "You've been studying me like a bug under a microscope and you don't like not being able to identify the species."

"I'm curious. It's the bane of my existence. But I've been told I'm not to offend you on threat of God knows what."

He sighed. "Elena. She's a little overprotective."

"Are you really a priest?" Forbes asked.

"I was when I was a younger man. I may still be considered a priest by the church. As far as I know, I've not been defrocked." He shook his head. "But years ago I decided I couldn't follow all the teachings blindly. I'm too willful. I have to do what I think is right, and that's considered sin and vanity. So in my heart I'm no longer a priest, and it's heart and soul that count."

"But you were a priest when Elena and you first met?"

"Yes, I was working with the rebels in the hills. I came from Miami, all full of zeal and vigor, with the intention of taking on the entire world. There was a lot to take on down here. Poverty, death, drugs, war.

Over the years I lost a good deal of the zeal." He smiled. "But I managed to hold on. There were always the children like Elena."

"You knew her as a child?"

"I knew all the rebels. She was ten when I came to Colombia. Her brother, Luis, was thirteen and her father, Frank Kyler, was still alive. Frank and I became friends. We didn't often agree, but I liked him. It was difficult not to like him." He grimaced. "Like me, he believed he was doing what was right, that he was needed. I respected that even if I felt he was wrong. You have to go where you're needed."

"And now you're needed to take care of Elena's son?"

"Elena took care of him herself for the first three years. She hunted and we grew our own vegetables and we just managed to survive. Then she decided this was no life for the boy, so she went to Medellín to earn a living and left him with me. It wasn't easy for her, considering how she grew up. She had no one to help her, and she won't even talk about those first months in the city. She did everything from waiting on tables to telephone sales to support us and to gather a nest egg to get us out of the country. She came home as often as she could." He poured more coffee into their cups. "And it was no chore for me to take care of Barry. He's a very special child. There are some children who give off a kind of radiance. Barry is like that." He sat down. "My only complaint is that he's a bit too solemn and old for his years. I guess it's natural since he rarely gets to play with other children. Elena was afraid it wouldn't be safe."

"You're hundreds of miles from Chavez's territory here."

"It didn't stop Elena from worrying. The boy is her whole life. She wouldn't take the chance."

"Why didn't she leave the country before this?"

"She couldn't risk earning money at the only profession she had been trained to do, and everything else paid a pittance. She had no money, no papers, and she would have had no way to protect Barry from his father if he'd discovered where he was. She was saving every peso she could get her hands on to get them away from here when Chavez found out about the boy. She had no choice but to move fast when that happened."

"If she'd broken with her guerrilla group, how did she manage to research Forbes?"

"She'd been hearing about him for years. He's something of a legend. I had maintained contacts with the group and made some discreet inquiries."

Galen looked down into the coffee in his cup. "You think he's Chavez's son?"

"I know he is. I'm aware of all the circumstances surrounding the boy's birth." He smiled. "You're very suspicious. You don't believe her."

"I believe he's her son. Anyone could see how much she loves the kid. But she could be trying for a free ride and a nice cushion in the U.S. for the boy. Life is rough down here." His gaze shifted to Dominic's face. "Or it could still be a trap. Though the scenario is getting fairly complicated. If you're bogus, then you're very good."

Dominic laughed. "I do believe you're reaching, Galen. Wouldn't it be a bit hokey to bring a priest into the mix? Besides, anyone can see I'd be terrible at subterfuge. I'm not clever enough."

"You're clever enough to be a teacher," Galen said.

"That's straightforward and doesn't involve deception. I promise you won't catch me setting a candle burning on the windowsill to tell Chavez you're here."

Galen smiled. "A candle in the window? You *are* out of the loop. Maybe you really are legitimate."

Dominic's eyes twinkled. "Or maybe I just said that to make you think I am. More coffee?"

"No." Galen stood up. "I believe I'd better check up on our Elena. She's been gone too long. Where's your bathroom?"

Dominic raised his brows. "I assure you that she hasn't slipped out the back door."

"But she might have passed out and hit her head. She lost some blood with that wound."

"Wound?" Dominic's smile faded. "She didn't tell me she was hurt."

"I stitched it up. She's okay. Where's the bathroom?"

"Beside Barry's room. I'll show—"

"Stay here. I'll take care of it." Galen was already halfway down the hall.

She didn't answer the first knock and he didn't wait for a second before opening the door.

She was sitting on the commode wearing nothing but jeans, staring down at the bra in her hands. She glared balefully at him. "Get out of here."

"In a minute." He took the bra from her and slipped the straps over her arms. "I thought you might be having a problem."

She went rigid. "I don't need your help. I can do this."

"But you might break my stitches." He fastened the hooks in the back. "I hate my efforts to be wasted." He took the blue oxford shirt draped over the towel rack, put it on her, and started to button it. "Why didn't you call Dominic to help you? A little too intimate?"

"Don't be an ass. He delivered Barry. I didn't want to worry him. I suppose you told him I was hurt?"

"Guilty." He fastened the last button. "He's a nice guy. I hope you're not leading him for a fall."

"You don't know what you're talking about. I wouldn't hurt him."

"Intentionally. Is he coming with us?"

"Yes. I suppose you object to that too."

"I didn't say that."

She glanced away from him. "You talk as if Forbes has made up his mind. Is he going to take us?"

"He hasn't said. He probably will. He's a good guy, an upright, decent family man, and you've hit him right on target. Isn't that why you chose him?"

"I chose him because I hoped I could trust him. You don't have to be afraid for him. I'm not going to cheat him. He'll get what he wants."

"I'm not afraid for him. He can take care of himself. My job ends when I deliver you to the U.S." He stood up. "I'd better get you some painkillers. That wound is probably throbbing."

"When we're safe on the plane. I can't run the risk of not being able to think clearly."

He opened the bathroom door. "Have it your own way."

She looked him directly in the eye. "Oh, I will."

He was smiling as he passed Dominic in the hall. "She's fine. She was having a little connection problem."

"Connection?"

"See if you can talk her into a painkiller."

He grimaced. "She's not an easy woman to persuade."

"Really? I never would have guessed."

Forbes was not in the kitchen, and Galen found him standing outside the door looking up at the tops of the trees. "We may have a problem. There's a strong wind coming up."

"We'll work our way through it."

"I don't know how. I was talking to Dominic and there's no level ground around here for at least twenty miles."

"Then we'll go twenty miles." He looked up at the trees. Forbes was right, the wind was definitely picking up. "Maybe. There's usually a way. I've got to get on the radio and tell my guys to start their approach." He paused. "If you're sure you want to go through with this. It's pretty clear you've made up your mind."

Forbes nodded. "I believe her. Every informant

who's reported to me has mentioned that Chavez is after her."

"But you can't be sure she's correctly judged the way he'll react."

"Then what have I lost? She's right: This chance is better than anything I've had so far. I've got to take it."

Galen shrugged. "Okay, then we'll get them out."

"I hope to God this wind is our biggest problem." Forbes gazed out into the darkness. "We've been lucky so far."

"Knock on wood."

"Chavez and his slimeballs can't win every game. Let me just win this one."

There was so much intensity in Forbes's words that Galen turned to look at him. "You'll never make it until your pension, Forbes. You're starting to care too much. That can be dangerous."

"You can't care too much." Forbes's voice was uneven. "Men like Chavez trample all over our lives and destroy our families, kill our children—" He stopped and then said, "Sorry. This means a great deal to me."

"You don't have to apologize." He paused. "Did I detect a personal note?"

Forbes didn't answer for a moment. "My son, Joel. He died of an overdose in his dorm room six months ago. I was so busy saving the world from drugs that I didn't even know he was experimenting. I should have known. I should have been close enough to him to explain what I knew, what I'd seen during these twenty-five years. Instead, I was chasing Chavez, saving other parents' kids." His voice roughened. "I have to take him down, Galen."

Don Quixote, tilting against the wicked world. Don Quixote, who'd received his own wounds.

"Hey, no problem." Galen turned away. "I don't like the bastard either. I'll get her and the kid out of here and you can tuck her away in a safe house."

"I'll take that as a promise."

Galen smiled at him. "Like I said, no problem."

Elena quietly closed the door of Barry's room and stood there looking at him. There was nothing more beautiful in the world than the sight of Barry sleeping. She would just take a moment to look at him and gain strength.

No, she had to move. There were things to do and not much time to do them. She went to the bureau and took out the photo album from the top drawer. Don't look at them. There were so many. Just take out some of the pictures and stuff them in the backpack. There were precious few things that she'd be able to take with her, but she couldn't leave the photos. They were too special. Barry at two with the icing of the chocolate birthday cake all over his face. Barry at three laughing as he splashed in the little plastic pool. Barry this year with the new bow and arrow set she'd bought him. How he'd loved that bow and arrow.

She moved over to the toy box. The toy bow was on top of the other toys. It was too big, she realized in disappointment. He would want to take his teddy bear, his favorite books, and the musical globe that Dominic had given him. There just wasn't room for everything.

"Mama?"

She turned to see Barry lying on his side watching her. "I didn't mean to wake you again. Go back to sleep, baby."

"What are you doing?"

"Just looking at your toys. Do you play with this bow every day?"

"Most days. I'm Robin Hood and Dominic is Friar Tuck."

"We're going on a little trip. Would you mind not taking it?"

"A trip? Is that the adventure?"

She nodded. "But it's in an airplane and we can't take much with us. I thought maybe your bear and the globe. Anything else?"

"I can't take the bow?"

"I don't think there'll be room for it."

He was silent a moment. "I guess I don't really need the bow. I can still pretend. Like you showed me, Mama. Remember? You said if you didn't have everything you wanted, you could pretend and sometimes pretending was better."

She felt a melting deep inside her. Don't cry. He mustn't think anything is wrong. It has to be an adventure. She cleared her throat. "What song is Dominic teaching you to play?"

" 'Yankee Doodle.' Shall I play it for you now?"

"It's the middle of the night."

"I'm not sleepy." His dark eyes were shining with excitement. "You're not sleepy either. I can tell."

"Well, we'd both better try to rest. Otherwise we'll be too tired to enjoy the adventure."

"Will you come and lie beside me?"

"For a little while." She moved across the room, knelt by the bed, and laid her head on the pillow. "If you promise to go to sleep."

"I will." He reached out and touched her hair. "You smell better now."

She chuckled. "I suppose I should be glad you were willing to take the risk."

"I don't care." He closed his eyes. "As long as you're here. I missed you, Mama."

"I missed you too."

"And I'm glad we're going on an adventure together. Though you have adventures all the time, don't you? Dominic says when you go away from us, you have adventures—"

"Not like this one. This one is special. Shh, don't talk."

He sighed. "Okay."

His breathing deepened to sleep fifteen minutes later, but she didn't move. Being here next to him was too sweet.

God, she was lucky.

"Tomaco," Gomez said. "I'm sending four men there now."

"She's been sighted?" Chavez asked.

"No, but I've run across a few people who said they've heard of a man, a teacher, who lives there." He paused. "Dominic Sanders. You remember him?"

"I remember him well."

"It seems he's become something of a missionary. He's teaching and caring for the needs of the people in the hills a short distance from Tomaco."

"And the child?"

Gomez shook his head. "No word."

But where Dominic Sanders was, he'd find the boy. Elena had looked on Dominic as almost a second father.

"Should I let you know when I hear something?"

He could feel the blood dancing in his veins. Every instinct was telling him that he was coming close. A man should obey his instincts. "No." He headed for the Land Rover parked by the side of the road. "I'm going to Tomaco myself."

Galen could hear the faint sound of the rotors in the distance.

"They're coming." He shaded his eyes against the brilliance of the rising sun. "Go watch the road, Forbes. Everyone for miles around will hear those rotors. You'd better go get the kid, Dominic."

"I have him." Elena, holding the child's hand, came up behind them, her gaze on the horizon. "You're sure it's them?"

"It's Carmichael." Galen turned to Dominic. "Get your gear. If they manage to land in this wind, we need to be off the ground and out in a few minutes."

"I'm not going."

"What?" Galen said.

Elena turned to Dominic. "You *have* to go. I told you it wasn't safe for you to stay here."

"And I told you that I've found a purpose here that I haven't anywhere else." He touched the little boy's head. "He won't need me anymore. There are people here who do."

"That's not the reason you're staying. You're going to try to cover our tracks. You're blaming yourself."

"Who else is there to blame?"

"There's no reason for you to feel guilty, dammit. It wasn't your fault."

He shook his head.

"I won't leave you here."

"Yes, you will." Dominic smiled. "Barry has to leave here and you have to go with Barry. Who else will protect him?"

"It's only a matter of time until Chavez finds this place. Someone will tell him that you were taking care of Barry. You know what that means."

"It means I go find another house, not another country."

She whirled on the little boy. "Barry, will you go and get me the little plastic case I left in the bathroom?"

Barry's expression was troubled. "Dominic is going, isn't he, Mama?"

"Of course he's going." She gently pushed him toward the house. "Get me the case." As soon as he was in the house, she turned back to Dominic. "You've been the only security he's ever known. He needs you. *I* need you."

"That was difficult for you to say, wasn't it?"

"I said it because I meant it. You've got to come. It's too dangerous for you to—"

"Too much argument." Galen stepped behind Dominic and gave him a quick karate chop to the back of the neck. Dominic grunted, his eyes glazing over. Galen caught him as he started to fall and eased him to the ground.

"Why the hell did you do that?" Elena jumped forward. "If you've hurt him, I'll—"

"I didn't hurt him. Not much." He met her gaze. "And it saved you from doing it. I bet you'd have given him a minute or so more before you chopped him yourself. Now when he wakes up, you can claim innocence." He scowled melodramatically. "It was that no-account Galen who did the deed. A pox on his evil soul."

"You can't be sure that I would—"

"Oh, then you weren't planning on doing it?"

She was silent for an instant and then grudgingly nodded her head. "But that's different."

"I understand perfectly. He's your friend, not mine. You have the right to kidnap him."

"It isn't safe for him to—"

"Carmichael's closer." Galen had turned away and was looking at the sky. "You'd better go get the kid while I give Dominic a shot to keep him under until we get to Medellín. Cook up some explanation for Barry why Dominic is going to be sleeping for quite a while."

She glanced at Dominic one more time and then hurried into the house.

"A helicopter," Chavez murmured. "Flying low. Interesting." And possibly detrimental to the hunt. He had thought Elena was alone and desperate, trying to find a cave in which to hide. If she had enlisted the kind of help who could supply a helicopter as an escape vehicle, the balance of power might have seriously shifted.

Gomez ran out of the hut. "I have the directions. Dominic's house is on the mountain road. About twenty minutes from here."

"Then let's get on the move." He lifted the binoculars to his eyes. "Have one of the men get the number on that helicopter and try to trace it." The craft was having difficulty, battered by the strong winds. It would be difficult for it to land.

Bad luck, Elena.

Chapter Three

"HE CAN'T MAKE IT." GALEN WATCHED AS CARMICHAEL made the third pass and then turned and headed away from the trees bordering the mountain. He lifted Dominic and put him in the back of the jeep. "Pile in and give me directions to that clearing."

"We should have tried that first." Elena lifted Barry into the passenger seat.

"Hindsight is always better, isn't it? I didn't want to parade you all over the countryside if I didn't have to." He raised his voice and shouted for Forbes.

But Forbes was already running toward him. "Two cars are coming up the mountain. One late-model sedan, one Land Rover."

Galen cursed and turned to Elena. "What are the odds?"

"In this area? The people are as poor as dirt. Most of them don't even have cars. It's got to be Chavez."

"Is there a way of going up and around the mountain without passing them?"

"No, the road runs out before it reaches the top. About five miles from here."

"Dammit. It's still the only way to go. Get in and start driving. Forbes, you sit in back with Dominic." He reached for the radio. "I've got to talk to Carmichael."

Chavez lifted the lid of the toy box and took out the bow on the top of the heap of toys. She had given his son these cheap toys. She had hidden him in this house and let him only know what she chose to tell him.

His son.

He flipped open the nearly empty album and saw a picture of Elena smiling down at a small boy. Damn her. He tore the picture in two and stuffed the half with the boy in his pocket.

"There's no sign of anyone around the house or in the forest," Gomez said behind him. "But the helicopter is still hovering nearby."

"And no one passed us on the road. They're still here. We just have to find them." His gaze returned to the toy bow in his hands. Chavez had been enjoying the hunt so much it had not fully hit home what that bitch had done to him.

He broke the flimsy bow in two and threw it aside. "Torch the place. Burn it to the ground."

Elena stopped the jeep. "This is as far as the road goes."

"At least there are no trees up here." Galen jumped out of the jeep and ran around the back. "Help me get this gear out, Forbes."

"It's still too windy for him to land," Forbes said. "He'll crash against the mountain if he tries."

"Then the mountain will have to come to Muhammad." He took out the gear in the back of the jeep. "Or something like that. We don't have any choice."

"What are you going to do?" Elena was beside them.

"Put on this harness." He threw two canvas harnesses at her. "And put one on Dominic. Carmichael is going to drop a line and pull us away from the mountain and then into the copter. The harnesses fasten onto the O ring on the line. Then it's up to them to use the winch to pull us up."

"He's going to pull us off this mountain into the air?"

"Do you have a better idea?" Galen tossed a harness to Forbes. "I wasn't expecting this many people, so I've told Carmichael to drop another harness with the line. It's good strong equipment. It's the same issue used by the Special Forces for difficult extractions."

Elena had finished putting the harness on the priest and was putting on her own. "Have you used them before?"

"Hell, yes. I never take a chance on everything going right. It usually doesn't." He checked the fastenings of all the harnesses before he waved to

Carmichael. "We have to stagger the ascent. You and Dominic go first. Forbes and I will clip on the second rung. I'll take the kid."

"Is Carmichael dropping a harness for Barry?"

"We don't have a harness that will fit him, so I'll tie him to me and hold tight."

"No, I'll take him."

"This wind is blowing up a gale and it's going to get worse when the helicopter is overhead. You're strong, but I'm stronger. It's a fact of life that men have more upper-body strength, and you're wounded. He's safer with me." He smiled. "And I know what would happen to me if I dropped him. I'd never make it onto that helicopter."

She didn't want to admit he was right. She didn't want Barry's safety depending on anyone but her.

But he *was* stronger. She had found that out when they struggled. With this wound she couldn't chance Barry being torn from her arms. "You're absolutely right. If anything happens to him, you won't survive either."

"Comforting." He went around to where Barry was still sitting in the jeep. Galen squatted down beside him. "Pretty exciting stuff, huh?" He smiled at the little boy. "Are you afraid?"

"No." He looked at Elena. "But Mama is worried."

"That's because she doesn't understand. She thought we were just going to take a plane ride. But it's going to be even better." He lowered his voice. "We're going to fly."

Barry's eyes widened. "Like Peter Pan?"

"You know about him? Of course you do. And Tinker Bell?"

Barry nodded.

"But we can't exactly flit like them. We have to have a rope to swing on. The helicopter is going to pull us along for a while and then bring us up. Your mama is going first, and then you and I are going to fly together."

Barry's gaze went to the edge of the mountain. "It's a long way down. Are you sure we won't fall?"

"Look at me." Galen held the boy's eyes with mesmerizing force. "We won't fall. I promise you. Like your mother said, it will be a grand adventure. Will you come with me?"

Barry stared at him gravely. "Mama will be safe? She won't fall either?"

"Your mama will be safe."

A sudden luminous smile lit the child's face. "When can we go?"

Galen laughed, stood up, and lifted him from the jeep. "Right now." He pointed to the helicopter, whose side door was opening. "You stand right here while I get your mother and Father Dominic fastened up."

"Can I help?" Barry asked eagerly.

"No, you just keep an eye on the helicopter for me."

Galen had practically hypnotized Barry, Elena thought in amazement. Talk about Peter Pan.

He grabbed the harness Carmichael· dropped, put it on, and then spaced a twenty-foot length from Elena's position before clipping his and Forbes's harnesses onto the line.

"Shit." Forbes's gaze was on the road. "Cars. Only a few minutes away."

"It might be enough time." Galen waved at Carmichael and then grabbed Barry and tied him securely to his body. "All set, lad?"

Barry nodded as his arms slid around Galen's neck. "I just hold on?"

He lifted his thumb to signal Carmichael. "You just hold on. See, there goes your mama. . . ."

Elena tried to keep an eye on Barry below her, but the wind was too strong. It was twirling her like a top as the helicopter lifted her and spun away from the mountain.

The figures looked like puppets dancing on the end of a cord.

Gomez lifted his gun. "I'll try for the gas tank of the helicopter."

"No!" Chavez struck his hand. "If the helicopter goes down, so does my son." He could feel the rage tear through him, choking him. "See if you can get a good shot at the woman. Blow her head off."

Gomez aimed carefully and then lowered the gun. "Too far away. And she's almost up to the helicopter door. If you don't want the chopper downed, I can't risk it."

They were almost gone from view. The bitch had stolen his son not once but twice. She had won.

No, he wouldn't accept that.

"Find out who helped her. Did you recognize any of the men?"

"No, but I'll check with the men in the other car. One of them might have gotten a better look."

He turned away from the cliff. "Do it. Find out who helped her. They're going to pay for what they've done."

Barry was laughing as they pulled him into the helicopter. "I flew, Mama." He hurled himself at Elena after Galen unhooked him. "Wasn't it fun? Can we go again?"

"Maybe someday. But not quite like this." She gave him a hug. "I'm glad you enjoyed it."

"I did." He turned to Galen. "Thank you very much."

Galen nodded solemnly. "You're very welcome. It was my pleasure." He shook hands with the two men who'd manned the winch. "Good job." He turned to Elena. "Tad Pullman and Dave Jebb, Elena."

She nodded. "Thank you."

Galen said to Barry, "Would you like to go up and meet the pilot who gave us such a great ride?"

"Please," he said eagerly. "Carmichael?"

"Yes, that's his name." He looked at Elena. "May I?"

She nodded curtly. Dominic was stirring and she didn't want Barry to be present when he found out what had happened.

Forbes was staring out the window down at the ground below. "Come here for a moment, Elena."

She went to the window. "What's wrong? Is there—"

Black smoke. Flames spiking up against the sky. "Dominic's house?"

"Yes," she whispered. All those memories of Barry's childhood—gone, destroyed in one cruel act. She closed her eyes for a moment until the pain subsided. "We're not going to tell Barry."

"I'm sorry."

"So am I. I have to break it to Dominic. He spent six years in that house. It was his home too." She sat down beside Dominic and leaned back against the fuselage. She could feel the craft vibrate against the muscles of her spine, and she shifted to ease the pressure. Her wound was throbbing again and she felt a little light-headed.

Hold on. She could let go soon. But it wasn't safe yet.

She closed her eyes and waited for Dominic to wake.

"You shouldn't have let Galen do it," Dominic said.

"It was done before I realized what was happening." Elena was silent for a moment. "But I won't lie to you. I would have done it myself. I was planning on it."

He shook his head. "You can't take people's choices away from them, Elena."

"I can if it means keeping them alive. I don't have that many people in the world that I care about. I won't let any of you be taken from me."

He smiled crookedly. "Even if it means taking us on one by one."

"Chavez burned your house. He would have killed you."

"I'm no novice at hide-and-seek. Remember all those years I spent with the guerrillas. I'm just a little out of practice."

"Chavez wouldn't have given you the opportunity to regain any lost skills. He would have tracked you down and butchered you. He'll do anything to hurt me now."

"Now?" He reached out and gently touched her cheek. "He's already tried hard to ruin your life."

"He didn't care before. It didn't mean anything to him. I was only an amusement." She added bitterly, "I guarantee he's not amused now." She took his hand, her voice vibrating with feeling. "I know you're thinking about not getting on that plane in Medellín. Please come with us. What would happen to Barry if I don't get through this? We need you."

"You have Forbes and Galen."

"They're strangers. They don't care anything about him. He's only a pawn to them." Her grasp tightened. "Come with us for a few weeks, a month. You've given me six years. Just give me a little more time."

"Elena . . ."

"I'm begging you," she said unevenly. "Just until Chavez is caught."

He sighed and then slowly nodded. "A few months. Then I have to get back."

"Thank God." She let her breath out in a profound sigh of relief. "And thank you, Dominic."

"Since when do there have to be thanks between us? Now, where is Barry? I've got to show him I'm alive and stirring."

She nodded at the front of the helicopter. "Galen has him."

He flinched as he rubbed the back of his neck. "Galen seems to be taking charge in a number of ways."

"Only until we get to the U.S. Then we're done with him. Forbes told me he only brought him into the picture to get us out."

"That may not be such a good thing. He seems to be a handy man to have around. You're going to be on unfamiliar ground and you're going to need help."

"Forbes will take care of things. We made a deal and he'll keep it." She glanced out the window. "I think we're descending. We must be landing in Medellín."

"So she persuaded him to come along." Forbes's gaze was fastened on Dominic and Barry, who were hunched over a game of checkers toward the front of the jet. "I wasn't sure she'd be able to do it."

"She would have moved heaven and earth to see that he wasn't left behind." Galen's gaze shifted to Elena, who was sitting by herself across the aisle. She was bolt upright, staring straight ahead, her muscles locked into place. "And she's got a damn strong will. I don't know how she's even managing to sit up." He stood. "But I believe it's time to pull the plug."

Elena stiffened warily when he crossed to stand beside her. "Yes?"

"Time to go to bed." Galen checked his wristwatch. "It will be at least seven hours before we reach the coast. There's a sleeping compartment and bathroom behind those curtains. Go and hit the sack until we get there."

"I'm fine here."

"Bullshit. You're just afraid you'll fall apart if you relax. Go on and lie down. I'll get some painkillers and bring them to you."

"I won't have Barry worried."

"He won't be worried. I'll take care of it. He'll be more worried if you collapse. He's going to an entirely new environment. He'll need you to be able to help him adjust."

"I'll be able."

"Right." He helped her to her feet. "If you get some rest. You don't look so good." He gave her a push toward the curtains. "Wash your face and try to get comfortable. I'll give you a few minutes."

"Your concern is touching."

"I'm not concerned. It's a matter of professional

pride." He moved down the aisle toward Dominic and Barry. "You were my assignment, and I have to make sure you're still alive and kicking when I bow out."

Elena moved her cheek, trying to find a cooler place on the pillow. There wasn't any coolness. So hot . . .

"Here I come. Ready or not." Galen had pulled back the curtains and entered the enclosure.

Elena sat up quickly on the bed. "What do you want?"

"Nothing to be alarmed about. Don't you remember? I was going to bring you something to ease the pain. You don't have to be defensive."

How else did he expect her to be, she thought hazily. Every minute that he was in the room she was aware of who he was, what he was. No, not what he was. She doubted if anyone knew what lay beneath the surface, but she knew he was dangerous and could be totally ruthless. Though he didn't look dangerous. He was lean and fit and his sparkling dark eyes held both humor and intelligence. Some women would have called him handsome. It wasn't until you studied him that you saw the threat.

He drew the curtains shut behind him. "Your cheeks are flushed. You probably have a fever. Unbutton your shirt and let me look at my handiwork."

She didn't move.

He came forward. "I need to change your ban-

dage and make sure you haven't broken any stitches."
He pulled two containers of pills out of his pocket.
"Then, if you're a good girl, I'll give you a couple
penicillin pills to fight the infection."

She stiffened. "I don't have to be a good girl.
Neither Forbes nor Dominic would let you withhold
medicine from me."

"It was just a turn of phrase." His gaze narrowed
on her face. "What did you think I meant?"

She didn't answer.

"You thought I was talking about sex." His lips
twisted. "You must be out of your head. I'm not that
hard up."

"Men don't have to like a woman or even find
her attractive to want to screw her. They only see
us—they use us. You know that."

"I don't know that. And I don't like to be lumped
in with the rest of mankind. It hurts my ego. Don't
generalize."

"Why not? You're generalizing about me, aren't
you? Whenever you spoke to Forbes about me, you
were thinking, *A woman like her*." She added fiercely,
"Well, I'm not like anyone but myself, and I value
who I am. You can hurt me and you can fuck me and
I'll still be Elena Kyler. Not some whore or worthless
piece of—"

"Shh," Galen said. "Hey, you're shaking so badly
you'll break my stitches."

He was right. Her whole body was shaking. Stop
it. Don't show weakness. Not in front of Galen. "I'm
not shaking."

"Sure you are. Perfectly understandable. You're not well."

"I don't need your understanding."

"That doesn't change the fact that I'm chock-full of it. It's one of my finest qualities. Now that we've established that I'm not going to rape you, unbutton your shirt. You're not showing me anything I didn't see back at Dominic's house, and considering your background, you can't be that shy."

"Considering what kind of woman I am?"

"That really seems to be bothering you."

"I have *value*."

"Who said you didn't?" He studied her face. "Or who acted as if you didn't? What happened to you in that prison?"

"Nothing that I didn't choose to happen. They wanted to break me. They didn't do it. They couldn't do it."

"You're telling me too much. It's the fever talking. You'll regret it when you're better." He sat down beside her and unbuttoned her shirt. "Just one look and then I'll get out."

She sat ramrod straight, staring over his shoulder at the wall.

"Not too much blood on the bandage considering the amount of movement, and the stitches held. Not that I'd expect anything else." He buttoned her shirt again. "You said that you'd been wounded before. How many times?"

"Badly?" She tried to think through the haze of heat and pain that was beginning to close around her. "One bullet wound in the leg when I was twelve. My father said it would never have happened if I'd been careful. Another in the left arm when I was sixteen. I'd learned by then, and that one wasn't my fault. A bayonet graze in my left side when I was twenty. This is the fourth."

His lips tightened. "Isn't it convenient that you can mark the rites of passage from childhood to adulthood by the wounds of war? I'm sure not many women can do that."

"And how did you mark your rites of passage, Galen?"

"You wouldn't want to know. I'll get some water for you to take the pills."

"I can get it myself."

"But then you wouldn't get the pleasure of having me wait on you." He disappeared into the bathroom and came back with a glass of water. He opened the containers and handed her the pills. "Swallow them."

She stared at him defiantly but swallowed the pills and set the glass on the table.

He paused before going through the curtains. "You have seven hours to nap and get that fever down. You wouldn't want me to have to carry you off the plane in San Francisco. Think how humiliating that would be."

"I wouldn't be humiliated. I'd take what I had to take from you."

He gazed at her thoughtfully for a moment. "You'd do anything for the boy, wouldn't you?"

"Anything."

"I could almost pity Forbes." He didn't wait for an answer before he went through the curtains.

Elena lay back down and took a deep breath. She felt exhausted and she wasn't sure if it was from the fever or dealing with Galen. She had thought he was like the mercenaries she'd known in the past, but he was much more complicated. It was strange that he had tried to stop her from revealing too much about herself because he'd known she would be ashamed of the weakness later. She *was* ashamed. She should not have babbled. Fever, exhaustion, fear of what was to come, horror of the past . . . She should still have retained control.

She would be stronger after she rested. She would push the thought of Galen out of her mind so that she could nap and be strong for Barry when she woke. She closed her eyes and tried to relax.

Christ, she hoped she wouldn't dream of Chavez.

"Is Elena all right?" Dominic asked as Galen dropped down in the seat beside him.

"Not exactly fighting fit." Galen glanced at Barry, who was now tucked under a blanket and sound asleep on a seat across the aisle. "But she won't admit it. I think she's been through more than she can handle right now."

"You're wrong. She can handle it," Dominic said. "I've never seen anything she couldn't work her way through, and I've known her since she was ten years old." He thought for a moment. "Well, once it was pretty close, but she found a way out."

"What happened?"

He smiled. "You'll have to ask her."

"Not bloody likely. She was with the rebel army when she was ten?"

"She ran messages from one village to another when she was younger than that. Her father didn't start training her until she was a little older."

"Nice."

"He wasn't the best father in the world, but as I told you, he had a good deal of charisma and he was an excellent soldier. A good teacher too. Elena was remarkably skilled in the arts of war by the time she was twelve. Sad . . ."

"Couldn't you stop it?"

He shook his head. "I was a guest in their camp. If I'd interfered, the rebels would have thrown me out. It was difficult for me, but I learned to compromise. I couldn't do everything I wanted, but there were things I could do. I was able to teach, give comfort and understanding and, every now and then, more concrete help."

"Like with Barry?"

A smile lit his face as he glanced at the sleeping child. "That was my joy and privilege. I couldn't give Elena everything she needed as a child, but I got another chance with Barry. I believe God finds ways to help us find our true path. When Elena needed help with Barry, I knew I'd found mine." His brows lifted. "You're asking a lot of questions. Why?"

"I'm plagued with a curious mind."

"And Elena is an intriguing woman."

"Since she tried to kill me a minute after we first met, it's difficult to think of her as a woman."

"Then why are you so angry at the thought of the way her father raised her?"

"I just don't like children being forced into grown-up games."

"As you were?"

Galen was silent a moment. "Are you fishing?"

"It's my nature. And my vocation." Dominic tilted his head, studying Galen. "You're an interesting man and probably better than you think you are."

He chuckled. "I couldn't be. Unless there's something better than perfection." His smile faded. "Dominic, I'm a cynical, selfish son of a bitch who's dabbled in more sin than you could measure in a lifetime. But that doesn't mean I'm all bad. I show up pretty good next to men like Chavez."

"Most men do."

"Don't you want to save his soul? What an opportunity."

Dominic shook his head. "I'd find it difficult to ask God to forgive him after what he's done to the people I care about. I suppose that's why I'm no longer a priest."

"But it makes you a hell of a lot more human." He shrugged. "Now, what about a game of checkers before Barry wakes up and needs your attention? It's going to be a long flight and I get bored easily."

"I've noticed a certain restlessness." He gazed thoughtfully at him. "What do you do to keep it at bay?"

Galen grinned. "I wouldn't want to disillusion you by telling you." He spread out the board. "I'll take the black pieces. Like to like, as my mum used to say."

"Time to get up."

Elena's eyes flew open to see Galen standing inside the curtains.

"It's okay. You have an hour before we land. Do you need any help?"

She shook her head and scrambled to a sitting position. "I'm fine."

"You're not fine, but you're probably better than you were. You were out like a light. How long has it been since you got any sleep?"

"I don't remember. It doesn't matter. How is Barry?"

"He slept a couple hours himself." He turned to go. "If you need any help in the bathroom, give a call. By the way, Forbes wants to talk to you."

She tossed the sheet aside. "I want to talk to him."

Fifteen minutes later she dropped down in the seat beside Forbes. "Where are you taking us?"

"That's what I wanted to talk to you about," Forbes said. "There's a place north of San Francisco in the wine country that we've used before as a safe house. It used to be a working vineyard, but it's deserted now. I've called and made arrangements to have a team pick us up at the airport and drive us straight there."

She stiffened. "What team?"

"DEA." He went on hurriedly. "I know you didn't want the government involved, but I can't protect you by myself. I've notified my superiors of the situation and they've agreed to go along with me. We got you out of the country without pulling in the agency, but I can't give you enough protection on my own."

She had known that would probably be the case. She didn't like it, but there was little she could do about it right now. "Do you know the men who'll be on this team?"

"I know the lead agent, and I've had the other three men on the team checked out and they came up squeaky clean. You can trust them."

She shook her head. "You trust them. I can't afford to trust anyone. I don't have the right. I'm responsible for Barry and Dominic."

"And I'm responsible for you."

"It's not the same." She paused. "You take me to this vineyard. I'm not going with anyone else."

"I had every intention of going along."

"No, you drive. You check out the vineyard. Your team can follow us."

"We always check out a safe house before we bring in a subject. Chavez hasn't had time to find out anything. There's no need to worry, Elena."

He was so sure, she thought in wonder. Didn't he realize she would never be safe until Chavez was dead? "You do the checkout yourself."

He shrugged. "If it will make you feel better. Don't you know this is almost as important to me as it is to you?"

"No, it's not. You want to catch a drug lord. I have to keep my son safe from him. There's no contest."

He hesitated and slowly nodded. "You're right. Your son is important. But so are all the other children this son of a bitch victimizes with his damn drugs."

"I can't think about them right now. I can't save the whole world. My job is to keep Barry safe." Her gaze went to Galen, who was talking to Dominic a few rows ahead. "Will you ask Galen to come with us?"

"His job is over. He doesn't like to work with federal agencies, and he's very expensive. I was lucky to persuade him to do the extraction."

"Will you ask him to come and just check over the security measures? He likes you. He might do it."

"I'm surprised you want him. He's not been exactly warm to you."

"I don't want him. But he knows what he's doing. That's enough for me. I'd use the devil himself if it meant keeping Barry safe."

"I'll keep him safe, Elena."

"Ask Galen."

He grimaced. "The private club again." He stood up. "I'll ask him, but I doubt if it will do any good." He came back five minutes later shaking his head.

"He said he was out of it and it was my job now. I told you that he wouldn't do it."

"It was worth a try." Galen was turning to look at her, and she defiantly met his gaze. He mustn't think she was pleading for help. I don't really need you, Galen. You were just an insurance policy. If I did need you, I'd find a way of getting you.

He suddenly smiled and she had the odd feeling he'd read her thoughts. She looked away from him. Forget Galen. Think about this safe house in the country. Think about finding a way to make sure Chavez hadn't gotten to any of those squeaky-clean agents Forbes had told her about.

Galen stood and watched Forbes drive the black sedan down the airport exit ramp, closely followed by the tan SUV with the DEA security team.

Gone. Job finished. Time to move on.

Forbes was smart and savvy and this operation meant too much for him not to be careful. Elena Kyler was tough and he'd pit her against almost any-one he'd run across. Let the two of them fight their battles with Chavez. He'd done his part in getting her out.

It was time to go fishing.

The idea left him with a curiously flat feeling. But then, it wasn't unusual for him to feel let down like this after a high-pressure job, and being around Elena had been like a shot of pure adrenaline.

Too bad Chavez might end up killing her.

He saw Elena bend her head to listen to something the kid was saying to her.

Not his business.

The black sedan was almost out of sight.

Oh, what the hell. It wouldn't hurt to make a few phone calls to Manero in Bogotá. . . .

Chapter Four

BARRY GAVE A RELIEVED SIGH WHEN HE SAW THE ROLL-
ing hills of the vineyard country. "This is better.
That city was . . . strange. Is this where we're going
to live?"

Elena could understand why he would think San
Francisco was alien. He had never been away from
Dominic's little house, and the first excitement of
seeing the city had faded quickly. Poor baby, he had
been assaulted with so many new experiences in the
last twenty-four hours. "No. This place belongs to
Mr. Forbes's company. We may not stay here long."

"Will we go on the airplane again?"

"Maybe." Her gaze was focused on the building
they were approaching. It was a two-story adobe hacienda with a red tile roof. Two rusty wrought-iron
balconies hung over a flagstone courtyard, and the
place appeared as old and worn out as the brown
vines of the vineyard. "You said someone has already checked the place out, Forbes?"

"Yesterday." He pulled up to the front door. "Stay here. I'll go inside and give it the once-over."

"We'll wait." Elena stopped Barry from jumping out of the car. "Not yet. We have to make sure there aren't any bugs or snakes inside."

"Very apt description," Dominic murmured.

Forbes came out of the house five minutes later. "It's okay."

"Go on, Barry." Elena opened the door for him. "We're going to be sleeping in one of those rooms with the balcony. Why don't you go find it for me?"

Barry jumped out of the car and ran inside.

"I'll go with him," Dominic said. "He's so excited he'll be jumping off that balcony."

"He's got more sense than that. I'll be there in a moment." Elena got out of the car. "Show me the back of the house, Forbes. What's that outbuilding?"

"Fermenting shed. It's where the vats are kept."

"Did you check it?"

"Of course. I went out the back way." He motioned to the men in the SUV and they began to get out of the vehicle. "I'm not incompetent, Elena."

"I know. But I want to see the shed."

He shook his head with exasperation but started around the side of the house. "Come on, see for yourself. And it's not a good idea for you to occupy the balcony room. You're too accessible."

"I didn't choose it because I thought it was romantic. If someone can climb in, I can climb out if I have to. It's always better to have an escape route. Don't worry, I'll know if someone tries to come in that way. I'm a very light sleeper."

"I don't doubt it." He opened the door of the fermenting shed. "Here we are. As you can see, it's empty. Satisfied?"

The sweet-sour smell of wine and wood assaulted her as she stepped into the shed. "Not yet." The room was large, and three wooden vats at least twenty feet high and ten feet wide lined each side of the room. The broken ruin of a catwalk ran over each line of vats. No access there. "Will you have a couple of your men get a ladder and check inside each of those vats?"

"I was going to do that."

"And then get rid of the ladder."

"Right."

"Thanks." She went down the row and looked in back of each of the six vats. "Now I'm satisfied." She came toward him. "Tell me about those DEA men who came with us."

"Bill Carbonari's been an agent for ten years. He has two commendations. Jim Stokes has worked with me for three years on various assignments. Mike Wilder served at the Mexican border for five years and was with Immigration before he became an agent. Randy Donahue has been with the agency for only two years, but he's sharp. Very sharp."

"I want you to introduce me to them. I want to know their faces and the way they move so well I'll be able to tell who they are in the dark."

"Why?"

She stared at him in surprise. "Why do you think? So I don't shoot the wrong man."

"Our job is to protect you. You're not going to have to shoot anyone."

"I want a gun. Galen never gave me mine back."

"Are you sure you—"

"I want a gun."

He nodded. "Okay, I'll have one for you by this evening."

"Thank you." She started for the house. "Now let's go meet your DEA friends."

"It's a television set, Mama." Barry's eyes were shining with excitement. "And there are cartoons and Bugs Bunny and a big yellow bird and—"

"Hold it." She held up her hand. "You found all of those in the first thirty minutes you were here?"

"Dominic gave me a remote." He held up the device proudly. "It's magic." He ran back across the room to sit cross-legged before the set. "You just press this button and you can find anything."

"Oh, dear." She smiled at Dominic. "You've created a monster. He'll never pick up a book again."

"It's only the novelty. When was the first time you saw a television set, Elena?"

"When I was nine. My father went to Bogotá to raise money for arms and we stayed for six months. It was interesting. There were so many things I'd never done. I'd never been to the movies or seen a circus or been to the zoo." She frowned, troubled. "And I've cheated Barry out of doing any of those things."

"He'll catch up."

"I should have found a way to leave before this."

"He's smart and happy and he's learned to use his imagination. Not many kids are that blessed in this technological age. So stop thinking you're a bad mother. You did what you had to do to keep him safe."

"You're supposed to work to give your children a better life than you've had yourself. I haven't done such a good job so far." She straightened her shoulders. "But that's going to change. I've got a chance now." She turned toward the door. "I'm going down to the kitchen to see what I can find to cook for supper. Do you think we can pry him away?"

"We'll do it. Want me to help with the meal?"

"No, I want one of us to be with Barry at all times from now on."

"You don't trust Forbes."

"I trust him. He just hasn't had the same experience as I've had. I've seen how Chavez can corrupt and change people. People you'd never expect to betray you." She could feel the bitterness surge through her. Don't think about it. It's in the past. All she could do was learn from the experience. "Barry will sleep in my room and we'll take turns being with him during the day. Okay?"

Dominic nodded. "As long as he doesn't make me watch those obnoxious Teletubby creatures. Otherwise, you're on your own."

She was smiling as she left the room and started down the tile staircase. Teletubby? What on earth was a Teletubby?

———

Eight miles.

Chavez could feel the burn as he ran down the path and then started up the steep hill toward the huge house the villagers called a palace. This was the best part of the run, the hardest, the most challenging. It was during these last yards that he knew the pleasure of triumph, the realization that he'd conquered every trace of weakness.

He could see Gomez waiting at the end of the driveway. He didn't stop, forcing Gomez to fall into step with him.

"It was definitely Forbes. A solo mission. No one in the agency knew anything about it until the woman was in the United States."

"Where in the United States?"

"I haven't been able to find out yet." Gomez was already getting short of breath. "Somewhere on the West Coast."

"If you've found out that much, then you can get me the rest. He wasn't alone. What did you learn about the helicopter?"

"It was rented by a mercenary, Ian Carmichael."

"And who hired him? Forbes?"

"Not likely. He's expensive."

"Then bring him in and find out."

"He seems to have disappeared off the face of the earth."

"Locate him. I want to know who else was involved." He had reached the outbuilding that contained his gym, and he stopped and allowed himself a deep breath. "It's been a week, Gomez. You haven't been efficient." He smiled. "And I think you're getting soft. Look at you huffing and puffing. Why don't you join me on the mats this morning?"

Gomez's eyes widened and he took a step back. "I have to get back to Bogotá. I've a lead on someone in the DEA's West Coast office who might know something."

"Then by all means hurry back to the city." He opened the door of the gym. "I'll have to make do with a young man I found among the paramilitary group." He gestured to the dark-skinned, beefy man who was sitting on a bench by the weight-training machine. "He's very strong and said to be good with weapons. What do you think, Gomez? Can he take me?"

"No."

"I don't believe he can either." He could feel the excitement tingle through him as he walked toward the man who was looking at him with eagerness. He liked that attitude. It boded well for the battle. "But he may make the morning interesting. . . ."

"Chavez has gone back to his place in the hills," Jose Manero said. "It's business as usual with him."

"He didn't come to the U.S.?" Galen asked. "You're sure?"

"Gomez has been the only one stirring. He's been to Bogotá four times in the last three weeks, and he's asking questions."

"But is he getting answers?"

"Maybe. I haven't been able to track him for the last day or two."

Galen stiffened. "Could he have left the country?"

"It's possible. He's being very quiet."

"Tell me about Gomez. He's Chavez's number one man?"

"If Chavez has such a thing. He likes to be totally in control. Gomez was a hit man in Caracas for four years before Chavez picked him up. He's not a genius, but he's canny and he has a healthy respect for Chavez. Chavez would like that. He doesn't tolerate rivals."

"Let me know if Gomez surfaces." Galen hung up. He didn't like the feel of this. Forbes had hoped Chavez would come running after Elena and her son, but sending a competent underling made much more sense to Galen.

Not his business. Call Forbes and warn him and then sit back and forget about it.

He flipped open his phone and dialed the directory. He was halfway through the dial when he hung up. What could he tell him? That his trap was going to be sprung by the wrong man? He didn't even know if Gomez was in the country. Manero hadn't been able to pin him down.

For all he knew, Gomez could be sitting fat and sassy somewhere in Colombia, not heading for that vineyard and Elena Kyler and her son.

There was a full moon shining over the hills. Elena leaned against the wall of the courtyard and took a deep breath of the fragrant night air. It smelled different from Colombia. Not damp or tropical or any of the things to which she was accustomed.

"Is the boy asleep?" Forbes had stopped beside her.

"Probably. Dominic is with him."

"And I take it you're not out here enjoying the scenery?"

"Actually, I am enjoying it. I was thinking it was different from Colombia."

"But you don't come out every evening to savor the differences. You go over this place like a sentry on duty."

"Habits die hard. I was a soldier from the time I was twelve. I didn't know any other life."

"Strange life."

"Galen wouldn't think so." Why had the thought of Galen popped into her mind? "You mean because I'm a woman? There were quite a few women in the rebel army. You have women in your army here in the States."

"But we poor males are still struggling to keep them away from the front lines." He paused. "And we don't send children to fight."

She shrugged. "It's all about what you become accustomed to." She looked back at the house. "You're disappointed, aren't you? You thought Chavez would be here by now."

"I hoped he would be."

"Perhaps he's on his way."

"No, my informants say he's still in Colombia."

"Then maybe you think I lied to you."

"No." He paused. "But you may have overestimated Chavez's reaction to you taking his son."

"That's one thing I didn't do. He'll come for Barry. It's only a matter of time." Her hands clenched. "Though I didn't think it would be this long either."

"You are so sure he'll find you?"

"Of course. There are too many ways he can get to people. Drugs, money . . . He'll find me."

"Then I suppose I should be flattered by your trust in my ability to keep you safe," he said ironically.

"I needed whatever help I could get. It's better to have you and a DEA team than to be on my own. The odds are stacked too high against me. I have to put an end to Chavez. I don't want to live like this, staking Barry out like a sacrificial lamb."

"I'd say you're the sacrifice. You stole the kid." He held up his hand. "I mean in Chavez's eyes."

"That's exactly how Chavez will see it. Which is why he'll come."

He hesitated. "I don't know how long I can keep a protective watch on you without proof there's need."

She stiffened. "You're going to leave me alone?"

"Not if I can persuade my superiors that we have a valid chance of catching Chavez."

"But you doubt that they'll go along with you."

"I'll do my best."

She had known this might happen, but she hadn't thought it would come this soon. Get over the shock. Think of a way to survive. "Will you still get false ID for Dominic, Barry, and me?"

Another hesitation. "I'm a federal officer and you're in this country illegally."

"And the deal is off if Chavez doesn't come calling." She lifted her chin. "I understand."

He stared at her for a moment and then muttered an oath. "You'll get your ID. Just don't tell me where you're going to go." He started to turn away. "But we won't worry about that yet. I'll see if I can buy more time. Coming in?"

"Not yet. I have to do some thinking."

"I guess you do. Sorry."

"Forbes."

He looked back at her.

"Thank you. You're a fine man. I won't forget you helping me."

He shrugged. "I like the kid. I don't want Chavez to get hold of him."

"He won't."

He smiled and strode back into the house.

He *was* a decent man and probably sticking his neck out for her. If bureaucracy worked here in the U.S. as it did in Colombia, the government would generally tie hands and punish initiative. The DEA was not going to help her. But, dammit, she'd had no one else to turn to. Chavez was in control of a massive operation, and people weren't standing in line to help a woman Chavez wanted dead.

Well, she was better off than she had been a few weeks ago. She was in the United States and soon she would have fake ID. She couldn't count on them catching Chavez, so she would have to go on the run. She was alone, but she was used to being alone.

What about Dominic? She had brought him here because she thought he'd be safer. Now he was as exposed and vulnerable as she. He would be better off away from her.

But then she would never be sure if Chavez was tracking him. Another problem.

Damn Chavez to hell. Even by staying his hand and doing nothing he'd managed to create torment.

"Chavez is still at the compound. The Delgados are paying a return visit to him. He gave a party for the Brothers Grimm and their wives three days ago," Manero said. "Gomez did not attend."

"Then where the hell is he?" Galen asked.

"No word."

No word. The answer repeated in Galen's mind after he hung up.

Manero was a good man and his sources were excellent. If he couldn't unearth information about Gomez, it meant that Gomez was planning something and was making sure no one got wind of it.

What was he up to? Where was he?

The immediate grounds were secure. Now for the fermenting room.

Bill Carbonari was standing at the rear door of

the house when she rounded the corner. "It's okay, Ms. Kyler. I checked it." He smiled. "What am I saying? You'll do it anyway."

"No offense."

"None taken." She could feel his gaze on her back as she walked down the path toward the fermenting shed. Carbonari appeared fairly alert and he was pleasant enough. She could sense a little resentment in the other three agents. She supposed it was a blow to their self-esteem that she didn't trust them.

She swung her flashlight from side to side as she walked down the aisle between the huge vats.

Nothing.

Nothing but the wooden cylinders and the sound of her own footsteps.

She stopped short, her gaze on the darkness behind the last vat. She had caught sight of something out of the corner of her eye.

Something gleaming, metal.

Shit.

Aluminum ladder.

There hadn't been any ladder in this room since that first night when she'd asked Forbes to check the vats.

There was one now, propped against the last vat.

She ran forward, kicked the ladder, and brought it crashing to the ground. She raced for the door.

A noise behind her, inside the vat.

She was outside, running for the house.

"Carbonari! Call Forbes—"

Carbonari was lying on the ground and a man was standing over him.

He whirled and blocked the blow she aimed at his head. "Dammit, stop trying to murder me. I'm here to help you."

Galen.

"By killing Carbonari?"

"All I know is that when I came on the scene, I saw him draw his gun and head for the shed right after you went inside. He didn't appear to be looking for wine."

"Someone's in the vat. I knocked down the ladder but they'll—"

"Hurry. Get the kid." He grabbed her arm and pulled her toward the house. "I'll bet Gomez will be driving up with reinforcements any time now."

"Gomez?"

"He's been camping out in the hills." He was climbing the steps two at a time. "I checked out all the nearby hotels and then went scouting for the last few days. I ran across them—surprise, surprise. Where's Forbes?"

"Second door on your right."

"And Dominic?"

"With Barry."

"Then get them out of the house and down to the vineyard. Avoid any of Forbes's men. I don't know if anyone besides Carbonari is on the take. Hide beyond the first rise of the hill until I come."

"What are you going to do?"

But he was gone, disappearing into Forbes's room.

She wasn't about to follow him. She had to get Dominic and Barry out of the house.

"I promised her they'd be safe, Galen," Forbes said dully.

"She will be safe, if we get out of here before Gomez shows up."

"I checked out Carbonari. I thought he was the best of the lot. What the hell are you doing?"

Galen was setting fire to the velvet draperies. "We need a distraction when Gomez shows up. You do the same in the kitchen. I want this whole place blazing."

"Why?"

"Would you want to face Chavez if you were responsible for letting his kid burn up? Gomez will have to try to get inside and make sure Barry isn't here." He glanced out the window. "Here they come . . . about three miles away. Move it, Forbes."

"It's burning, Mama," Barry whispered, his eyes fastened on the hacienda. "The house is burning."

"Shh, I'll explain later, baby. You just have to be very quiet. Okay?"

Where was Galen?

She would give him a few minutes more and then she would have to start moving Barry and Dominic out of this field and toward the road.

No, not the road. She could see the headlights of a car racing toward the house.

Gomez.

"Come on, Forbes." Galen turned toward the door. "Time to get out of here."

"I can't leave my agents. They may be wounded and unable to respond." He thrust the phone into his pocket. "I've notified San Francisco to send backup, but there's no way they'll get here in time. I have to check on my men."

"Listen, why didn't they come running in here when they saw the fire?"

"It's been only a few minutes. They can't all belong to Chavez. I won't believe that."

"I'm not saying they do. But there could have been another agent on the take, and it's easy to surprise someone if you work side by side with him every day."

"I know that."

"Then let's get the hell out of here. Or do you want Elena to be caught by that son of a bitch?"

Forbes hesitated and then headed for the back door. "Let's go."

"Good. We go alongside the house and then head for the vineyard."

The thick smoke poured out of the house. Galen's eyes stung as they raked the area and then the road.

The headlights were closer, but they still had time.

"If I'm not there in a few minutes, get Elena out of here," Forbes said.

Galen turned to see that he had stopped at the corner of the house. Shit. "Don't be an idiot."

"The smoke will cover me, and I know exactly

where they're stationed. I have to make sure. I won't leave them for Gomez. They're my responsibility."

"It's your responsibility to stay alive," Galen said roughly. "Don't be a fool. Don't take the risk."

"I'll be careful."

"For God's sake, it's not even Chavez."

"Get Elena out." Forbes darted around the side of the house.

Galen started to go after him and then stopped with a muttered curse. No time.

The lights of the oncoming car were closer. Too close.

Galen took off at a run for the vineyard.

Shots. Behind him.

Galen's hands clenched at his sides.

Christ.

Forbes's head was almost blown off by the barrage of bullets.

My God.

Elena quickly buried Barry's head in her shoulder and looked at Dominic. "Did he see it?" she asked unevenly.

"I don't think so." Dominic's lips tightened. "I wish I hadn't."

She wished she hadn't seen it either. She felt sick.

"Let's get the hell out of here." Galen was suddenly beside them. "Gomez will be at the house any second and it won't be long until they start searching the fields. My car is parked over that hill, in the trees."

"Forbes—"

"Move."

She was already moving, keeping low and pushing Barry ahead of her.

And trying to forget the sight of Forbes's head exploding.

Galen didn't speak again until they were in his car and driving down the road that led to the highway. "How's Barry?"

"Scared." Her arms tightened around the little boy on her lap. "But he's being very good, aren't you, baby? He'll be fine."

Barry didn't speak, only nestled closer in her arms.

God, she hoped she was telling the truth. Ever since his birth she'd protected him from the violence she had lived with all her life, and now in one night he had been exposed to this horror. "Where are we going?"

"I'm taking you to a friend's apartment in the city for the night. He lends it to me when I come to town. We'll make a decision once we've had time to think."

"Forbes," she whispered.

"I couldn't stop him. He wanted to make sure his men were okay."

She glanced down at Barry. He seemed to be too stunned to pay attention, but she still kept her voice down to a whisper. "It was one of his own agents. It was Wilder. I didn't see any of the other men, but I saw Wilder raise his gun."

"And I'm sure he'll be well paid."

"I . . . liked Forbes."

Galen's lips tightened. "So did I."

"No pursuit yet," Dominic said from the back-seat as he looked through the rear window.

"We'll be on the freeway in a minute," Galen reassured the priest. "I think we're okay."

She didn't feel okay. She felt scared for Barry and Dominic and, yes, for herself. It was a terrifying world where a decent man like Forbes could be butchered by those he trusted. Why am I even surprised? she wondered wearily. It was no different from the world she had known all her life.

But it was different. During these few short weeks she'd begun to believe they could have a better life. Maybe it was still possible.

A hope that shone that bright was hard to surrender.

The apartment was a penthouse that overlooked the bay, and it was the most luxurious place Elena had ever seen. The living room was exceptional: beige velvet couches, deep burgundy carpets, and one wall that was all window.

"Several bedrooms with baths." Galen gestured to the south wing. "Why don't you find a cozy place for the three of you while I make a pot of coffee?"

Cozy? That was the last term she'd use for this place, Elena thought wearily. Barry's grasp was tight on her hand and his eyes were wide with wonder. He'd been through too much tonight. So had they all. "I'll be back to talk to you after I put Barry to bed."

"I thought you would. This place is kind of big. I'll leave a trail of bread crumbs to the kitchen."

"I'll find you." She moved down the hall. "Come on, Barry. Time to get to bed."

"This is a strange place." Barry's eyes were big as he gazed over his shoulder at the glass wall. "Can you see the whole world from here?"

"No, only the city and the bay."

"Does Galen own the city?"

"Nobody owns it. Or maybe everyone does."

"Oh."

He didn't speak again while she got him undressed and tucked into a king-size bed in one of the guest rooms. He was too quiet, she thought worriedly. She sat down beside him on the bed. "Okay?"

He nodded and closed his eyes.

It wasn't okay. "Barry, bad things happened tonight, but we're all safe now. Nothing can hurt you."

His eyes opened. "Who did it, Mama?"

"Bad men."

"Why?"

"It's hard to explain. Bad men do bad things."

"It was burning. . . ."

"I know." What could she say when he was almost in shock? "But we're safe now."

"You're sure?"

"I'm sure." She pressed a kiss on his forehead. "I'd never let anything happen to you. Don't you know that?"

He didn't answer for a moment. "This was an adventure, wasn't it?"

"I guess some people would call it that."

"I didn't like this adventure, Mama."

"Neither did I. Sometimes adventures aren't very much fun."

"I didn't know that."

She could feel the tears stinging her eyes. He was already absorbing lessons she had wanted him never to learn. "There are wonderful adventures too."

"I guess so." He turned over and closed his eyes. "Mr. Forbes wasn't in that fire, was he?"

"No."

"Good. I was worried. He's a nice man."

"Yes. Go to sleep, love."

"I will. I don't want to be awake right now."

Because being awake was more frightening than the oblivion of sleep. "And in the morning everything will be bright and beautiful and all the adventures will be happy ones."

"I hope so. . . ."

He dropped off to sleep five minutes later, and Elena carefully covered him with the sheet and rose to her feet.

Dominic was waiting in the hall. "I'll sit with him for a little while. He may not stay asleep. He's had a rough night."

"So have you."

"Well, I admit that it's not every man who's burned out of two houses in the space of a month." He smiled. "Go on and talk to Galen. I'll take good care of Barry."

"You always have. Better than I've done. Maybe I should have—"

"Go." He gave her a push down the hall. "You must be upset if you're dealing in should-haves."

She took a deep breath. He was right. It was no time to be looking back when she had to find a way for them all to survive. "Watch him. He may have nightmares. I'll be back as soon as I can."

Chapter Five

"How's the boy?" Galen asked as she came into the kitchen.

"Not good." She sat down at the granite-topped table. "But he didn't see Forbes killed. I was afraid he had."

"He saw enough to disturb most kids." He poured her a cup of coffee and sat down across from her. "Don't try to smooth things over. You need to be up front with him."

"He's five years old."

"And you want to protect him. But you may not be able to do it. It's better if he knows that you'll always tell him the truth. Truth is important to kids."

"And you're an expert?" she asked sarcastically.

"At most things. Drink your coffee."

She lifted her cup to her lips. "Why did you come to the vineyard tonight? I thought you were going fishing."

"So did I. I've always had problems with letting

go. At first, I was only going to keep a watch on Chavez and see if he made any moves."

"Why would you do that?"

He looked down into his coffee. "Ben Forbes and I go back a long way. I liked him. I thought it wouldn't hurt to keep an eye on things. Then, when Gomez went incommunicado, I decided to go up to the valley and see if there was a stakeout."

"Why?"

"I had a hunch. I believe in hunches."

So did Elena. "And then you came to the house to warn us."

"But I got there when things were already starting to happen. Carbonari had evidently found a way to let some of Gomez's men into the fermenting shed and didn't like the idea of you getting in the way."

"I wouldn't have suspected anything if they hadn't left the ladder propped against the vat. It was stupid of Carbonari not to put the ladder away and then put it up again later."

"I wonder if the fermenting shed caught fire." Galen tilted his head. "It would be pleasant to think of Gomez's men in that vat, slowly roasting."

"You'd like to kill them?"

"Oh, yes." His gaze narrowed on her face. "And you're studying me, analyzing my responses, looking for an edge. That's fairly amazing after what you've gone through tonight."

"It's because of what I've gone through tonight." Her hand tightened on her cup. "I have to find a way to keep Barry and Dominic safe. They won't be safe for long in this place."

"Don't be so scornful of Logan's pad. It has top-notch security. Billionaires are prime targets for kidnappers and terrorists, and he's very careful of his family." He added, "But I agree that penthouses aren't the best safe houses. There's only one way out and that's down."

"You could always arrange another helicopter pickup."

"You almost smiled then."

"Did I?"

"Yes, but it's gone again." He leaned back. "Go ahead. Ask me."

"Ask you what?"

"I'm not going to make this easy for you. You've already been a pot of trouble for me. I want the words."

She was silent for a moment. "I'm alone here. I need help."

"You could call the DEA."

"Forbes tried that. I won't make that mistake again." She paused. "I need your help. You have contacts and experience. You could keep Barry safe—if you wanted to do it."

"And what do I get out of it?"

She met his gaze. "Anything you want. Tell me and I'll find a way to get it for you."

He said nothing for a time, then, "How can I resist an offer like that?"

Galen was angry. His expression hadn't changed and his tone was as mocking as ever, but she sensed the anger was there. "You're not supposed to resist it. You want to be paid; you'll be paid. You're not being reasonable."

"I'm not, am I? I'm glad you called that to my attention."

"So what do you want?"

"I'll decide later. Maybe I'll run across some old enemy you can knock off for me. You wouldn't mind doing that, would you?"

"I'd mind."

"But you'd do it."

"It wouldn't come to that. You'd want to make your own kill." Her lips tightened. "What do you want to know? Could I do it? Of course I could do it. My father used to send me out to clear the way before the troops moved out."

"Clear the way?"

"Find and kill any snipers or sentries who might be waiting. He taught me well. I was very good at it."

"Bully for him." He got to his feet. "You know, I don't think I would have liked your father."

"I loved him."

"That makes it worse. Go to bed. I have some phoning to do."

"You're going to help us?"

"I thought we'd already established that fact. Yes, I'm going to help you. I have a ranch in southern Oregon that should fit the bill as far as security is concerned. I buried the paperwork on the place and it should be extremely difficult for anyone to find out I own it."

"But not impossible."

"Nothing is impossible. It only gives us an edge and a little time to make plans. I have a contact who can probably tell me when Chavez is getting close." He stared her in the eye. "And you're going to do everything I tell you to do. That's the only way I play the game."

"If I think what you're doing is right for us."

He shook his head.

She bit her lower lip. "All right. If you don't do anything stupid."

"It will be difficult, but I'll try to restrain myself." He added, "And for your cooperation, I'm going to give you a bonus."

"A bonus?"

"Chavez. I'm going to give you Chavez's head on a platter."

"Why?"

"I'm very irritated with him. A few years ago he killed two of my men, and I didn't like that. But that was business and they knew the risk they were taking. Forbes was different. Forbes was more . . . personal. I think it's time Chavez took the fall."

"You may be disappointed. Chavez didn't come after Barry himself as I thought he would."

"I'm not surprised. Barry may be important to Chavez, but Chavez is smart and wouldn't risk his neck if he could risk someone else's. But Gomez failed. It's not likely Chavez will trust anyone else again. I think he'll come this time." He smiled grimly. "And Forbes would be disappointed: Chavez is not going to survive to spill his guts to the DEA." He paused. "Not that he probably would have anyway."

She stiffened. "What do you mean?"

"You'd have killed him. You wouldn't have chanced him bribing himself out of jail. And you wouldn't have risked Barry being drawn into any messy courtrooms. The answer? Kill the son of a bitch."

"You didn't tell Forbes you thought I'd do that."

"Why should I interfere? I had no desire for Chavez to live to a ripe old age in some cozy jail." He moved toward the door. "Good night. Don't be afraid to go to sleep. You're safe here. Logan's alarm system is awesome, and I'll be up most of the night."

She stared after him for a moment before getting up, going to the sink, and washing out her cup. It was strange to think that after all these years of caring for herself, she was putting her life into someone else's hands. Strange and a little intimidating. Galen was too perceptive, and his will was as strong as her own.

But he didn't have her motivation. He didn't have Barry. She could do anything if it meant keeping Barry safe, and that made her stronger than Galen.

She would be able to handle him.

"Forbes is dead," Gomez said.

"And you have my son," Chavez said. "Of course."

Gomez hesitated. "We'll have him soon. There was a little problem at the vineyard."

Chavez smothered the surge of rage. "Problem?"

"She must have been warned. They set fire to the place and were gone before we got there."

"How could she have been warned? Unless you were so exceptionally clumsy as to have been spotted."

"We were careful. I had bribes in place with two of the DEA team members. It should have gone smoothly."

"Don't tell me how it should have gone. Where is my son? Does the DEA still have them in custody?"

"We don't think so. I've been in touch with Carew, our contact at the agency, and he says the agency is in the dark about where she is now."

"As much in the dark as you are?"

"I think I know who got them away from the vineyard," Gomez said hurriedly. "We caught up with Carmichael in Rio. It took a little time, but he talked. Sean Galen got them out of Colombia and delivered them to San Francisco. If the DEA didn't pull her out of the safe house, Galen has to be the one who did it."

"Why? It appears to me that an orangutan would have had enough brains to take my son away from you."

Silence. "He's the only person she knows in this country. He's our strongest lead."

"Then follow it. Dig until you unearth everything about Galen. Find out where he took them." He lowered his voice to silky softness. "And don't phone again and tell me you've failed me, Gomez. The minute you zero in on them I want to know about it."

"It may take a little time. Galen works alone. It will be hard to—"

Chavez hung up on him.

Whining bastard. He didn't want excuses. He wanted his son.

And the chance to savage Elena Kyler until she begged him to kill her.

He drew a deep breath and tried to rid himself of the anger. Two more days and the Delgados and their network would be in his pocket. Then he would be free to finish this business with Elena himself. He should have known better than to rely on Gomez to take care of her. He was the only one strong enough to defeat the bitch. He had done it once and he would have no problem doing it again.

Elena lying on the mat, her eyes blazing up at him.

The memory gave him a burst of pleasure that was part sexual and part heady triumph. He was almost glad Gomez had failed. He had forgotten the sheer enjoyment of making her submit to him. He had never felt stronger or more the conqueror than in those last days with her. It would be good to have a little quality time with Elena before he cut her heart out.

"It's beautiful." Elena looked out at the blue mountains in the distance. "I've never seen anything like this. It's so . . . wild."

"And Colombia isn't?" Galen leaned out the window and punched in the number on the electronic gates. "But I know what you mean. Barrenness has a power of its own."

"It's not really barren," Dominic said. "A little stark. Is it your ranch?"

"Yes." Galen drove through the gates and they swung closed behind the jeep. "I occasionally come up here to relax."

"Livestock?"

Galen shook his head. "Too much commitment. You have to take care of livestock. Or hire someone else to do it, and then I'd have to have them report to me. A regular Pandora's box. It would defeat the purpose of coming here to relax."

"When was the last time you came here?" Elena asked.

He thought about it. "About three months ago . . . I think."

"Then you must not need to relax very often."

He shrugged. "I get bored."

She stared at him appraisingly. "I bet you do."

"What's that supposed to mean?"

"Nothing." Her glance shifted to the ranch house. "This place is huge."

"I never liked to rough it. I did too much of it when I was a kid."

"Where was that?"

"In Liverpool. And other places." He parked in front of the long wraparound front porch. "My mum always believed that if one place was good, the next was sure to be better." He got out of the jeep. "Come on, Barry. I'll show you the barn. There's a hayloft you'll appreciate."

"Later," Elena said. "I want to take a look. You

can never tell what kind of creatures may be in that hay."

"It's clean." A man dressed in jeans and a denim shirt had come out of the house. "When Galen called, I went to town and bought a few bales."

Elena went rigid.

"It's okay," Galen told her quickly. "This is Judd Morgan. He's sort of the caretaker here. He's harmless."

He didn't look harmless. He appeared to be in his mid-thirties, was tall and lean, and gave the impression of whipcord strength. Pale blue eyes were deep-set in a face that was planed, chiseled, and hard. Very hard.

"How do you do?" Morgan said. "I assume you're Elena Kyler. The boy will be all right. I cleaned out the barn two weeks ago, and the only varmints are the kittens and Mac, my German shepherd. He's gentle."

"A puppy?" Barry's eyes lit up.

"Well, not exactly a puppy. He only acts like one."

"This is Dominic Sanders," Galen said solemnly. "He was once a priest. I brought him here to save your soul."

"I'll let him practice on you. I'm a bigger challenge." Morgan shook Dominic's hand before turning his gaze on Galen. "Any news for me from Logan?"

Galen shook his head. "Not yet."

"Damn." He turned back toward the house. "I'll show you to your rooms. It's a surprisingly nice place considering Galen's lack of good taste."

"Mama, may I go to the barn?" Barry asked.

She couldn't resist the eagerness in his expression. "For a little while. You need a bath before dinner."

"He'll have plenty of time." Galen took his hand and they turned away. "I'm planning a gourmet meal for our first night. Perfection doesn't happen without effort."

"Neither does modesty," Morgan murmured.

"Come on, Barry. This denigration of my sterling character isn't for your ears."

Morgan led Elena and Dominic into the house. A cathedral ceiling gave the living room an open, airy look and the chenille-upholstered furniture provided a contrasting coziness.

"Five bedrooms, four baths on the second floor," Morgan said. "Game room, library, kitchen, dining room, living room, and several other rooms on the main. Do you want the grand tour or to see just your bedrooms?"

"The bedrooms," Elena said.

Morgan nodded and led them toward the staircase. "The first bedroom on the right has a smaller adjoining room. I thought you'd want to take that one for you and the boy."

Elena nodded. "That will be fine."

He threw open the door and stepped aside. "Galen said to get all of you enough clothes to see you through your stay here. They're already in the closets and chests. I had to rely on Galen's eye, so blame him if they don't fit." He gestured to a door across the hall. "Your room, Mr. Sanders. If either of you has any problems or questions, let me know. I'll see you at dinner." He turned and left them.

"Interesting man." Dominic was looking after him. "And an interesting contrast between him and Galen."

Like a granite slab and a glittering mirror, Elena thought. Either one could damage you under the right circumstances. "I don't like Galen not telling us about Morgan."

"You would have objected to having anyone you didn't know here. Maybe he thought it would be more reassuring if you met him first."

Reassuring was not a word she'd use in connection with Judd Morgan. "He obviously lets him have the run of the place. He may trust him, but I have no reason to."

"Galen hasn't been wrong yet. Give him a chance." Dominic crossed the hall and opened his bedroom door. "You know, I like this place. It reminds me of our house."

Except that it was ten times bigger. But she knew what he meant. There was a simplicity of design and an air of comfort that was homelike. She liked it too. Much better than Logan's luxurious penthouse where they'd spent last night. "It's very nice."

She closed the door and went over to the window. She could see the large barn from here, and it looked as neat and well cared for as the rest of the property. A barn and pets and enough ground for a child to run. Their stay here might not be so bad.

Her gaze lifted to the surrounding countryside.

You could see for miles and miles. Was that why Galen had bought this property? She'd received the impression from Forbes that Galen's past had been shady at best and he was extremely wary. So wary that even when he relaxed he needed to know what was coming toward him?

My God, was she feeling sorry for him? It was good for her and Barry that he'd lived a life that had made him build this stronghold. She mustn't think beyond that truth.

Barry came running into the house an hour later.

"Mama!"

"Here." She came to the head of the staircase. "Did you enjoy it?" She could see that he had. Straw was sticking out of his hair and his expression was glowing. "How many kittens were there?"

"Three." He ran up the stairs. "But the dog . . . Mac. He rolled over and let me rub his belly."

"What an honor." She smiled and gave him a hug. "Looks like you rolled over a few times too."

"Galen and I had a straw fight, and he threw me on top of the stack. Then I couldn't fight anymore because I was laughing. He said he was making duck orange for dinner and I could help. I've never eaten that, have you?"

"No."

"I've got to hurry. Where's the bathroom? He said I couldn't touch anything in his kitchen until I had a bath."

She nodded at the suite. "In there." She followed

him into the bedroom and gestured to the bathroom. "I'll get you some clean clothes from your room. It's right through that door. Our rooms are connected."

"Good." Barry's tone was abstracted. "I have to wash my hair. Galen said that if he saw even one piece of straw, I was out of there. Will you help me?"

"Of course." Every other word he'd uttered had been about Galen. "I'll see that you pass inspection. You like Galen?"

"Sure. He makes things . . . different."

He meant exciting. Why wouldn't he think Galen was some kind of magician? He'd flown through the air with him and then been whisked to the top of a great city. Now Galen had given Barry the elements of every boy's dream: a dog and cats and a hayloft.

He was staring at her, troubled. "You like him too, don't you?"

One word and she could turn him against Galen. This affection that Barry was beginning to feel for him could be dangerous. Galen might be something of a magician, but after all the sleight of hand and wondrous tricks, he would vanish and leave Barry alone and empty. But how could she say that word when Galen had single-handedly banished the fear and uncertainty she had sensed in Barry since the fire at the vineyard? She owed him a debt, dammit. "Why wouldn't I like him?" she asked lightly. "After all, he's going to teach you how to cook me a fancy dinner."

"Come on, young man. Time for bed." Dominic stood up from the table. "Your face is going to fall into that chocolate mousse if you don't stop nodding."

"Tired . . ." Barry stood up, yawning. "I stirred the chocolate, you know."

"It's been called to our attention," Dominic said. "Several times." He turned to Galen. "A great meal. I've never had better, even in the finest restaurants in Miami."

"Of course not," Galen said. "I told you I was a master."

Judd Morgan snorted. "It's getting thick in here. I need some air."

"And leave me with the dishes?"

"I'll help," Barry said.

Galen shook his head. "I believe in specialized labor. You've done your bit. I have you scheduled for omelette duty at breakfast tomorrow."

He yawned again. "Okay."

"Let's go," Dominic said. "You're about to fall asleep, and you're getting too big for me to carry up those stairs."

Elena watched Dominic and Barry leave the dining room before she rose to her feet. "I'll wash the dishes."

Morgan shook his head. "My job. Galen cooks. I clean up." He started to stack the dishes. "Though if he didn't have a great dishwasher, I'd take you up on it."

"Then I'll help," Elena said.

"No, you won't. I like to work alone." He carried the dishes into the kitchen.

"He's not rejecting you. He's telling the truth. He likes to do everything alone," Galen said as he stood up. "That's why he likes staying here at the ranch. You can't imagine a more solitary existence. I guess it's his artistic temperament."

"He's an artist?"

He nodded. "There's an oil painting of his in the library that's remarkable."

"I would never have guessed."

"Well, I grant you that he doesn't look the part. What would you think he does for a living?"

"I don't know. Maybe the same thing that you do."

He smiled. "Close. But Judd was more specialized."

"You appear to get along very well."

"We understand each other. In many ways we're a lot alike."

She shook her head. "You're nothing alike."

"You don't think I'm the artistic, solitary type?"

"I don't know what type of person you are." She studied him. His expression was slightly mocking, but his dark eyes were sparkling. "Do you?"

"I know exactly who I am. I just dislike sharing it with all and sundry. Do you want to see Judd's painting? Or maybe you've had a look around already?"

"No, just the upstairs." She followed him from the room. "This is quite a place. I'd think you'd use it more often."

"I get restless." He opened a paneled door. "This is the library. It's the one room Judd totally approves of."

Books. Books everywhere. "So do I." She went into the room and caressingly touched the leather spine of a book on the shelf closest to the door. "You couldn't get a room with this many books wrong."

"You like to read?"

"I love it." She went around looking at titles. Everything from classics to how-to manuals. "When I was a kid, there was no way I had access to TV or movies, but my father managed to get me thousands of paperback books over the years. That's all I needed."

"No, that's not all you needed. Tell me, were you on the reward system? Shoot a sniper, read a book?"

She flinched. "You don't understand. My father wasn't a heartless monster. He came to Colombia as a mercenary with the rebels and he stayed as a patriot. He met my mother and he learned to love her and her country. He wanted to change things. He believed in what he was doing."

"Did you believe in what he was doing?"

"I believed in him."

"Would you let your son be taught the things he taught you?"

She didn't answer for a moment. "My father did the best he could. After my mother was killed by government troops, he became obsessed with the cause. Defeating them was worth any sacrifice. He couldn't give it up, and he was left with me and Luis to raise. He wanted to keep us with him."

"Where is Luis now?"

She looked away from him. "He's still with the rebels."

"I take it you're not close."

"No." She touched another cover. "*Macbeth.* Do you like Shakespeare?"

"Culture? Me? I bought the entire stock from an estate auction."

"Really?"

"Why should that surprise you?"

She stiffened as a thought occurred to her. "It only surprises me you feel it necessary to lie to me."

"Why do you think I'm lying to you?"

"Aren't you?"

He was silent a moment. "I did buy the library at an estate auction. But I examined every book on those shelves before I made my bid. I do like Shakespeare. He understood human frailties. Are you satisfied now?"

"No, because I think you lied so I wouldn't feel uncomfortable. You don't have to feel sorry for me. I've led a rough life and I haven't had any formal education, but I'm not ashamed of what I am or what my father was or what I've had to do to survive. I'd match my—"

"Shh." His fingers were across her lips. "I don't feel sorry for you. I'm not that stupid. You're probably a hell of a lot better educated than I'll ever be. I was kicked out of more schools than you can count on both hands. I didn't even crack a book until I was fifteen. I was the most ignorant rowdy on the face of the planet. If I wasn't honest, it was my built-in camouflage coming into play."

She turned her head away to avoid the touch of his hand. He was warm and hard and her lips felt—

She drew a deep breath and stepped back. "Why? You don't care what I think about you."

"It appears I do. What a surprise." He nodded at the wall behind her. "That's Judd's painting."

As she turned around, she felt a surge of relief that he'd changed the subject. She didn't like what she was feeling. The sexual tension had emerged out of nowhere, and she wanted to snuff it out.

The painting. Look at the painting.

It was a small landscape of the hills surrounding the ranch. But the talent and power of the picture wasn't small. Its effect was like a stormy burst of lightning. "It's wonderful."

"It reminds me of an El Greco. I don't tell Judd that because he'd be insulted."

She remembered what Morgan had said after dinner. "Because he likes to do things alone. And in his own way."

Galen nodded. "We all like to be considered unique. And he is unique, of course."

She nodded. "Is he going to have an exhibition?"

"Not right away. He's been concentrating on his art only since he came here, and he has to create a body of work. Besides, he has to stay out of the limelight for a while."

"Why?"

"He wants to stay alive."

"I . . . see."

He smiled. "How tactful. You don't see at all. Judd used to do sanctions for the CIA. He was exceptionally good and they chose him to take out a general in the North Korean government. Unfortunately, his

superiors decided that it was a mistake and that the
man who did it should have his head served up as a
sacrifice to diplomacy. Judd objected. Can you imagine that?"

"So he's hiding out?"

"Until my friend Logan manages to pull some
strings in Washington to take the heat off. He's got a
lot of clout, but it could take some time." He
glanced at her. "But you needn't worry about Judd
being around Barry. He won't hurt him."

"I'm not worried. I believe I should be a decent
judge of character by now. What someone does is
not necessarily what they are."

"And vice versa."

"Aren't you running a risk helping him?"

He shrugged. "I always liked Judd." He took her
elbow. "I'll show you the rest of the house. The
game room's kind of fun. I don't suppose you play
pool?"

"No."

"Didn't think so. Not that many pool halls in
the jungle. We'll start lessons tomorrow. I'm a fantastic teacher."

"Is there anything you're not fantastic at?"

"Can't think of anything." He opened another
door. "You're going to like this. It's right up your—
What's wrong?"

It was a gym. Mirrored walls and metal equipment.

And the mat lying on the floor.

"You're white as a sheet. What the hell is wrong?"
The mat.

"Nothing." She moistened her lips. Stop shaking. You were just caught off guard. She took a deep breath. "I'm . . . tired. I need to go to bed."

"Not until you tell me what—" He stopped as he saw her expression and said roughly, "For God's sake, get out of here."

"I will." She ran out of the room and up the stairs. She barely made it to the bathroom before she threw up. Stupid to be this feeble. After all she'd gone through, to have the sight of that blasted gym turn her into this quivering weakling. It was the shock. She hadn't been in a gym in the last six years. She hadn't realized all those memories would come flooding back to her.

The mat.

She felt the sweat break out on her forehead.

Jesus.

The mat.

Chapter Six

ELENA'S HAND CLENCHED THE BANISTER AS SHE STARTED down the stairs. The house was in darkness, but there was enough moonlight streaming in the windows for her to dimly make out the shape of the furniture in the living room.

And the hall leading to the gym.

She could do it.

One step at a time.

She reached the bottom of the staircase and paused for a moment, the muscles of her stomach twisting.

Don't think. Just do it.

But she had to think, that was part of it. She couldn't block it out or he'd win.

She moved slowly down the hall.

The mat.

She could see it in her mind.

And Chavez's face above her.

No.

She leaned against the wall and breathed deep. Her heart was pounding hard, painfully. Get it over with. Just a few more steps and she'd reach the door.

She was there. She searched blindly for the knob and threw the door open. Go in. Look at it.

The mat.

She went forward and stood over it. It didn't mean anything. It was only a piece of cloth and padding. It was nothing.

So she could leave. She didn't have to stay here.

If it didn't mean anything, why was she shaking as she'd done when she had malaria? Why were the tears running down her cheeks?

Run away. Forget it. She didn't have to do this.

Yes, she did. If she ran away, he would win.

Stay until the pain went away. That's all she needed to do.

She backed away until she felt the cold mirrored wall touch her body. She sank to the floor.

Look at it. Remember. He can't hurt you unless you let him.

Dear God, she wished she could stop shaking.

"Come on," Galen said roughly. "You're getting out of here."

She looked up to see him standing before her.

He held out his hand. "I don't know what the hell you're doing, but I'm not standing around and watching you."

She shook her head and wrapped her arms more

tightly around her body. Jesus, she was cold. "Go away."

"You've been in here over an hour and I'm tired of being patient and understanding. I'm not going to wait any longer."

"I don't want . . . your . . . understanding. None of your business. Go away."

"It's my house and, as long as you're here, you're my business. I run the show, remember? Now, come on, we're getting out of here."

"Have . . . to stay . . . here."

He gazed at her for a moment. "Shit." He dropped down beside her and leaned against the mirror. "Okay, we both stay."

She shook her head. "Alone. I have to do it alone."

"Bullshit." He tossed her his handkerchief. "Stop crying, okay?"

"I'm not—"

"Just shut up. I've had a rough night. I don't know what's happening to you, but I don't like it. And I don't like feeling like this. I want to go to bed and forget about you."

"Do it."

"I can't. If I could, do you think I'd be sitting here in the dark in the middle of the night?"

"Go away."

"I'm not going away. If this is something you have to do alone, it's going to have to be another time. So stop communing with that damn mat and let's go get a cup of coffee."

"I'm not commun—" Anger surged through her. "You make me sound like a crazy woman."

"Crazy? If you've got some weird fixation for mats, heaven forbid I object."

"You don't under—" She struggled to her feet. "What an asshole you are." She moved toward the door. "Leave me alone, Galen."

It wasn't until she was out in the hall that a relief that made her go limp replaced the anger. She reached out blindly for the wall.

"Easy." Galen's arm was around her, supporting her, leading her toward the kitchen. "Don't fight. You might hurt me."

"Asshole." She was still shaking and felt as weak as a kitten. They both knew she was in no shape to hurt a cockroach.

"You keep calling me that." He pushed her down in a chair at the table and turned on the light. "It's not very polite. If you keep on doing it, I'm not going to pick you up from the floor when you shake yourself off that chair. Stay here. I'll get a throw from the sofa."

She should get up and leave. In a minute. As soon as she was stronger.

He was back, tucking a sage chenille throw around her. "Better?" He turned away. "You don't have to admit it. After all, I interfered with your hair-shirt detail. I'll get you a cup of coffee. It's already made."

The throw did feel warm and soft, and her coldness was beginning to subside. "It . . . feels good."

"I thought so."

She watched him pour steaming coffee into two cups. "Why was the coffee already made?"

"I was in the living room when you came downstairs. You didn't look so good. I thought you might need it." He brought the cups to the table. "I didn't realize you'd decide to set up camp in there."

"You should have left me alone."

"You were in pain. I have a problem with that." He sat down across from her. "You're still in pain."

"I'm *not* in pain. I won't let him hurt me again."

"Okay. Okay. Drink your coffee."

She knew she couldn't hold the cup steady. "In a little while."

"Whatever." He looked down into his coffee. "I don't suppose you'd like to tell me what's going on with you?"

"No."

"That mat is bothering you. We could drag it outside and start a bonfire. I'll supply the match."

She shook her head.

"I could let Judd draw a bull's-eye and use it as a target. You'd be doing him a favor. He's probably out of practice."

She stared at him in exasperation and then a hint of a smile touched her lips. "Asshole."

"Okay, you're better. Drink your coffee."

He was right. Her hand was no longer shaking. She lifted the cup to her lips. The coffee was hot and strong and it tasted good going down. She set the cup down and leaned back in the chair. "Why were you sitting there in the dark?"

"You ran away. You were scared. But I knew you wouldn't allow yourself to cower in your room."

"And you were curious?"

"You might say that."

But it wouldn't be the truth. She knew he had waited because he wanted to help her. And he had helped her. He had broken the hold the trauma had on her with flippancy, making light of the agony she was going through. It had made her angry, and the anger had freed her.

Had he known what he was doing?

Probably. He was clever and perceptive and he knew how to manipulate people and situations. He had chosen to manipulate this one to try to help her.

He was studying her expression. "You're not going to start bristling, are you?"

"No."

"I heard sometimes it helps to talk about it."

"Did you?"

"I promise not to blackmail you."

"You couldn't. It was important only to me."

"Not to Dominic?"

"I never told him. It would have hurt him."

"Then that could be why you reacted like that. Maybe if you let it out . . . It won't hurt me. You wouldn't care if it did." He shrugged. "Only a suggestion."

He could be right. She would try anything to avoid falling apart again when she went back into that gym. "You'd be bored."

"But it might save me some late nights waiting for you to wander downstairs for a midnight tryst with that dumb mat. You'll be going back, won't you?"

Her hands clenched her cup. "I can't let him win. I can't let him make me afraid."

"Chavez?"

She didn't answer for a moment. "I didn't think it would affect me like that. I thought I'd put it all behind me."

"Did you have an affair with Chavez?"

"Affair?" Her lips twisted. "Chavez doesn't know how to have a relationship with a woman. He chose his wife as a meek slave and childbearer. His mistress is the same, except I understand she's very talented sexually."

"And you?"

"He found me different. At first he was amused, and then he wasn't amused at all." She stopped. What the hell. Let it all out. She wasn't ashamed. Why should she hide what had happened? "I was nineteen, and the situation with the rebel band I belonged to had changed. They had begun taking money from Chavez to finance the cause and in exchange they protected him. He was distributing drugs among the soldiers, gaining influence, using us as puppets. I hated it. My father had died the previous year and I was thinking of breaking with the group and leaving Colombia. But I waited too long. I was very good at my job and I was respected. Chavez heard about me and thought it would be interesting to take a woman to his little playground."

"Playground?"

"Chavez likes to consider himself a conqueror.

When he was in his teens, he was a soldier with a paramilitary group. He was a good soldier, brilliant with weapons and very strong. He liked it. He found the idea of being a killing machine very appealing. But the money wasn't good enough and he left the army for the drug trade. He wanted the best of both worlds." She moistened her lips. "Now he keeps himself fit at a gym he had built on his property in the hills. It's a fine gym, with every exercise machine you could think of. But a machine isn't a man. He needed combat to give him the rush he needed. So he invited or coerced or paid members of the different rebel groups to come and spar with him. He had no trouble besting most of the fighters he paid to come to the gym and give him a workout."

"What happened to the ones he couldn't beat?"

"He kept them there until he could defeat them. Most of them died. But, then, most of the others died too. Fighting to the death made him feel exhilarated. He said there was nothing like knowing you had that power over another human being."

"He took you to this gym?"

"Took me? I was delivered to him by my own people. I was paid for with a tidy bundle of cocaine."

"Nice."

"I was there for three weeks." She was beginning to shake again. Get it over quickly. "He found me a . . . challenge. Every night he'd come into the gym and fight me—unarmed combat. Karate, judo, street fighting . . . It didn't matter how dirty. Whatever worked. The only rules were the length of the session. Two hours. If he got me down and pinned me, he would win. I wouldn't let him do it. He couldn't beat me. I couldn't let him win." She drew a deep breath. "But there was one way he felt all-powerful. After all, I was a woman. Every time I was still standing at the end of that two hours, he'd have me tied down and he'd rape me."

"Son of a bitch."

"That's exactly what he is. He had to win." She stopped. Don't break down. Get it over with. She was near the end. "It was . . . hideous. The first few times he did that to me I was too stunned to think. Then I tried to pretend that I was giving up and he was getting the better of me. I guess it was too sudden. He knew I was faking it. He brought in a young boy—he wasn't more than fourteen—and he fought him in front of me. He killed him. He told me that every time I tried to cheat him he would do the same thing." She swallowed hard. "Oh, God, I knew I'd die if I couldn't get out of there. That would be a final victory for him." She paused. "But I let it go on and I tried to be patient. I took it slow, very slow. Our bouts gradually became closer and closer, and he was sure it was only a matter of time before he'd triumph. I even made sure I was compliant to every sexual whim. He began to take me for granted."

"Dangerous."

"Then one night I let him win. I had to do it. It was the only way to disarm him. I'll never forget his face. . . . I knew the next time we fought, he wouldn't be satisfied with taking me down. He'd want to kill me. The fun had gone out of it for him. I was right. Before he left he told me that the next session he'd introduce something new. Knives." She drew a shaky breath. "That night I escaped and hid out in the hills. I kept away from our group, but I managed to find Dominic. He'd been told a lie about me and that I'd left the area, but he was still searching for me. He gave me money and told me he'd meet me in a month in Tomaco."

"But you found out you were pregnant?"

"I wouldn't admit it to myself until I was almost four months. I didn't think God could be that cruel."

"You could have had an abortion."

"No, I couldn't. That wasn't an option I was able to accept." She looked down into her cup. "But I was planning on giving him away after he was born. I hated those months. My swollen body and his child inside me . . . It was as if he'd finally found a way to beat me."

"And when Barry was born?"

"I wouldn't even look at him. Dominic took care of him after the birth while we were trying to find a home for him. Then one night, when Barry was about six weeks old, Dominic was down with the flu and I had to care for the baby." She paused, remembering. "I sat there rocking him and he smiled at me. I know they're not supposed to really smile at you at that age, but Barry did smile. It wasn't like any other smile I'd ever seen. I think God wanted him to tell me something."

"That you should take care of him?"

"No, that he was his own soul and deserved a chance." She smiled tremulously. "It's a beautiful soul, Galen. From the beginning he was full of love and joy and wonder. There's nothing of that monster in Barry."

"I believe you."

"You don't really know him. He's . . . special."

"And you're afraid Chavez would change him?"

"No. Barry has a strong, loving nature, and I don't believe it can be twisted. But what Chavez can't conquer, he destroys. Barry's only a little boy. I don't know if he could survive him." She drew a deep breath. "But he's not going to have to try. Chavez isn't going to get his hands on him."

"How did Chavez find out about Barry?"

"Dominic kept contact with someone in the rebel group. He still believes a lost soul can be saved. We were betrayed."

"By whom?"

She didn't answer for a moment. "My brother, Luis. He works as an informant for Chavez now."

"So much for family feeling."

"Family feeling doesn't stand a chance against a kilo of cocaine. Luis has been on drugs for years."

"Chavez again."

"Yes."

"It must have been tough for you."

She nodded. "I loved Luis. You can't just turn feeling off and on. God knows I've tried." She pushed her chair back. "I'm going to bed. Good night."

"Good night." He rose to his feet and followed her out into the hall. "Try to have pleasant dreams."

"Sometimes you can't control your dreams."

"You surprise me. I thought you could control everything these days."

She looked back over her shoulder. "Don't try to make me feel better about the way I behaved tonight. I know you probably think I was weak."

"No, you were human. There's nothing weak about you." He met her gaze. "Everyone's entitled to let their guard down occasionally."

"When do I get to see you do it? Never mind." She started up the stairs, then she turned to face him as she reached the landing. "You've been kind to me tonight. I . . . thank you."

"Oh, for God's sake. All I did was listen."

"No, you did more than that. I'll remember."

"See that you do. You never can tell when I'll decide to collect. I don't suppose you're going to be sensible and stay out of that gym from now on?"

She shook her head. "I have to face it until it doesn't hurt me any longer. That time with him is still dominating me, twisting my life, changing what I am. I didn't realize that until tonight. I have to find a way of freeing myself."

"Then I guess I'll have to think of a way of speeding up the process. All this lingering gloom depresses me."

"You have nothing to do with this."

"That's what I keep telling myself." He met and held her eyes. "It's not working."

She went still. She couldn't tear her gaze away.

"Go to bed." He turned away. "I have to go wash those cups. A man's job is never done."

She gazed after him. What had happened in that last moment of contact? He hadn't touched her, hadn't said a word that wasn't simply meant to comfort her. Yet that single glance was enough to cause a wave of heat to tingle through her. It shouldn't have happened. Particularly not tonight. She had been mentally reliving that period of sexual horror and brutality, and she should have felt only revulsion, as she had with other men. But it had happened, which meant that the chemistry between them must be as strong as that bitter memory.

Forget it. She was too weary and confused to think about sex and chemistry and Sean Galen. The realization that she was still crippled by that memory had come as too much of a shock. She had been lying to herself. She had thought in the years after she'd escaped from Chavez that she'd gradually healed herself. It was clear she still had a long way to go.

She started up the stairs again.

But she would get there. She couldn't let Chavez win. During those last days when she had pretended to be defeated by him, she had been filled with self-doubt and bitterness. There had been times when she had wondered whether the pretense was reality.

That could be fatal when she met Chavez again. He would take advantage of every doubt, every weakness. And if there was still a lingering poison in her system from that horror, he would pounce on that as well.

There would be no weakness. She had discovered

it in time, and she would make sure she exorcised any hint of it before she had to confront Chavez.

Shit.

Galen turned the water at the sink on full blast.

That's the way to do it, my man. Give her a hand up, listen to a story that had made him want to draw and quarter Chavez, and then let her know you want to jump her and do the same thing. He was lucky she hadn't come back down those stairs and given him a karate chop.

He deserved it.

Hell, it had been bound to happen. The sexual tension was a constant undercurrent since the night they'd met, and he'd been fighting it tooth and nail. He didn't even know if Elena had been aware it was there until tonight. He hadn't wanted her to know. If he ignored it, it might go away, and that would be best for both of them. He preferred to keep his relations with women light and enjoyable, skimming on the surface, and there was nothing light about Elena. She was too intense, and she filled him with a mixture of emotions that ranged from protective pity to admiration to exasperation. Sometimes in the space of a few moments. He didn't need this. He didn't want it.

He rinsed out the cups and put them on the drain.

Okay. Solve the problem and get her out of here. If he did it fast enough, he might be able to keep from making a move on her they'd both regret.

He sat down in a kitchen chair and dialed Manero. Although it was late, he picked up immediately.

"What's the word on Chavez?"

"Still in Colombia. The Delgados left this morning, and I've been told the departure was very cordial."

"And Gomez?"

"No sign of him." He paused. "But there have been questions about you buzzing around the grapevine."

"What kind of questions?"

"Oh, tender, caring little inquiries. How to get to you? Who to pay off to bring Chavez your head? Where you might be? You must have been stirring things up."

"I've been a little busy." He thought for a moment. "Make sure you let Chavez find out my phone number. It will make him feel like he's getting somewhere, and I want to encourage his initiative."

"Chavez doesn't need encouragement."

"The tiger always needs to feel he's the only predator. It makes him careless about any pits that might be dug for him. Call me if Chavez moves out." He hung up and leaned back in his chair. Keep cool. The rage he had felt as he listened to Elena was still strong. It had been a long time since he'd wanted to kill a man this much, and hatred caused a man to make mistakes.

Come on, Chavez. I'm waiting for you.

Barry was laughing.

Elena smiled as she started down the stairs. He and

Dominic must have awakened before her this morning. He sounded like he was having a wonderful—

The laughter was coming from the gym.

She stopped in shock and then slowly continued down the steps and the hall.

"Barry?"

"Mama, come quick. I'm turning somersaults."

"I see you are." She stood in the doorway. Barry and Galen were on the mat, and he was helping the little boy flip over. She held tight to the doorjamb. She wanted to snatch Barry up and carry him out of there. She wanted to kill Galen.

"Watch me, Mama."

Galen met her gaze. "Yes, watch him, Mama. He won't hurt himself. The mat will cushion him. That's all it's meant to do." He turned back to Barry. "Okay, now we try a handspring."

"Are you watching, Mama?"

She moistened her lips. "I'm watching, Barry."

She watched him for another ten minutes. She watched him do somersaults. She watched him do handsprings. She watched him collapse into giggles when Galen slyly raked his ribs and tickled him.

Galen finally set him on his feet and gave his behind a swat. "Enough of this horseplay. We'll put in another session tomorrow. Go wash your hands and get into the kitchen. We've got work to do."

"I know. Omelettes," Barry said as he ran to Elena. His cheeks were scarlet and his dark eyes glittered with excitement. "Did you see me? I did the last handspring by myself."

"You were wonderful." She kissed his forehead. "A regular acrobat."

"I *like* this place." He ran down the hall toward the bathroom.

"Let's get it over with fast." Galen got to his feet and reached for a hand towel draped on one of the machines. He dabbed at the perspiration on his forehead. "Barry will wonder where I am."

"You're an interfering bastard."

"Yes. I told you I didn't like clouds hovering over me."

"I wanted to throw up when I saw Barry on that mat."

"It was chancy." He wiped the back of his neck. "I decided I had two choices if I didn't want to see you tearing yourself apart. I could hang up the mat on the wall with a picture of Chavez pinned to it. Then we'd all take turns with darts—or maybe bowie knives—until the mat was no more. It would have been like the effigies I heard the Allies had of Hitler and Tojo during the Second World War. That plan really appealed to me, but it might have been too violent with Barry around." He tossed the towel back on the machine. "So I decided to replace a bad memory with a good one."

"It wasn't good."

"But it wasn't a nightmare. You liked seeing Barry happy." He started for the door. "You may not have felt defeated by your bouts with Chavez, but I think the rape was different. That got to you. But you're wrong. What happened on that mat wasn't a defeat for you; it was really a final victory. Chavez didn't mean to do it, but he gave you the grand prize. He gave you Barry." He passed her and went down the hall. "I've promised Barry a workout every morning. I think he'd like you to be there. Can you do it?"

She wanted to say no. She had been filled with dread and horror and the desire to snatch Barry and run away with him. Those minutes had seemed to last forever.

But they hadn't been impossible to endure. It might get better.

Replace bad memories with good.

"I can do it."

"The telephone is in the name of Desmond Sprull, phony address in Las Vegas," Gomez said. "We can't trace Galen by the number."

"And since you don't know where he is, you can't get close enough to put a trace on his calls," Chavez said. "It's a wonder you were even able to get that number."

"We'll find him." He paused. "He has a friend, John Logan. We could possibly discuss the matter with him."

"You mean force the information out of him? Logan has influence in high places. All we need is to have the government making noise. Our informant tells us the DEA is raising enough stink about the death of those agents at the vineyard." Chavez paused. "But he might be in contact with Galen. Bug his office and his home. Let's see what we can come up with."

"Logan has good security. We may not—"

"I don't want to hear about problems. I want to hear about answers." He pressed the disconnect button.

He looked down at the telephone number on the pad in front of him. Technology was a wonderful thing. The conquerors of old had their weapons and Chavez had his. He could dial this number and be talking to Galen in seconds. A phone call might be all it would take. Offer most men enough money and they would give Chavez anything he wanted. Galen didn't have that reputation, but it was only a matter of finding which button to press.

He wouldn't dial that number. Not yet. Galen had interfered with his business and helped that bitch steal his son. He didn't want him to walk away without suffering. He'd give Gomez a chance to locate him first.

And then perhaps he'd invite him to his gym for a little workout.

Chapter Seven

"GOOD MORNING." JUDD MORGAN TURNED AWAY from the cabinet and smiled at Elena. "Would you like a cup of coffee? I'd offer you something to eat, but Galen is very territorial about his domain. I'm a junk-food addict. I have to sneak in here and have my Frosted Flakes."

"I'd like coffee." She glanced at his bowl and the box beside it. It really was Frosted Flakes. "I'll get it. If you're really sneaking, you don't have much time. I think Galen and Barry are almost finished with his lessons."

"Sounds like he's having a great time. And he learns fast. He's been at it for almost a week, hasn't he?"

She hadn't thought Morgan was even aware of what was going on in the gym. She had scarcely seen him except at lunch and dinner. "Yes, he's getting better every day." She poured her coffee. And she was getting better too. Every session was easier for her to watch. This was the first morning she had felt that it wouldn't be running away for her to leave the gym. "Galen is quite a taskmaster. He never gives up."

"No, he doesn't." He took a bite of his cereal. "But he won't hurt the kid."

"That's what he said about you."

He paused with his spoon in midair. "He told you about me? He must trust you. He's been damn careful about hiding me here. But, then, you're one of his orphans too, aren't you?"

"I'd hardly refer to either of us as an orphan."

"Neither would Galen, but I believe somewhere deep in that convoluted mind of his, that's the way he thinks of us. He's a problem-solver, and we each have a problem." He took another bite of cereal. "He struggles against it, but it's his nature. As for me, I couldn't be more pleased. To hell with pride. That little quirk of his saved my neck. He whisked me out of that jam in the nick of time."

As he had whisked Elena away from that mountain and then the vineyard. "Have you known him long?"

"About five years. We met on a job in Sydney and we've run into each other several times over the years." He pushed his bowl away. "He has contacts and heard I had been set up for a fall and gave me a ring. I was only minutes ahead of the squad that was sent to take me out."

"And he brought you here?"

"He thought it was pretty safe. They didn't know

we were that close friends." He grimaced. "Neither did I. I wasn't even sure if I was going to act on that phone call."

"But you were glad you did."

"Hell, yes." His lips twisted. "I just wish Logan would get on the stick. I'm getting edgy."

She changed the subject. "I saw your painting. I liked it."

"So do I. I like everything I'm doing here. I was tired and ready to quit the game anyway." His gaze narrowed on her face. "But you aren't, are you?"

"What do you mean?"

He shrugged. "I grew pretty good at interpreting body language over the years. You're not hiding, you're waiting."

She hadn't even realized he'd been studying her. "So?"

"Nothing. Do anything you please. Play any gambit. But make sure Galen comes out of this in one piece."

She stared at him curiously. "And what would you do if I didn't?"

"I owe him. What do you think?"

She had never seen a more chilling smile. "Then it's a good thing that I've no intention of letting anything happen to him, isn't it?" She stood up. "Thanks for the coffee, Morgan."

"My pleasure."

She left the kitchen and went down the hall toward the gym.

Waiting, not hiding.

Judd Morgan was as perceptive as Galen, but she wasn't quite as ruthless as he thought. She wasn't so filled with hate that she'd sacrifice the innocent with the guilty.

Or would she? When the time came, would she stop at anything to rid their lives of Chavez? He had hovered over her like a hideous gargoyle, always there, always a threat. She didn't want him to have that kind of power over her any longer.

Barry's session was over only a few minutes after she returned to the gym, and he streaked by her to go upstairs and wash up. Galen stopped her as she started after him. "You left. Everything okay?"

"I heard Morgan in the kitchen and went to get a cup of coffee. I need caffeine to get my day started."

"If you felt the need for outside stimulus, you must be getting better."

She nodded.

"Thank God." He grinned at her. "I'd have been truly chastened if I was wrong. Though, of course, it doesn't happen often and everyone is entitled to one mistake in a millennium. Still, it would—"

"Hush." She couldn't help smiling. He was as flushed and gleaming as Barry had been, and the energy level was even greater. She had the sudden urge to reach out and rumple his dark hair as she did her son's. Not a good idea. "Next you're going to throw a quote from your mum at me, and I'm not up to that."

"Why not? You've had your caffeine." His stride was springy as he headed toward the staircase. "Well, did you bond with Judd?"

"Not exactly."

He stopped at the hesitation in her tone and turned to look at her.

"He warned me not to let anything happen to you."

"Understandable. He's a bit protective. He knows what a weak, fragile being I am."

She snorted.

"But I'm curious why the subject came up."

"He said I wasn't hiding, I was waiting."

"Ah, Judd is a bright man. He'd understand the distinction."

"You didn't talk to him about Chavez?"

"I told him he was looking for you and the boy. No, I didn't tell him that you were going to find a way to rid yourself of Chavez permanently. But he might have figured it out if he'd run across those afternoon workouts you put yourself through in the barn."

She stiffened. She'd tried to keep those exercise sessions private.

"It's my job to know where you are at any given time," he said, answering her unspoken question. "Those workouts are pretty strenuous. How is your wound?"

"Healing."

"I figured it was or I would have stepped in." He gave a mock sigh of relief. "I'm glad I didn't have to do it. I value my neck. You're a truly fearsome woman."

"And you're full of bull."

"But of the most entertaining variety." He stopped with one foot on the steps. "I'll tell Judd not to hold you responsible if Chavez gets lucky. I knew what I was getting into."

"But you wanted to solve the problem. What is it with you? Are you so bored that you have to get involved with everyone around you?"

"I'm not bored. Not this time," he said quietly. "I find you very . . . stimulating."

She inhaled sharply. He had moved away from lightness to disturbing gravity in the space of a heartbeat. She looked away from him. "I solve my own problems, Galen."

He nodded. "That's why you're trying to get stronger. How are you with weapons? Have you lost any of your skills in the past six years?"

She shook her head. "I grew up with guns and knives. That's something you don't lose."

"But you do lose the edge in hand-to-hand combat. It's something I'll have to think about." He started up the steps two at a time. "Right after my shower. Turn on the oven and preheat it to four-fifty, will you? I'm making biscuits this morning."

She stared after him. It was hard to contend with all that energy and boundless self-confidence. She often felt as if she had come too near a lightning bolt. She had meant to establish her independence and also tell him she had no intention of making him a victim. It hadn't happened. He had caught her off guard and she had become defensive.

Later.

She sighed as she went into the kitchen to turn on the oven.

Elena was sound asleep in the hammock on the porch.

Galen carefully closed the screen door behind him and paused a moment, gazing down at her. He hadn't seen her this vulnerable since that night at Tomaco. When she was awake, she always seemed totally alert and wary. No, that wasn't quite true. There were moments with Dominic and Barry when she looked soft and sort of . . . glowing. It had been hard to keep his eyes off her.

The glow was not there now, but her cheeks were flushed from the heat. Her lips were relaxed and slightly parted and her body was—

Better not think about her body.

Better stop staring at her entirely. He had come out here to track down Judd, who was standing at the corral fence a short distance from the porch. So get down to business.

He kept an eye on her as he moved silently across the porch and down the steps.

She didn't stir.

"I'm going to try to paint your damn corral. It's got some interesting contrast lines and lights and shadows," Judd said as Galen reached him. "But you could have provided me with some horses. What's a corral without horses?"

"Empty?" Galen leaned on the fence. "Look at it this way. Anyone could paint a corral teeming with horses. It's been done. You'll be interpreting the loneliness, the progress of time, the cowboy myth without his old pal—"

"I'm beginning to feel ill."

"Then I'll let you make up your own reasons." Galen gazed out at the mountains. "I have a favor to ask, Judd."

"Besides doing the dishes?"

"I realize you don't like to get your valuable hands chapped, but someone's got to do the day-to-day drudgery. I have to save myself for bigger things."

"Knock it off, Galen."

The flippancy dropped from Galen like a discarded shirt. "I want you to work out with Elena."

"What?"

"I want you to spar with her. Hand-to-hand."

Judd glanced at Elena sleeping in the hammock. "No way."

"She needs it."

"You mean you want me to teach her some moves?"

"No, she might be able to teach you a few. She just needs the practice."

Judd's brows lifted skeptically. "She's a woman. I have a problem with beating up women."

"Give her a chance. She might surprise you."

"You were in the Special Forces too. And you've done a hell of a lot more hand-to-hand than I have in the last few years. You do it."

"That's not an option."

"Why not?"

He didn't speak for a moment. "Because she'd

know right away that I want to get my hands on her in a different way."

"Oh."

"So will you do it?"

He shook his head. "I'm not used to holding back. I could kill her."

Galen looked back at Elena. It was clear she was in a deep sleep. . . .

What the hell. "Do you have your switchblade on you?"

Judd stared at him with narrowed eyes. "What are you up to?"

"Just a little test. Do you?"

"In my pocket."

"Take it out, but don't spring the blade yet."

Judd took the knife out of his jeans. "What now?"

"Put your arm around my neck from behind."

Judd locked Galen's neck from behind. "This is dangerous," he murmured. "I've got a lot of smothered resentment for all those dishes I've been washing."

"Now release the switchblade."

The sound was a smooth metallic *click*. "Why? Do you want a shave? That's not—"

Galen pushed him aside, whirled, and held up his arm to ward off the attack.

Elena's hand was coming down on the back of Judd's neck.

Galen grabbed her wrist. "Hold it. It's okay. Just a demonstration."

Elena started to struggle and then stopped. "The

hell it was." Her eyes were dazed and she shook her head to clear it.

"She was asleep." Judd was staring thoughtfully at Elena. "Sound asleep."

"Until she heard something unfamiliar and then caught sight of you holding me in a headlock. Battle instinct. We've both seen soldiers dead to the world respond automatically when an enemy comes near." He released Elena and stepped back. "She was fast, wasn't she?"

"And you were stupid," Elena said coldly. "I could have killed Morgan."

"If I hadn't been expecting you." He turned to Judd. "That was a shuto blow aimed at the back of the neck. If it had landed, you'd have been permanently crippled or dead. Are you still worried about hurting her?"

"Hell no." He snapped his switchblade shut and jammed it into his pocket. "Let her look out for herself."

"Who said I didn't?" Elena glared at Galen. "What's happening here, dammit?"

"You evidently impressed Judd as being too gentle to defend your life and limbs. I just gave a little demonstration to show him he wouldn't need to bother his conscience about it. You'll do it, Judd?"

He nodded slowly. "In the gym tomorrow morning?"

"Late afternoon. Barry takes his nap then," Galen said. "And not the gym. The barn."

"You've got it." Judd moved toward the house. "But I only do those damn dishes every other night."

"If you insist. But be careful, I'd take it badly if you accidentally killed her."

"You can't have it both ways."

"Sure I can."

"Will you talk to me?" Elena said to Galen through her teeth as Morgan disappeared into the house. "What's all this about?"

"You need hand-to-hand practice. Judd has graciously agreed to act as your sparring partner. You'll find he's very good."

"And what if I don't want his help?"

"Then I went to the trouble of getting you two together for nothing. I hate it when a plan doesn't come together."

"And I hate it when someone makes plans without consulting me."

"Don't you need the practice?"

"Yes."

"And wouldn't it be foolish not to take advantage of a willing and able partner?"

She scowled at him.

"And why wouldn't I assume you'd do anything necessary to get ready for Chavez?"

"You could have asked me."

"I wasn't sure I could get Judd to cooperate. Then I would have had to disappoint you."

"I've been disappointed before."

"I know." He met her gaze. "And it makes me sad. I didn't want to be the one to do it again." He started for the porch steps. "Are you going to use Judd?"

"Yes." She grimaced. "But you're the one I should have chopped. If you're looking for a problem to solve, go look somewhere else."

"But you're such great material." His dark eyes were twinkling as he glanced over his shoulder while opening the screen door. "And I should call your attention to the fact that you didn't chop me. You did your damnedest to save my neck. Does that mean you're growing fond of me?"

"It means I was half asleep."

"Crushed again. Oh, well, better my ego than my larynx." He disappeared into the house.

She gazed after him with exasperation. He should have consulted with her. It was true that he'd done her a favor enlisting Morgan to spar with her, but that didn't mean he had a right to assume control. He was bulldozing ahead, providing what he thought she needed, manipulating the people around him.

But it hadn't been bulldozing to arrange for her sessions to be in the barn instead of the gym. She was getting less traumatized about that nightmare setting every day, but Galen had realized she wasn't ready to be thrown into combat in those surroundings. He had displayed an understanding and sensitivity for which she was deeply grateful. What the hell kind of man was he?

She shouldn't think about him. He was too disturbing both mentally and physically. Lately she had found herself watching him instead of her son during those morning sessions. At first it had been an objective admiration of his quickness and the almost animal grace with which he moved. She wouldn't lie to herself and claim what she was feeling now was still objective. The heat was too strong to be anything but sex.

She instinctively shied away from the thought. Not with Galen. Not with anyone. She couldn't face it. Accept what Galen offered and don't get involved. Don't ever let yourself willingly do what Chavez made you do. Run away, keep up your guard. . . .

Run away?

She stiffened as she realized what she was thinking. Good God.

"You're all sweaty," Barry said. "And you've got straw in your hair. Have you been playing in the barn with Judd again?"

"Yes." She brushed a kiss on his forehead. "What have you been doing?"

"Galen went into town and bought me a keyboard. Dominic says it will work just like the piano I had at home."

"That will be fun for you."

"Can I come and watch you next time you're in the barn?"

"I don't think so."

"I let you watch me in the gym."

Barry would be frightened silly if he saw those workouts. Judd Morgan was good, innovative, and totally ruthless, and her response was equally unrestrained. It had been a valuable eight days and she felt almost at her old level of competence. "Sometimes grown-up games can be kind of scary."

"But you told me I had to face scary stuff, and most of the time that made it go away. Remember when I thought there was a monster under my bed? We got down and looked."

"Maybe after a few more sessions I'll let you come." She changed the subject. "Will you play me 'Yankee Doodle' after I get out of the shower?"

He shook his head. "I have to practice. I forget. . . ." He frowned. "It seems like a long time since we left Tomaco, doesn't it?"

She nodded. "A lot of things have happened." She headed for the shower. "I'll be out in ten minutes and you can show me that keyboard."

"Okay." His reply was abstracted. "If it's a scary game, why do you play it?"

"It only seems scary."

"Then let me come and watch."

Good heavens, he was being stubborn. Or maybe it wasn't stubbornness, she thought suddenly. "Are you worried about me, Barry?"

"You shouldn't do stuff that could hurt you."

"And you're trying to protect me?"

"I just want to go with you."

She strode across the room and cupped his face in her hands. "Nothing is going to happen to me, love. There's no monster that could hurt me in that barn. There's only me and Judd and a haystack."

"You had a cut on your arm yesterday."

She hadn't thought he'd noticed. "It was a scratch. You get scratches all the time."

His eyes were glittering with unshed tears. "But I don't want you to get them. Ever."

She hugged him close. "I can't promise you I won't be hurt, just like you can't promise me you won't fall off that corral fence you were climbing this morning." She paused, searching for words. "We try to take care of ourselves, but things happen. Then we have to get up and dust ourselves off and try again. Otherwise we'd never know what it is to get to the top of the fence. Didn't it make you feel good when you did that?"

He nodded. "I could see clear to the mountains."

"I didn't stop you from climbing that fence, did I?"

"No."

"Because I didn't want you to be scared of it."

A sudden smile illuminated his face. "You wanted me to look under the bed."

She smiled in return. "You've got it. And you didn't find any monsters ready to knock you off that fence, did you? Well, I have fences of my own to climb, and I can't be scared or I'll never get to the top."

He was silent a moment. "You stood by the fence while I climbed it. Maybe I could go along in case you needed help."

"Maybe." She laughed. "I'm pretty good at climbing fences these days, but I can always use a little help." She gently pushed him away from her. "We'll see, Barry. Now go and find Dominic. I have to shower."

He ran toward the door and looked over his shoulder with an impish grin. "Yes, you do." He wrinkled his nose. "Phew."

She was still smiling as she turned on the shower. He was changing, growing more independent and responsible every day. Galen's influence? Possibly. Or maybe it was the result of the events of the last few weeks. She was just lucky that they had not made him timid as she'd first been afraid they would. Fear could be a terrible thing.

But you told me I had to face scary stuff, and most of the time that made it go away.

Her smile faded. Easy words to say, not easy words to live by. Yet she believed those words or she wouldn't have spoken them.

I have fences of my own to climb, and I can't be scared or I'll never get to the top.

She was scared. Chavez had damaged her confidence and ripped and scarred her.

Time hadn't healed her yet.

It had already been six years. How much longer would she have to wait for some miraculous transformation to take place? It wasn't her nature to sit back and take no action once she realized a problem existed.

She closed her eyes and let the warm water pour over her. She didn't want to take action. Not this time.

Not this way.

———

Galen was sitting on the couch in the living room, reading, when she came into the room. He glanced up from his book. "I thought you'd gone to bed. Something wrong?"

"Yes. Can we go out on the porch?"

"Sure." He rose to his feet. "The kid okay?"

"Barry's fine." She moved toward the front door. The moon was shining, but it was better than the bright lights in here. What a coward she was being, she thought in disgust. It wasn't as if—

"What do you want?" Galen said from behind her.

"You're a problem-solver." She moistened her lips. "I have a problem."

"So?"

"I want you to screw me."

There was no sound for a full minute. "I beg your pardon?"

"You heard me."

"Turn around. I want to see something apart from the back of your head."

She took a deep breath, braced herself, and turned around. "Then look at me. What do you see?"

His eyes were narrowed on her face. "Beats me to hell."

"This . . . is difficult. I never thought I'd— Will you do it?"

"Why?"

"I haven't been with a man willingly since Chavez took me. I've just realized that's a victory for him. I won't let him have it. I won't let him scar me like that."

"Wonderful." Galen's lips tightened. "Makes a man feel really wanted."

"I can't help it. I have to be honest with you."

"Why me? Why not go knocking on Judd's door?"

"There's been something . . . You know it. I thought it would be easier with you."

"Not the greatest compliment I've received."

"I didn't mean to make you angry." Her voice was shaking. "Maybe this wasn't a good idea."

"Oh, don't back out now. It's just getting interesting."

"Stop it. Just say yes or no." Her chin lifted. "I'd actually rather you said no. This . . . scares me."

"Oh, shit." The anger disappeared from his expression. "Just when I'd managed to whip up some authentic resentment for this insult to my ego." He took a step closer but didn't touch her. "You always manage to disarm me, dammit."

"I didn't mean to hurt your ego." She looked away from him. "I didn't think you'd mind. It wouldn't be unpleasant. I'd do anything you want. Just ask—"

"Shut up." His hand covered her lips, then moved down to her throat. "You *are* scared. Your heart is beating like crazy."

It wasn't entirely fear that was causing that response. "I told you I was. I want to be honest." She looked back at him and met his gaze. "I have to do this. I taught Barry that you have to look under the bed if you think a monster is there."

"I'm not sure what that makes me." He smiled. "But I'm not going to be under the bed. Your pulse just jumped under my thumb."

"You're going to do it?"

"There wasn't any question about our coming together from the minute I first put my hands on you." His thumbs rubbed up and down the sides of her neck. "I'm just a poor male unable to quench my lust."

"Thank you." She was having trouble breathing. "Where? The hammock?"

"God, no." He grinned. "I'm lousy in hammocks. I've never mastered the knack." He was leading her inside and up the stairs. "Bed. My bed. It will make me feel less insecure."

"Bull."

"You think I'm not insecure? You tell me I have to solve your problem and then call me a monster." He opened his bedroom door and drew her inside. "It's enough to make Casanova quake. I'll have to overcome the sheer—"

She stiffened as she saw the bed.

"It's going to be fine," Galen said quietly. "Nothing to it. Piece of cake."

"No."

"Maybe not." His grasp tightened. "But we'll get through it together. You set the pace."

"That's going to be difficult for you." She tried to smile. "You always say you like to run the show."

"In a situation like this, the woman is always in command."

"I never found that to be true."

"Because you've never been in a situation like this." He lifted her palm to his lips. "Or have you?"

She could feel heat spread from her palm up her inner arm. "I wasn't a virgin when Chavez took me. When I was sixteen, there was a man. No, he was more of a boy. I . . . enjoyed it."

"Bless him. Then we have something to build on." He released her hand, and his fingers went to the buttons of her shirt. "No sex since Chavez?"

"No. The guards at the prison—I broke their necks."

"Good." He undid a button. "Then I won't feel obliged to go back and do it for you."

"Why should you want to do that?"

"I'm feeling amazingly protective of you." He undid another button. "I want to fight your dragons."

She inhaled sharply as his fingers brushed against the top of her breast. "You are."

"All your dragons."

"So much for my being in control."

"You're in control." He took her hand and put it on his heart. "Feel it? You did this to me. You have power. You make me feel weak and strong and everything in between."

His heart was beating hard against her palm, sending a ripple of vibration through her. "You're being . . . very kind to me."

"The hell I am." He opened her shirt. "We both know I've been wanting this."

"But I'm not . . . You may not like it."

"I'll like it." His eyes were glinting with sudden

humor as he raised them to look at her. "If you don't break my neck."

Incredibly, she found herself smiling.

Replace bad memories with good.

She knew that the memory of the guards would never be quite as bitter after tonight. "I wouldn't do that."

"Good." He dropped down on the bed. "Then let the play begin."

"I don't want you to . . . I'm . . . damaged. I want you to get something out of this, and I'm not sure how to make sure of that. It's not fair to you." She moistened her lips and said unevenly, "I could pretend. I'm good at pretending."

He drew her down beside him, leaned over her, and slowly, carefully spread her short hair on the pillow. She had never realized what an intimate gesture that could be. Suddenly she was aware only of the darkness and the heat and his eyes glittering down at her. He whispered, "Don't you dare."

Chapter Eight

"IT WASN'T GOOD FOR YOU, WAS IT?" ELENA STARED into the darkness. "I cheated you."

"It was good." He pulled her closer. "And it will get better."

"I told you that I should pretend."

"I've never been fond of fakes. I like the real McCoy." He kissed her temple. "My ego again. When we finally make it, I don't want there to be any doubt about it."

"You were . . . very good. I think."

"Thank you. I value your opinion." He chuckled. "Even though you have only a sadistic son of a bitch and a young kid to compare me to."

"Do you want to do it again?"

"Definitely. But not right now. I'm enjoying holding you too much."

"You are?"

"Yes. I like touching, and I've wanted to have

my hands on you for a long time." He stroked her back, from her shoulders to her buttocks. "You have wonderful muscles, strong and smooth. . . ."

She lifted her head to look at him. "That's a weird compliment."

"I like strength. I think it's sexy."

"I wasn't very strong tonight."

"Sure you were. You had the strength of your convictions and determination." The tips of his fingers grazed lightly up and down her spine. "You were bloody wonderful."

"And you're lying."

"No, it doesn't all have to be about frantic urgency. There's truth and trust, and you gave me both of those. I feel honored." He playfully pinched her butt. "Of course, frantic urgency can be nice too. We'll work on that."

She stiffened. "You're acting as if this is a long-term project."

"Am I? I sometimes have difficulty letting go even after I've solved a problem. But I'm sure you'll make sure I don't get too possessive."

"I will. I have to do that."

"But that's down the road a bit." His smile faded. "I think it's time I had a progress report. How was it for you?"

"Scary. At first, I wanted to fight you."

"I know. I felt your muscles tense."

"But when I managed to relax, it was better."

"Did you think about him?"

"Yes, of course." She swallowed and blocked

out the memory. "Not toward the end. He was gone then."

"Why?"

"I was distracted."

"Hallelujah." He chuckled. "Distracted is good. Though I never thought I'd be grateful for that description of my sexual expertise." He gave her a quick hard kiss. "Now all I have to do is worry about distracting you from step one."

"It may never be good for you."

"Don't be a pessimist." He paused. "If it was never any better than it was tonight, it would still be worth it. Remember, you told me that men just think of women as vessels. Do you still believe that?"

Not Galen. She'd learned a good deal about him tonight. His patience and humor and the protectiveness that had enveloped her like a velvet cloak. He had taken a long time to arouse her and a longer time to try to keep her from being frightened when he'd entered her. "Maybe not all men."

"Maybe?"

"Okay, not you."

"Because I'm truly exceptional," he prompted.

She suddenly smiled. "Because you're truly too egotistical to let any woman pigeonhole you that way."

He sighed. "Cut to the quick. Now you have to say something nice about me to soothe the wound. Do you like my body?"

She studied him. "Yes, I like it." He looked hard, totally masculine. He was without an ounce of fat and far more muscular than she'd dreamed. A patch of dark hair thatched his chest. "You have nice muscles too."

"Touch me."

She didn't move.

"Touch me," he repeated. "I'm going to touch you. Everywhere. Every place. Tonight. Tomorrow." He took her hand and put it on his chest. "Every time I get the chance. Not around Barry, but whenever else the opportunity presents itself. I'm going to pet you and nuzzle you and enjoy the hell out of it." He rubbed her palm up and down on his chest. "And hope that you'll enjoy it too."

"I'm not used to being fondled."

"All the more reason. So you'll have to bloody my nose to keep me from doing it." He guided her hand down to the tight muscles of his stomach. "And even then I'd still be thinking about how it would be to do it, and you'd know exactly what was on my mind. Do you like the feel of me?"

Her hand was tingling as he rubbed it against him, and her breathing was becoming shallow. She closed her eyes. "Yes."

"Yes," he repeated softly as he moved her hand again. "How I love that word. . . ."

Galen waited until the screen door closed behind Elena before he went into the barn.

Judd was without a shirt, dousing his head under the water running from a pump. He scowled as he looked up. "No more favors."

"How is she doing?"

"Too good." He toweled off his hair. "Better than me. She could have downed me twice today but didn't. Do you realize how humiliating that is?"

"You'll survive. She's sharp?"

Judd nodded. "She's ready. I'll give her one more session and cut her loose." He paused. "But can she take Chavez?"

"That's the question. I called Manero and had him do a little in-depth questioning of a few of the survivors of Chavez's little games. There weren't many, and they survived only because Chavez grew bored with them. He's very, very good."

"She's waiting for him. You could go after him yourself."

"I've been thinking about it."

"Not too hard." He grinned. "You've been a little busy for the last week."

"Shut up."

"Whatever you say." He reached for his shirt. "Hey, I'm glad you got lucky."

Galen ignored the comment. "Don't cut her loose yet."

"Why not?"

"I want you to keep her occupied for as long as possible. She's thinking, planning, and I'd bet she's trying to get a scenario together that would protect Barry and Dominic and still give her the result she needs."

"Has she talked about it?"

"No."

Judd's eyes twinkled. "Not even in the wee, intimate hours of the night?"

"That's not what we talk about."

"Astronomy, great literature, cloning?"

"Don't cut her loose, okay?"

"I'm taking some punishment."

"Four more days."

"She may decide herself to cut the sessions off." He started buttoning his shirt. "Or maybe not. I've noticed she's pretty distracted around you these days."

Distracted. Funny that Judd had used that word. No, not funny at all. "She won't cut short any preparation available to her. Not when it concerns Barry."

"Then I'm in the driver's seat." He pretended to think. "Now, what prize can I ask in return . . . ?"

"Judd."

"Okay. Four more days." Judd tucked his shirt into his jeans. "But I'm going to be far too exhausted to do any of the cleanup around here."

"Thanks, Judd." Galen left the barn and headed for the house. He had bought a little time, but he didn't know how much. Elena was definitely not predictable.

Hell, and nothing about his relationship with her was predictable. He felt as if he were trying to walk on water and at any moment he could plunge in over his head.

But, God, it was worth it.

"We're getting close," Gomez said. "We've uncovered the paperwork on a house Galen owns in New

Orleans. We checked it out and he wasn't there, but we were able to pinpoint the man who buried the paperwork. Samuel Destin, an attorney. If he did the work on that property, then he may have done the same on another. If he didn't, he may know who did."

"Have you located Destin?" Chavez asked.

"He's in Antigua. We're on our way."

"Be very persuasive, Gomez."

"He's there with his wife and little boy. We don't anticipate any trouble." Gomez hung up.

Yes, it was often easier to use the wife and children of a target to gain information, Chavez thought. He had done it himself on many occasions.

Destin had a son.

He felt a sudden surge of anger. He also had a son, but he'd had no opportunity to teach and guide him as Destin had. It must be the ultimate thrill to mold a human being in your own image.

His son . . .

She couldn't take her gaze off Galen's hands as he poured the coffee. Powerful hands, nails cut short, the fingers long and graceful and capable. She felt the heat move through her as she remembered how capable.

"Dessert?" Galen asked.

She looked up to see him smiling at her. Bastard. He knew exactly what she was thinking. "No, thank you."

"Sure? It's apple pie. Barry cut the dough for the crust."

She smiled at her son. "Then I'll have to try it."

"I'll help." Barry jumped off the chair and ran after Galen into the kitchen.

She heard them laughing and chattering.

"He likes Galen." Dominic paused. "But not as much as you do."

She stiffened. She had been waiting for him to make a comment. He knew her too well not to realize what was going on between her and Galen. He would have had to be blind, she thought ruefully. Galen had never made any physical move toward her in anyone else's presence, but he had kept his promise. He never lost an opportunity to touch her, and she had moved from wariness to anticipation. Admit it: not anticipation, lust. Her whole body readied when he walked in the room.

"Don't look so apprehensive," Dominic said. "I'm not judging you. I know what kind of hell you've been through. If Galen helps, I'll be grateful to him." He hesitated. "But I admit I'm worried. You really know very little about him. He's a complicated man and not the most stable."

She knew what an understatement that was. "I'm not looking for a lifetime commitment, Dominic. I may never see him after we leave here."

He still looked troubled. "Forgive me. It's none of my business."

"Yes, it is." She reached over and covered his hand with her own. "We're family."

He smiled. "We are, aren't we?" He returned the

pressure of her hand before releasing it. "Did I tell you Barry has a new tune he wants to play for you on the keyboard?"

"Jesus." Galen rolled over, bringing her with him. His breathing was labored as he fought for air. "Or should . . . I say, eureka."

Oh, God, she was shaking. Elena's fingers dug into his shoulders. "Don't talk."

"Have to talk—happy." He hugged her close. "Am I damn good or what?"

"Don't flatter yourself," she said unevenly. "It's just an orgasm."

"It's a home run, a touchdown, a first million on Wall Street."

"And you're giddy as a loon."

"Yep." He hugged her close. "See, it didn't take so long. Nothing wrong with you that Galen couldn't fix."

"The master problem-solver." Her smile faded. "Challenge met. Problem solved."

"No way." He snuggled her closer to him. "Just a giant step. It's going to take a long, long time to perfect the process."

How long? she wondered suddenly.

You really know very little about him.

Yet she felt as if she did know him. She knew his body and his wit. She had laughed with him and shared danger. But she knew what Dominic meant. Did you ever know anyone until you knew what made him what he was?

He lifted his head. "What's wrong?"

As usual, he had sensed what she was feeling. "What could be wrong?"

"Tell me."

She looked away from him. "It might be nice to know a little more about the man who gave me my first orgasm."

"Nah, mystery men are always more sexy." He studied her. "You mean it."

"I realize I have no right to pry into your—"

"Shut up," he said roughly. "You want to know something. Pry."

"Why do you do this kind of work? You seem to have plenty of money. Why take the chances?"

"It's what I do. I get bored. I tried to quit a few years ago and nearly went bananas. I have no calling. I can't paint pictures like Judd. I'm just a provider and a problem-solver."

"You get restless."

"Did you ever consider that you might too?"

She shook her head. "I have an anchor. I have Barry."

"I envy you." He added lightly, "As my mum used to say, there's nothing better than a steadying influence."

"Did she?"

His smile faded. "No, I never knew my mother. I grew up in an orphanage. They found me in a cardboard box in an alley."

She gazed at him, shocked. "Then all those pithy little quotes are lies? Why?"

He shrugged. "It started when I was a teenager. I

think I was drunk at the time. The irony appealed to me. Putting all those homey bits of wisdom in the mouth of a woman who didn't give a damn for me . . . Later it just got to be a habit."

"You don't know what she was facing. Maybe she had to give you up."

"No."

"I almost gave up Barry."

"Did you drop a newborn baby in an alley when the temperature was below freezing?"

"She did that?"

"Oh, yes. She obviously wanted me to die. But I fooled her. I became the healthiest, meanest little son of a bitch that ever came out of Liverpool." He sighed. "And now I'll never be able to quote my dear old mum to you again. It's going to put a crimp in my conversation."

"I'm glad. I don't want to hear about her." She wrapped the sheet around her and stood beside the bed. "Unless you want to name that price we talked about."

"Price?"

"I told you I'd do anything you wanted me to do. I wouldn't mind killing your dear old mum."

"My God, you're furious." He laughed. "I should have known you'd go all soft and sentimental over the thought of a wee babe out in the cold."

"Don't be ridiculous. I'm *not* soft."

"I know." He took her hand and brought it to his lips. "That's what makes this such a golden moment."

She felt a melting deep inside. "Damn you."

He turned her hand over and kissed the palm. "And we've had a good many golden moments, haven't we?"

"A few."

"Damned with faint praise." His eyes were twinkling as he looked up at her. "Come back to bed before you start calling me an asshole again."

"It's time I went to my own room."

"Just a little while," he coaxed. "No sex, just cuddling."

She hesitated, then lay back down.

His arms enfolded her. "This is good," he whispered. "Would you really have put down dear old mum for me? Now, I think that's caring."

"Be quiet." She nestled her cheek in the hollow of his shoulder. "It was only a fleeting impulse. Even as an infant you probably deserved to be thrown out in the cold."

"Stung again." He stroked her hair. "I don't like the idea of you charging out to defend me anyway. It offends my sense of gallantry." He paused. "I'd be happier taking the initiative myself."

"With your mum?"

"No, with Chavez."

She stiffened.

"Shh." His hand moved to massage the taut muscles of her nape. "I don't like to talk about it either. But I don't want you making a move without our discussing it."

"What's to discuss?"

"You know it's only a matter of time until Chavez appears."

"You said you'd be told when that was likely to happen."

"I will. But why wait like sitting ducks? Why not let me go hunting and take Chavez down?"

"No!"

"Why not? It's the sensible thing to do. It will keep any fight with Chavez away from you and Barry." He paused. "You were planning on leading him away from Barry, weren't you?"

"I didn't say that."

"It's much more reasonable to let me do it before he even has an inkling where you are. Then, if he takes me down, you and Barry still have a chance to run."

"It appears I'm not that reasonable." Her voice was uneven. "Or that callous."

"Think about it. I was going to do it without telling you, but it's safer if we coordinate our strategy and—"

"I'm not going to think about it. This is my life and my fight."

"What about Barry?"

"I'll protect Barry. I'd never risk him. I'll find a way to do both."

He was silent a moment. "I can do this, Elena. I'm very, very good. Stay with Barry and let me take care of Chavez."

"Do you think I don't want to say yes?" she asked fiercely. "I want him dead. It shouldn't make any difference to me who kills him. But it does, dammit. It does."

"Why?"

"Because I— It does."

"Clear." He chuckled. "Could it be you're beginning to care a bit for me? Yes, that must be it."

"Why would I care anything about an asshole like you?"

"Well, it might be because you sense that I'm willing to throw my heart out on the ground and let you trample on it."

"Stop joking."

"Who's joking?" He brushed her temple with a kiss. "It's a surprise to me too, but I find I'm bloody helpless around you. I feel like a mooning kid again. But don't let it worry you. I'm a very patient bloke and I know you have a few problems to work out."

"Don't let it worry me? How generous of you. But you tell me that—"

"I thought you should know. I don't know where it's going to go or how far it's going to take us, but I don't believe in holding things back."

"Particularly when you want to run out and get yourself killed."

"That wasn't my intention. I'm not into last hurrahs. I was merely—"

"I don't want to talk anymore." Her arms tightened around him. "And I'm tired of cuddling."

"Sex? Glad to oblige." He rolled her over. "Even when it's a form of escape, sex is good." He smiled down at her. "But I have to warn you, there's going to come a time when I'm going to call it something else."

———

He was asleep.

Elena carefully moved Galen's arm from around her shoulders and slipped out of bed.

She paused a moment, gazing down at him. He was sprawled on his side, and yet he still possessed that catlike grace even in sleep. Most people appeared defenseless when sleeping, but Galen didn't. He looked as if he was only resting, waiting for the opening bell so he could spring up and once again enter the fray.

Stop looking at him. Get out of here. Tonight he had confused and frightened her. She had been so absorbed in pleasure that she hadn't thought of anything beyond sex; she didn't believe Galen had either.

Or, if he had, she supposed he was thinking about "solving her problem." Maybe whatever Galen felt for her was impossible to separate from the effort he'd put into helping her. In six months he'd probably be involved in another project and forget she existed.

And what about how she felt about him? She instantly shied away from that thought. She wouldn't allow herself to feel this softness whenever she was around him. She had Barry and Dominic, and they were more than enough hostages to fortune. She was weakening too much already. If she hadn't been weak, she would have let him go after Chavez. No one was more important than Barry, and it made no difference who killed Chavez.

But she hadn't been able to let Galen go on the hunt.

Which meant it was getting close to the time she must go on the hunt herself.

"Your helicopter pilot, Carmichael, is dead," Manero said. "And it wasn't easy. If he knew anything you didn't want Chavez to know, then you'd better regroup."

"He didn't," Galen said. "Chavez was bound to have found out it was me who snatched Elena and Barry. When did it happen?"

"I'm not sure. Maybe four weeks. He was in Rio before he disappeared. They just found the body in a village outside the city."

Four weeks. Then Chavez had definitely had time to get a massive search under way for Galen. He'd hoped for more notice. "Chavez is still in Colombia?"

"Sitting like a fat cat on the top of his hill. I told you I'd let you know when he made a move."

"Okay, okay." He had thought about this eventuality and it was time to run a check. "There are a few people who could tell him where I might be located. John Logan, Sam Destin, and Paul Russell. I need to know where they are and if they're having any problems. Tell them about Chavez. Warn Destin and Russell they'd better go underground for a while. Logan can take care of himself. They probably won't touch him."

"I usually don't work outside South America. A man has to have his specialty."

"But you have contacts everywhere. I don't have time to get anyone else. I'll pay double."

"Why didn't you contact Destin and Russell before?"

"With enough money, even honest men can be bought. I didn't want them to have time to think about selling me out."

"I like money too."

"But you're an honest man in your way. Bad for you, good for me."

Manero sighed. "Double?"

"Double."

"Give me the background info."

"You know about Logan. Paul Russell buried the paperwork on this place. Sam Destin referred him to me. Destin lives in New Orleans. Russell's home base is San Francisco. Destin won't be difficult to find, but Russell's in trouble with the IRS and he floats around. You can usually reach him through his mother, Clara Russell. She works for Macy's."

"Right. I'm on it."

"Thanks, Manero." He hung up.

Shit. He had liked Carmichael. Galen had warned him to get out of South America when Carmichael dropped them in Medellín. Why the hell had he settled in Rio? He should have— Stop thinking about him. Carmichael had known what he was getting into when he took the job. He had realized how powerful Chavez was in South America and had made a mistake and paid for it. This wasn't the time for Galen to dwell on Carmichael's mistakes. He had to be sure not to make any of his own.

Time was running out.

It might have run out already.

"Problems?"

He turned to see Elena standing in the doorway. "Not yet." He stood up. "Come and help me make dinner. Barry's deserted me since Dominic's been teaching him to play that keyboard. Just can't get reliable help these days."

"You're holding something back."

"Carmichael's dead, presumably killed by Gomez." He started for the kitchen. "But he didn't know anything important. We're still safe."

"Chavez?"

"Still in Colombia. Like this apron? Judd bought it in town." He tied on a gaudy green apron with dancing red chili peppers wearing ballet tutus and blue tennis shoes. "He thinks I won't wear it."

"It's perfectly ridiculous."

"Yep, but I don't feel threatened. My masculinity overcomes any challenge. Besides, it makes me smile." He took out a frying pan. "I need a smile now. I liked Carmichael."

"I'm sorry. Was he a good friend?"

"No. But I'd known him for a long time."

She was silent a moment. "He's dead because of me."

"He's dead because he didn't get the hell out of Dodge. You shouldn't feel guilty."

"I do feel guilty." She stared directly into his eyes. "But it wouldn't stop me from doing it again. I can't worry about anyone but Barry. I can't let anything else matter."

"You're not talking about Carmichael. I scared you last night, didn't I? I knew I would." He got a paring knife out of the drawer. "Get those red potatoes out of the bin, will you?"

"Are you listening to me?"

"Of course I am. You're scared you may feel something for me and you're warning me that you might have to sacrifice me on Barry's altar." He got the potatoes himself. "It doesn't matter. I've known that all along. We'll get through it. Barry has the edge, but give me another six months and you'll be surprised what inroads I'll make."

"Galen, I don't want—"

"You're going to say we shouldn't sleep together again. Don't be hasty. You like sex these days. You like me. I won't be discouraged no matter how far you distance yourself, so we might as well enjoy. Right?"

"Wrong."

"Okay, I'll compromise. Just until we hear Chavez is on the move."

"It's not fair."

"You're worried about my tender feelings?" He grinned. "No problem. Maybe I'll get tired of you. You know how restless I am."

She was silent for a moment and then smiled with an effort. "You really do look ridiculous in that apron."

"Just for that you can peel the potatoes." He handed her the paring knife. "Sit over there at the table where I can watch you."

"You don't trust me to do it right?"

"It's not that," he said quietly. "It just makes me feel good to look over and see you. It . . . warms me."

"Damn you, Galen."

"Don't get all misty. Can't help it. My mum always said I was an optimist who—oops."

"Oops, indeed."

"It's going to be difficult not relying on old Mum."

"Who knew you were an optimist."

He nodded. "And that I believed in enjoying the moment. So sit over there and let me enjoy this one. Okay?"

She gazed at him with a multitude of expressions flitting over her face before she slowly moved over and sat down in the chair he'd indicated. "Bring me those potatoes."

Chapter Nine

"Mrs. Russell?"

"What is it?" Clara looked over her shoulder at the two men who'd appeared from beneath the staircase. Her hand tightened on the keys she'd gotten out to unlock the door of her apartment, her fingers moving to the pepper spray on the key chain. Her son had given it to her six months ago and told her to use it if she had any trouble. Paul was always worried about her working nights in the city with all those creeps around. These men didn't look like creeps. She knew expensive suits when she saw them. She had worked in Menswear at Macy's for years before they transferred her to Shoes. They didn't look like IRS either. They were too . . . slick. Both were dark-haired and swarthy. Maybe Mexicans. The Mexicans seemed to be taking over California. "What do you want?"

"May we come in?"

"No. Who are you?"

"Carlos Gomez." He smiled. "I need to see your son."

Maybe they *were* IRS. She stiffened. "I don't know where he is. I haven't seen him in years."

"I don't think that's true. We need to talk."

"No, we don't. Find him yourself."

Gomez took a step closer. "You're being uncooperative. That's not very smart."

"Get the hell out of here." She raised the pepper spray. "I don't want you—" She gasped as Gomez ducked to one side and closed his hand on her wrist, numbing it. The key ring fell to the floor. "Get the keys. Open the door," Gomez said to the smaller man as his other hand covered Clara's mouth. "Quick."

She struggled, her foot lashing out and connecting with Gomez's shin. She heard him grunt as her teeth bit down on his hand.

"Shit." He pushed her inside the apartment and slammed the door. "Bitch." He punched her in the stomach and then backhanded her across the face.

The pain. She couldn't breathe. She sank to her knees, gasping. She could see him towering over her through a dark haze.

Gomez smiled. "Now, let's begin again. I need to see your son."

"We need to talk, Galen." Judd Morgan was standing in the door of the library. "Got a minute?"

Galen nodded and tossed his book aside. "What's wrong?"

"It's been several months and Logan hasn't been able to get the agency off my back."

"He'll do it."

"But how long will I have to wait? I like your ranch, but I don't relish feeling like a prisoner while those bastards in Washington are running around free. I'm tired of waiting. It's time I did something on my own."

"What?"

"I'm thinking." He smiled crookedly. "When I decide, you'll be the first to know. I'm not whining. I just wanted you to know I'm not your problem any longer." He turned and started toward the door. "Is it okay with you if I stick around here until I've made up my mind?"

Galen nodded his head.

"Good," Judd said gravely. "Because I can't wait to see you in that apron again. Did I tell you how cute you looked?"

"Destin, his wife, and their child are dead," Manero said. "Destin's car went off the road into the ocean in Antigua."

"When?"

"Yesterday. Suspicious circumstances. I have a man in San Francisco on the way to contact Clara Russell. She didn't answer her phone."

"Contact, hell. Get her out of there. Tell him to hurry." He hung up the phone. It might be too late already. He'd only met Clara Russell once, but he got the impression of a tough, hardworking, home-loving woman who was a little too loyal to her son for her own good.

It had been only one day since Destin died. But Chavez's men would move fast. Chavez was behind them, goading them on.

They were getting too close to Elena. He had to sit down and run through the possible scenarios to see if he could find a solution.

"The woman phoned Paul Russell," Gomez told Chavez. "We're supposed to meet with him in two hours. She was very convincing. He won't be suspicious."

"It took you a long time to break her," Chavez said.

"Seven hours. She was very stubborn. Mothers usually are, aren't they?"

"Yes, indeed," he said with a note of irritation. "Let's hope her son won't be as obstinate. I'm getting impatient."

"I'll be calling you back within five hours." He hung up.

Five hours. Excitement began to course through Chavez. In a short time he'd have the information he needed to find his son.

And that bitch who had stolen him.

"Chavez is on the move," Manero said. "He left Colombia in his private jet two hours ago."

"Jesus." Galen had known it was coming, but the news still exploded like a thunderbolt. "Clara Russell?"

"My guy just found her in her apartment. He wished he hadn't. Messy. I don't know anyone who would have withstood that kind of punishment without spilling everything they knew. What do you want me to do now?"

"I'll get back to you." He hung up and got to his feet. They had to move. Now.

He took the steps two at a time. "Elena!"

She looked up from the book she was reading with Barry. "What is—" She stopped as she read his expression. "It's happened?"

He took a step nearer and knelt by Barry. "Time to have another adventure. Want to camp out in the hills?"

Barry's eyes lit up. "Really?"

"Really." Galen swatted him on the butt. "Now, go and tell Dominic. We're all going."

Elena rose to her feet as Barry ran out of the room. "How much time do we have?"

"I'm not sure. Chavez left Colombia two hours ago, but Gomez is ahead of him. At any rate, we're out of here. Better pack quick."

She went to the closet. "I'm almost packed." She took out her duffel and reached up and got her gun from the top shelf. She tucked it into the duffel. "Now I'm completely packed."

"That's what I like. A woman who's always ready," Galen said. "I suppose I should have expected it of you."

"Yes, you should."

"But I ask myself if you were ready for an emergency exit or if you were planning on taking off on your own."

"One reason is as good as another."

"No, it isn't." His lips tightened. "But we'll let it go for now. Get Barry and Dominic. I'll go tell Judd we all have to get on the road."

"He's coming with us?"

"Would you rather leave him for Chavez? He'd enjoy questioning him; it would be a real challenge trying to break someone like Judd."

"Yes." She started toward the door. "But he'd enjoy breaking you more. Remember that."

Judd was shoving his cases into the bed of the pickup but looked up as Elena and Galen came out of the house. "I'm going to run my dog and the kittens over to your nearest neighbor and ask him to keep them for a while. Have to take care of the pets with company coming." He carefully stored the box with the three kittens on the floor before whistling for his German shepherd. Mac jumped into the cab and Judd started the ignition. "I'll meet you at the camp."

Galen nodded absently as Judd drove away.

Elena barely heard Judd as she threw Barry's keyboard into the trunk of the car. "You're absolutely sure he's on his way?"

"I'm sure. Gomez left a trail of bodies behind

him to find this place, and Chavez left Colombia a couple hours ago. It's reasonable to assume he found out what he wanted to know."

"He's coming. . . ." She stared at the mountains. Chavez would soon be here, coming down that road. From the moment Galen told her about Chavez she had felt numb, frozen. She'd waited for this moment for six years, and now that it was here she was almost in shock. And she was feeling fear, she realized. She hadn't expected to be afraid. She had thought the hatred would be violent enough to overcome any fear. Yet memory of that other time was weakening her. Block it out. Fear was the enemy. Chavez would feed on it. Don't give him the chance.

"Elena."

Her glance shifted to Galen's face. "Do you have any explosives?"

He smiled. "You're thinking of blowing up my house with Chavez in it?"

"Yes."

"I don't have any explosives. It's not something I keep on hand when I'm here. So my house is safe from you."

"I would have found a way to pay you for it."

"I was joking. But I can see your sense of humor is seriously impaired at the moment."

"Are we really camping out?"

"For a little while. I know those hills, and there are a hundred little pockets for us to hide in. I sent Judd up a few days ago to set up a camp where we would be safe and could still observe the ranch.

I don't think Chavez will suspect we're sticking around. He's too used to people running from him. I want to make sure Chavez is really here."

"So do I." She looked back at the hills. "So do I. . . ."

"They're not here?" Chavez got out of the car in front of the ranch house. "What do you mean they're not here? You've failed me, Gomez."

"They were here. There's fresh food in the refrigerator. Clothes in the closets." Gomez held out a children's book. "This was in one of the bedrooms."

"But they're gone. She got away again?"

"We checked the barn and the entire area around the house."

"*Damn* you."

Gomez took a hurried step back. "He must have been tipped off."

"You said that about the vineyard. It was because you didn't move fast enough." He looked up at the hills. "Search the foothills."

"They wouldn't stay here if they knew we were coming. They're probably halfway to Portland by now."

"Search anyway. She was a guerrilla. She'd be comfortable in the hills."

"We'll have to wait until tomorrow morning. It's getting dark. The men I have here aren't trackers. They'll only blunder around. We'll need the daylight."

Chavez's hands clenched. "Daybreak. I want every man out there by first light." He turned to look at the hills.

Are you there, Elena? I'm coming for you, bitch.

He turned toward the house. "I'm going to go through Galen's personal papers and see if I can come up with anything. Did you check for booby traps?"

Gomez nodded. "It's safe."

"Safety is a very fragile thing." He started up the porch steps. "You might keep that in mind, Gomez."

"A tall, muscular man, not bad-looking, gray at his temples." Galen adjusted the powerful binoculars. "Is that Chavez?"

"It sounds like him," Elena said. "Let me have the binoculars." She slowly lifted them to her eyes. Jesus, she didn't want to see him again. She forced herself to look at the man standing on the porch.

Power. Strength. Cruelty.

The mat.

She hurriedly lowered the binoculars. "That's him."

"Then you were right: Barry did draw him here," Galen said. "I wasn't sure a selfish bastard like him would actually come after the kid."

"I was sure. Coming after him was all about self-ishness. He wants to play God." Her lips tightened. "Not with my Barry."

"Easy." His hand clasped her shoulder. "Your muscles are in knots."

"How do you expect me to feel?" She drew a deep breath. "When are we going to leave here?"

"Tomorrow morning." He lifted the binoculars to his eyes again. "I count eight men in those two cars. They seem to be settling down at the house for the night. Remind me to burn the bedsheets when we return. Come on, let's go back to camp." He started down the slope. "I'll check on them again later."

She took one more glance at the ranch house before she slowly followed him back to the encampment.

Barry was sitting beside Judd Morgan. "Judd's teaching me how to whittle, Mama. Did you see his big knife?"

She had a memory of that switchblade pressed against Galen's throat. "Yes, I've seen it."

Judd smiled. "I won't let him use it. That's advanced play." He glanced at Galen. "See anything interesting?"

"What I expected to see. There are a few animals out there. Nothing to worry about, but it wouldn't hurt for us to take turns on guard."

"I'll take first watch," Elena said.

"I wasn't going to insult you by leaving you out of it," Galen said. "But you take second watch. That way you can get Barry to sleep first." He went over to the cave. "I don't think we'll light a fire tonight, so I'll have to see what I can come up with in the way of cold rations. I'm sure I can concoct something perfectly splendid."

————

Galen's digital phone rang as they were finishing up the meal.

"Where are you, Galen?" A deep voice, heavily accented.

Galen tensed. "Chavez?"

Elena's gaze flew to his face.

"Yes, I'm getting impatient. I want my son. Give him to me."

"Screw you." He got up and moved out of the cave and beyond Barry's hearing. "You don't have a son. He belongs to Elena. It's going to stay that way."

"It won't stay that way." He paused. "I was very angry at your interference and I wanted you punished. But I'm a reasonable man and I know how to cut my losses. I'm willing to pay to have my son turned over to me. Five million dollars. You set up the terms of the drop-off."

"No way."

"Ten million."

"We're not trading, Chavez."

"I'll go higher."

"And you'll get the same answer."

"The bitch isn't that good a lay."

"I'm terminating this conversation."

"Think about it. I'll give you my phone number."

Smother the anger. They might be able to use it. He took out his pen and pad. "What is it?"

Chavez rattled off a number. "Be reasonable. I'll get him anyway. If you hand him over, you become a very rich man."

"No deal." He hung up.

"What did he want?"

He turned to see Elena and Judd standing behind him.

"What he's wanted all along. Only he offered to pay for him." His lips twisted. "The last offer was ten million, but he would have gone higher."

Judd gave a low whistle. "That's impressive money. It would cause a lot of men to turn traitor. You may have a tough time keeping the kid if he's spreading that kind of money around."

"You took his phone number down," Elena said to Galen.

"Oh, for God's sake, I thought we might need it. Did you think I was hedging my bets?"

"No." She looked away. "I don't know what to think."

But she had doubted him for that moment. What else could he expect? From the moment she had learned Chavez was on his way, she had changed. She had gone back into the battle mode she had learned from childhood—wary, tense, trusting no one.

It hurt, dammit. "No, I'm not going to take the damn money."

Judd glanced from one to the other and changed the subject. "Who takes first watch?"

"I do," Galen said curtly. "I need some space."

He walked away.

Elena could see only one guard circling the house.

She crawled slowly, silently, grasping the rifle with her left hand.

There wasn't much brush in this level meadow-land, and she had to keep low and move with pains-taking care.

The lights in the office were burning. Chavez was probably trying to find a way to trace them.

Once she reached the barn, it would shelter her until she had a look around. She would have to take out the first guard, and she'd already spotted an-other man at the corral. If she took him out too, then she might be able to get to the house.

Her gaze was fixed on the window of the study as she crawled forward.

I'm coming, Chavez. Do you feel it?

She could imagine him in her sights, sitting at the desk shuffling papers. No, don't think about it. Just do it. She had to distance herself, as her father had taught her. Just do the job and the—

A heavy weight dropped on her.

She struggled over onto her back, reaching for her pistol.

"No," Galen whispered, pinning her down. "You shoot me and Chavez's men will all run out here, and Barry won't have a mother. Is that what you want?"

She froze. "What are you doing?"

"I'm trying to stop you from getting yourself killed."

"Get off me. I'm not going to get myself killed. I know how to do this. My father sent me out to—"

"You've told me. But that doesn't mean you can take down Chavez when he's being guarded by fif-teen men."

"There are only eight men."

"That's what I thought. The others must have arrived after dark. Where were you headed? The study? There's a man around the corner and one inside with Chavez. They're all over the place, and they're pretty good. I almost got caught when I was scouting the area."

"Scouting? When?"

"When I was supposed to be on watch. Do you suppose you're the only one who hoped we could end this thing with one bullet? It's no good, Elena. I was going to tell you the chances were nil, but when I came back to camp you'd already left."

"Let me go."

"Not until you tell me you'll go back to camp."

"The only thing I'll tell you is that if you don't get off me, I'm going to break your ribs and then crush your nuts."

"Oh." He studied her face for a moment. "What a persuasive woman you are." He released her. "Now what?"

"We go back to camp. I'm not stupid." She turned and started crawling across the meadow. "But don't you ever strong-arm me again, Galen."

"It seemed the only way to catch your attention. Now I suggest we shut up until we get back to the hills."

It was several hundred yards before they came to the first straggly trees that signaled the start of the foothills. Galen pulled her to her feet. "Where did you get that rifle?"

"I took it from Judd's truck. I thought he'd have one. I wasn't sure I could get close enough to use my thirty-eight."

"You were planning this ever since you knew we were staying here tonight."

"Evidently you were too. I was wondering why you didn't want to leave the minute you found out Chavez was really here."

"And I knew you'd jump at any chance to get to Chavez. I wanted to beat you to it." His lips twisted. "We think too much alike. Like Forbes said, the private club."

"Privacy isn't a bad thing," Judd said as he stepped out of the trees. He held out his hand to Elena. "My property, please."

She handed him the rifle. "Sorry. I needed it."

"You could have asked."

"Would you have loaned it to me?"

"No." His hand moved caressingly over the barrel. "I have a very special relationship with this rifle."

"It's a Heckler and Koch PSG1, right? Specially modified?"

"Yes."

"I didn't think you would lend it to me. That's why I didn't ask you."

"Makes sense. But don't do it again or you'll regret it. I don't give second warnings." He turned and strode ahead of them in the direction of their camp.

"He meant it," Galen said. "That rifle has been part of him for a long time."

"I needed a rifle. And I'd do it again. But it

didn't do me any good anyway. I was hoping . . ." She shrugged. "It didn't happen. So we might as well pull up stakes and head out. I want to get Barry somewhere safe."

"He won't be safe anywhere now, Elena."

She knew that was true. Now that Chavez was here in the United States, it would be only a matter of time until he found them. "Safer. Do you have any suggestions?"

"He's probably been tipped off about my place in New Orleans. I have an idea of a place that might work for us, but I don't want to involve any of my friends directly, because it's going to get nasty."

"Where are we going?"

"You're going to leave it up to me? Amazing." His tone was faintly sarcastic.

"I'm a stranger in this country."

"You seem to want to do everything else on your own."

She whirled on him. "What do you want me to say? I did what I had to do."

"And you did it alone," he said through his teeth. "You couldn't ask for help. You couldn't ask me to go with you."

"I'm not used to asking for help."

"That's pretty clear. What have I got to do to get through to you?" He grasped her shoulders and shook her. "You are *not* alone. Do you hear me? Let me help. You're not alone."

He didn't understand. There had been moments since they left the ranch when she'd been too terri-fied to think. She had been alone too long, and she was afraid to act except in the way experience had taught her.

"*Trust* me, Elena."

"I trust you."

"Not enough. Not enough to break through that glacier you've had around you since Chavez appeared on the scene."

She stared at him helplessly.

He shook his head and his hands loosened. "Lost cause."

"I'm . . . sorry."

"Me too. It's going to make everything a hell of a lot harder." He checked his watch. "I have to make a few phone calls and see what I can do about finding a safe haven. I've already set tentative plans in motion in case this happened. There's a small airport near here where we can get a hop to Portland and then a jet from there." His lips twisted. "After all, I have to live up to my reputation as the great provider."

She had hurt him. He was being flip, but the pain was there. She wanted to reach out and comfort him as she did Barry, but she couldn't seem to move. "Thank you. I know it's difficult for—"

"For God's sake, shut up." He drew a deep breath and tried to temper his tone. "We'll let everyone sleep for another hour or two while I make sure we have a place to go."

"You didn't tell me where we're going."

He turned away. "Atlanta."

Chapter Ten

THE COTTAGE ON THE LAKE WAS RUSTIC BUT SPACIOUS, and the surroundings were absolutely beautiful, Elena thought. The hills and woods and the lake itself were spectacular.

"Hey, come back here."

She turned to see Judd running after Barry as he streaked toward the lake. "Barry!"

"I've got him." Judd scooped Barry up and tucked the giggling child under his arm. "Come on, brat. If you're so set on jumping in the lake, I'll see if I can find something you can wear for a swimsuit. Does he swim, Elena?"

"Like a fish," Dominic said. "I taught him in the creek a short distance from our house."

"Then you'd better come along and keep him in line," Judd said as he set Barry down and started unloading the car.

Judd seemed to be doing a good job, Elena thought. He'd kept Barry cheerful and busy on the long cross-country flight that brought them here. In fact, it surprised her that such a solitary man as Judd had made so much effort to care for Barry.

He looked up and caught her gaze. "I like kids," he said quietly, as if he had read her mind. He took a duffel and grabbed Barry's hand. "Come on, let's get you unpacked."

She turned to Galen. "Whose house is this?"

"Joe Quinn. He and Eve Duncan took their kid to Hawaii for a couple months. They said I could use the house while they were gone. It's secluded, and I thought Barry would like the lake." He picked up the other two suitcases and closed the trunk. "I'm sure you can't wait to scout around and make sure it's safe, but be back by dinner." He turned toward the house. "I've already contacted David Hughes, who provided the security people I've used before in Atlanta; they'll show up tomorrow morning for you to vet. I wouldn't want you to take one of them down by mistake. Hughes would be most upset. I figure Judd and I can handle the security of the cottage, but we need some good men to patrol the woods and lake. They won't be obtrusive."

"You seem to have thought of everything. Do you have a key to the house?"

"No, but I have a talent." He carried the cases up the steps to the porch, where Barry and Judd were waiting. He tried the door and then knelt before the lock. A few seconds later the door swung open. "Piece of cake. Remind me to tell Quinn that his security sucks." He waved Judd and Barry into the house and then went inside himself.

"Judd is getting along very well with Barry," Dominic said from behind her. "It makes me feel a little useless."

"Don't be silly." She turned to face him. "Judd and Galen are new and different to him. He'll come back to us when the first shine wears off."

"I wasn't complaining. I know it's natural, maybe even healthy. I was just stating a fact. You may not need me any longer. Perhaps I should go home for a while."

"I'll always need you, Dominic." She reached out and grasped his arm. "And there's no home to go back to."

"I could build again. I'm needed there, Elena."

A surge of fear went through her as she realized he was serious. "It's not safe. What if Chavez has a watch on the area?"

"That's not likely."

"I don't want to take the chance. Not with you, Dominic." She stepped closer and laid her head on his chest. She whispered, "I don't know what I'd do without you. You and Barry are my family."

"I'm not going to run out on you yet, and I'm not talking about leaving you permanently. You and Barry mean too much to me." He gently patted her shoulder. "But I had to tell you what I'm thinking. I can't stay where I don't have a purpose, Elena." He pushed her away. "Now, I'm going to go swimming with Judd and Barry. Why don't you come with us?"

"I'm going to scout the area. I want to be familiar with every cove and tree."

He smiled. "That's what Galen said you'd do. He knows you better than I do."

"No, he doesn't."

He shook his head. "Maybe not in experience, but his instincts are very good. He knows you're obsessed."

"So do you, Dominic. We've been together for so long." She grimaced. "And why are we talking about Galen? You told me we didn't really know him."

"Things are changing." He turned and started for the house. "Chavez is on the other side of the country. It will take him a little while to regroup and send out his search dogs. We probably have some breathing space. Why don't you take a little time off and relax?"

It had taken them only five hours to get to this lovely, peaceful spot. If Chavez found out where they were, he'd be on them like a vulture. "I can't."

He glanced at her over his shoulder. "No, I can see you can't," he said sadly. "It's too bad."

"They're not in the hills," Gomez said. "But the man I sent to scout out the area reports that there's a small airport about eighty miles from here. He's questioning the personnel there now."

"If Galen reached an airport, then we've lost him. He's not going to let himself be traced." Chavez glanced with frustration at the pile of papers on the desk. No leads. Nothing.

"We'll continue to try," Gomez said.

"You're damn right you will," Chavez said. "There's no way I'm giving up. I still have a few cards to play."

He took out his phone and started to dial.

"Mama, look at me, I'm going to dive into the water!"

"I'm watching."

Barry jumped onto the tire Judd had tied to a branch of the oak tree close to the lake. Then Judd pulled the tire back several yards and let it go. The tire swung out over the water, and a whooping Barry jumped from the tire into the lake.

He surfaced, sputtering. "Did you see me?"

"I would have had to be blind not to see you," Elena shouted. "And deaf too."

"I'm going to do it again."

He swam to the edge of the lake and Dominic helped him onto the bank. "Watch me."

"Only a couple more times. It will be dark soon."

But it wasn't dark yet, and the setting sun gilded the water with beauty. Jesus, it was peaceful here. In spite of her tension, she had not been able to ignore the sheer blessed tranquillity of the surroundings during the last three days.

"Pretty." Galen dropped down beside her in the porch swing. "I like porch swings."

"You have a hammock on your porch at the ranch."

"Hammocks are for dozing. Porch swings are

for socializing. I can imagine the two of us sitting
here listening to the birds and the creak of the swing
for the next fifty years or so."

"I can't."

"Because you're too tied up in knots to imagine
anything." He reached out and took her hand. "Don't
stiffen up. I just want to hold your hand. I'm not trying to lure you back into my bed." His thumb rubbed
the pulse point at her inner wrist. "I'm not sure you
wouldn't break into pieces if I made love to you."

"I'm not that weak."

"Heaven forbid I accuse you of that." He started
to play idly with her fingers. "No weakness. You
won't permit it."

"I can't permit it. I can't concentrate on anything but Chavez now." Her gaze shifted back to
Barry in the water. "I was weak all those years ago. I
was so afraid after he finished with me every day. I
was tied up and helpless and I knew he'd be back the
next day and it would start again. I wouldn't let myself cry, but I couldn't stop shaking. The only time I
didn't feel weak was when we were fighting. But I
knew if I let the fear come to the surface then, I'd
die."

"We're all afraid sometimes."

"I can't afford to be now. I have Barry."

"And me." He lifted her wrist to his lips. "Don't
forget me."

There was no danger of her doing that. He was
always there, talking, moving, disturbing her. He
was disturbing her now.

"Your heart's beating faster." He brushed his lips back and forth on her wrist. "I have to point out that sex is known to be a great relaxer."

"But I might break apart on you."

"I'd risk it."

"I can't risk it."

He looked at her. "If I kept on, you'd change your mind."

"Possibly. But I'd resent it."

"I know." He kissed her wrist and then placed it back on her lap. "What a dilemma for a sex-starved man. I suppose we'll just have to sit and swing and think about the next fifty years. Shh," he said as she started to speak. "I said think, not talk. Don't worry. You can't commit if you don't talk."

The creak of the swing was very soothing, and Galen's presence was restful too. He had turned off the sexual charge as if he'd flicked a switch. What an incredibly complicated man he was, she thought. Complicated and perceptive and with a seemingly limitless range of talents and potential. It was an amazing—

Galen's phone rang.

She tensed.

"Easy." He punched the answer button. "Galen."

Elena could feel his muscles tauten. "No way. Talk to me."

"Who is it?" she asked.

"Chavez."

She went cold. "He wants to talk to me?"

He nodded. "But we're not going to give him what he wants. You don't have to talk to him."

"Yes, I do. Give me the phone."

"I can deal with him."

"Give me the phone."

He hesitated and then handed it to her. "Two minutes and then you hang up."

She scarcely heard him. "I'm here, Chavez."

"I need to know where *here* is, Elena. You've been leading me on a chase."

He sounded so close, as if he was only yards, not hundreds of miles, away. He's not close, she told herself. He can't hurt me. He can't hurt Barry or Galen. "Go home, Chavez. You're not going to find us."

"Your voice is shaking, Elena. You're afraid, aren't you?"

"I'm not afraid of you."

"You're lying. I always knew when you were afraid. It always made the contests more interesting. Because you were fighting yourself as well as me. But the fear won out, didn't it? In the end I beat you."

"You didn't beat me."

"Of course I did."

"I pretended, you son of a bitch. And you were so conceited you were fooled."

A silence. "That's not the truth."

"Yes, it is. Can't you tell the truth when you hear it?"

"You *puta*."

"No, you wanted to break me and make me your whore, but I didn't let you. You lost, Chavez."

She could feel his anger vibrating through the

phone. "If you're telling the truth, that only makes me want to find you all the more. We have unfinished business. I'm almost as eager to get my hands on you as I am to find my son. You remember what it felt like to have my hands on you?"

The ropes cutting into her wrists, his hands running over her body. Don't think about it. "I've forgotten. And you'll never get Barry."

"I'm going to change his name. I'll give him mine. Little Rico."

"No."

"Yes. After all, he's my child. I'll be the one who tells him what to do or not do."

Smother the fear and the anger. "Why did you want to talk to me? You don't actually think I'm going to tell you anything."

"I wanted to hear your voice. It brings back such pleasant memories." He paused. "And I have someone here who wants to hear your voice too. I'm giving the phone to him now."

"Elena?"

Oh, my God. She closed her eyes. "Luis."

"You've got to do what he says." Her brother's voice was broken. "I can't stand any more pain. He says he'll kill me."

"Why should I care? You betrayed me, Luis. You told Chavez about Barry."

"I couldn't help it. I was hurting. I needed a hit. Dominic shouldn't have told me. He kept it from me all these years. He shouldn't have told me. I didn't want to do it."

"But you did it. You didn't care about me or Dominic or Barry. All you cared about were those damn drugs." She blinked back tears. "Well, I can't care what happens to you now. I have to worry about the people you served up to Chavez."

"You do care." His voice was desperate. "Remember when we were children? All the good times . . . Help me, Elena."

"By giving up my son? You've got to be crazy."

"I couldn't help what I did. You were always the strong one. You never understood. I can't stand pain, Elena. They'll hurt me."

"I'm sorry, Luis," she whispered. "I can't help you."

"You have to—"

He broke off as Chavez took the phone.

"What a hard woman you are, Elena," Chavez said. "He really sounds pitiful. Doesn't he touch your heart?"

"You might as well let him go." She tried to steady her voice. "What made you think I'd give up Barry for a man who betrayed me? Do you think I have any feeling left for him?"

"I thought it was possible. You're an unusual woman, but surely you have a certain softness for the brother you grew up with. You shared danger and good times. Yes, you probably feel something for him."

"I feel nothing for him."

"Then you won't mind if I toy with him, will you? He's a weakling, but maybe he has a little of

you in him. This may take longer than you think. I'll
have him call you back after I see just how weak he
is." He hung up.

Luis . . .

She thrust the phone at Galen. "He . . . had my
brother talk to me."

"So I heard."

"He's going to hurt him." She tried to keep her
lips from trembling. "I don't care. I don't care anything about him. He deserves it."

"Yes."

"I tried to get him off drugs. I did everything I
could. He wouldn't listen. It's not my fault. . . ."
Tears were running down her cheeks. "I can't do it,
Galen. I can't help him."

"I know." He pulled her into his arms. "Shh, I
know."

"You don't know." Her hands clenched his shirt.
"I cared about him. I think I still care about him. I
don't want to, but he made me remember—"

"What's wrong?" Dominic was frowning as he
climbed the porch steps. "What's happened, Elena?"

"Luis . . ." She pushed Galen away and wiped
her eyes with the backs of her hands. "Chavez has
Luis with him, Dominic."

He stopped in shock. "Luis."

"He's going to hurt him."

It took Dominic a moment to recover. "But Luis
helped him." He shook his head as if to clear it.
"That won't make any difference, will it? Sometimes
I forget how evil Chavez is."

"I don't."

"Can we save him?"

"Not without giving up Barry. And you know I can't do that."

"There has to be something you can do."

"He's using Luis to bait a trap. He wants Elena as well as Barry," Galen said. "If she tries to go after Luis, he'll snap the trap. Besides, we don't even know where he is."

"Could he still be at the ranch?"

Galen shook his head. "I called the DEA as soon as we got to the airport and told them where Chavez could be located. He'd left the ranch by the time they got there."

"You didn't tell me that," Elena said.

"The DEA wasn't as good as a bullet, but I thought they might buy us time until he bought his way out of jail."

"You should have told me."

"Why should I give you bad news? I hoped we'd get lucky."

"Too much to ask."

"Is Chavez going to call back?" Dominic asked.

"Yes." Elena rose to her feet. "I'm going down to the lake to Barry. I need to . . ." She wanted to be close to Barry, to touch him.

She hurried down the steps and down the path.

"I want to roast Chavez over a slow fire," Galen said as his gaze followed Elena. "How close were she and Luis?"

"Very close as children. It was the two of them

against the world. Later they grew apart. Her father openly favored Elena, and that hurt Luis and made Elena feel guilty. Luis wasn't a bad boy. He was just weak. When he got on drugs, Elena did everything humanly possible to help him. Every time she'd turn her back, he'd be back on them." Dominic shook his head. "It's a terrible thing Chavez is doing to both of them."

"I don't care what he's doing to Luis. The bastard betrayed her."

Dominic nodded. "I'm sure he had no intention of hurting Elena."

"I'm not sure about anything." Galen stood up. "Except that after she thinks about it, she may decide to try to do something to help that son of a bitch. Even if she doesn't, I don't want her torturing herself because she had to choose between her brother and her son. I don't want any tinge of guilt touching her."

"What are you going to do?"

"I have a few options open." He gazed at Elena sitting on the bank talking to Barry. She was smiling, but he could see the strained tenseness of her muscles. He had never seen her completely relaxed, totally content. Christ, he wanted to see her like that.

"I want to help," Dominic said. "After all, I'm to blame for trusting Luis in the first place." His lips twisted. "I wanted him to change, to come to us and start a new life. Instead, I almost ruined Elena's life. I have to make amends."

"I'm drowning in all the guilt bubbling around here," Galen said. "You were only guilty of bad judgment, and Elena isn't guilty of anything. Luis wouldn't be in this situation if he hadn't betrayed her in the first place. She knows that, rationally, but her emotions may be a different matter." He turned to go inside. "If I can use you, I will. But you're not as qualified as Judd in this kind of situation. Your morals would get in the way."

"Second fiddle to Judd again." Dominic grimaced ruefully. "I'm not as gentle as you might think. Let me help."

"I'll let you know." Galen glanced at Elena again. She was looking past Barry at the setting sun, but he knew she wasn't seeing it. She was thinking about her brother and the load Chavez had dropped on her shoulders.

Time to get to work. He'd make some calls and then, later tonight, after Elena had gone to bed, he'd talk to Judd.

"You're going to go after him?" Judd shook his head. "Let Chavez put him down. The sniveling bastard deserves it."

"You're probably right. In any event, I'm going to scout around to make sure Luis is really in dire straits before I decide whether or not to go in."

"Go in where? You know where Chavez is?"

"Miami, or near there. He went there directly from the ranch. Manero just found out he's cruising around the coast on a yacht called *The Prize*."

Judd's gaze narrowed on his face. "And how do you know that?"

"I called Manero the minute I heard Chavez was on his way to the ranch. I told him to get a man out there to monitor the situation and to track Chavez when he left. He came through for me."

"How long have you known this?"

"I've known he went to Miami since the day after I got here. As I said, Manero just found out about the yacht."

"And you didn't tell Elena." It was a statement, not a question. "You were afraid she'd try to go after him again."

"I didn't want to take the chance. I think she'd do anything to put an end to this threat to Barry."

"She won't be pleased."

"I don't care. I want her safe." His lips twisted. "Jesus, is that too much to ask? She's never been safe in her life."

"You want me to go with you?"

"I may need help."

"Good God, you're admitting you're not all-powerful? What's the world coming to?"

"Will you do it?"

"It will be difficult. A yacht isn't like a house. They can see you coming."

"It can be done."

"When?"

"Tomorrow night."

Judd was silent a moment. "I'll think about it."

"I won't go in unless I believe we have a chance."

He nodded. "I know you're no amateur. It's just that I have a good deal to live for right now. I don't want to blow it."

Galen turned to leave. "Let me know."

Judd grinned. "You'll be the very first."

The mat.

Elena woke up screaming.

Just a dream.

She was panting and drenched in sweat.

She got out of bed and went to the bathroom and splashed water on her face. Then she changed her nightshirt and went back to bed.

No, there was no way she could relax. Her heart was still beating so hard she felt suffocated. She needed air.

A moment later she was on the porch and taking deep, cool breaths.

"Okay?"

She looked over her shoulder to see Galen standing in the doorway. "I needed some air."

"Couldn't sleep?"

"Oh, I slept," she said. "Nightmares."

"About Luis?"

"Yes. He was on the mat, and Chavez was hitting him and hitting him and hitting him." She drew a deep breath. "Luis was never good at hand-to-hand. My father and I both tried to teach him, but he didn't want to learn. Maybe the life we led was too rough for him. Maybe if he'd grown up in a stable family situation, he'd have been different, happy. Everyone should have the chance to be happy."

"If they don't try to take that chance away from someone else."

"You're right. I know you're right." Her teeth bit into her lower lip. "But I can't just sit here while Chavez is torturing him. I have to help him. After he's free, I can turn my back on him, but not now."

"What about Barry?"

"You and Dominic will keep him safe."

"Oh, so I'm the one who is supposed to stay here and baby-sit?"

"Yes. Luis isn't your responsibility. I want only one thing from you. I need to know where Chavez is."

"And you think I can find out?"

"Sure." She tried to smile. "You're the great problem-solver. You can solve this one, can't you?"

"Maybe."

"Try." Lord, she was cold. She crossed her arms over her breasts. "Please. Find him. I don't want to have nightmares like that for the rest of my life."

"You won't. Go back inside."

"You'll do it?"

"There's not much I wouldn't do for you." A smile lit his face. "Fight a dragon, tilt at a windmill, explore a wilderness . . ."

She loved that smile. She never wanted to stop looking at him when he smiled at her. "Just a location."

"You don't understand. You have to make me stretch my capabilities. Next time I want a challenge." He opened the screen door. "Now scoot back to bed. I have some thinking to do."

She didn't move. "Will you . . . sit on the porch swing with me?"

He went still. "Why?"

She didn't want to go inside. She didn't want to leave him. "It would be nice. I feel a little . . . It would be nice."

He took her hand and led her toward the swing. "Yes, it would." He pulled her down beside him and put his arm around her. "Cuddle up. It's a little chilly."

But he was warm and strong and smelled of lemony cologne. It was good sitting here and not thinking of anything but the creak of the swing and how comforting it was to have him hold her. "This is very nice of you. If you want . . . we could go in later and have sex."

He chuckled. "No, we couldn't. That's not what you need right now. You keep trying to pay me. How long is it going to take you to realize that times like this have their own value to me? Of course, that's only when I'm not being a sex-driven pig."

"Or an asshole."

"You're smiling." His hand gently massaged the side of her neck. "That's a good sign. Now, close your eyes and I'll tell you about my life as a smuggler in the Orient back when I was young and dashing. Of course, I'm still young and dashing, but maybe not quite as foolhardy. I remember one time when I was trying to find a ship to Shanghai . . ."

Chapter Eleven

CHAVEZ'S CALL CAME THE NEXT MORNING.

"Did you have a good night?" he asked after Galen gave her the phone. "I'm afraid poor Luis didn't. Of course, I slept very well indeed."

"I'm not going to give you Barry." She paused. "But he's not the only one you want. I'll meet you, if you like. Don't you want another chance at me?"

"So much that I'm almost tempted. Almost. But I have to have my son first. Once you're dead you won't be able to tell me where he is. Then I'd have to negotiate with someone else."

"Maybe you'd get lucky and be able to keep me alive. I'm sure you'd much rather torture me than Luis."

"Much. But there are small satisfactions. He looks a bit like you around the eyes. Give me my son."

"Let me talk to Luis."

"I'm afraid he's not able to communicate at the moment. Perhaps the next time I call." He hung up.

"He wouldn't let me talk to him." She handed the phone back to Galen. "He said he couldn't talk."

"He could be lying," Judd said from his seat across the room.

"I know that." She drew a deep breath. "Just find Chavez for me, Galen." She went out on the porch. She tried to make her face expressionless as she saw Barry sitting in the swing with Dominic. "Hi. Are you hungry?"

"No." Barry was gazing at her, troubled. "You look sad, Mama."

"No, I'm fine. I thought maybe we'd take a walk by the lake. I heard wild geese when I was out here last night."

"Sure." He jumped down from the swing. "I'll go tell Galen that I can't help with breakfast." He ran past her into the house.

"It's getting harder to keep things from him," Dominic said. "He's a smart boy, and all this bouncing around would make anyone suspicious. You may have to talk to him."

"And what am I going to tell him? That his father is a monster and wants to kill his mother?" She shook her head. "My job is to protect Barry."

"And Luis?"

She shook her head. "I don't know. Chavez wouldn't let me talk to him."

"I'm ready." Barry opened the screen door. "Galen said he had to do some business this morning anyway and I could come back and help with brunch.

That's half breakfast, half lunch." He ran down the porch steps. "Let's go see the geese."

"Well?" Galen asked Judd.

"You may not be handling this right," Judd said. "I've been thinking about it, and maybe we should be more patient. Chavez doesn't seem to be in a hurry to kill her brother."

"Which won't be particularly good for Luis."

He lifted his brows. "Do we care?"

"No, but Elena does. And she won't be patient."

"True." Judd stared thoughtfully out the window at the lake. "Chavez is playing on her emotions. He's counting on her breaking down."

"Not counting—betting on a long shot. He knows how tough she is."

"Then he may be as desperate as she is."

"Are you going to help me or not?"

Judd nodded. "But we don't go for it tonight. Tomorrow. I want to think about it a little more."

Galen shrugged. "Why not? Tomorrow."

Chavez looked down in disgust at Luis Kyler sprawled unconscious on the bed.

Weak vermin. He could see nothing of Elena in her brother. He had lied to her about that. Such a weakling shouldn't be permitted to live. Only the strong should inherit the earth.

"We've not been able to trace Galen yet," Gomez said behind him. "We're going through reports on his friends and associates." He glanced down at Luis. "Will we still need to find them?"

"Keep on looking." He turned away from Luis. He had been grabbing at straws when he brought Elena's brother into the bargaining. He would have to think of some way to use him other than as a trade. He had no faith that she would give in to save her brother. He would not do it for his own brother, and she could be almost as strong.

But not as strong. She had lied about pretending to let him defeat her. That couldn't be the truth. He would not accept the idea that she had not only defeated but also fooled him.

For the past two nights he had begun dreaming about having her back in the gym. Wonderful, exhilarating dreams of triumph.

They *would* come true.

The phone rang at eleven-forty that morning.

Elena froze.

"Chavez." Galen handed her the phone.

"I don't know how much more Luis can take," Chavez said. "Give me the boy."

"We've already discussed this." Her voice was shaking. "No deal."

"You're upset. I think you're weakening." He paused. "And you'll be even more inclined to save him if you see what kind of punishment you're inflicting on him. Yes, I believe we should arrange to bring you and Luis together. Let me see. Suppose I take your brother to Orlando two days from now? The garden of the Kissimmee Hotel. The bench beside the koi pond. Ten A.M."

"Do you think I'm an idiot?"

"Oh, he'll be alone. I understand Galen called the DEA on me when I was at the ranch. Do you think I don't know that he could have a truckload of agents at the hotel to try to catch me? It wouldn't be smart to place myself in that position."

"Then what's to stop me from taking Luis?"

"The fact that I'll have a very fine marksman stationed nearby with his sights on Luis. He leaves the garden, he's dead."

"And that same shooter could take me out."

"That's your problem. I'm sure you can work it out to your satisfaction."

"I won't be there."

"After another two nights of worrying about dear Luis? I think you will." He hung up.

"He's bringing Luis to the Kissimmee Hotel in Orlando. Ten A.M. two days from now," she said. "He thinks I'm softening. He wants to show me his handiwork. He says Luis will be alone."

"Not likely."

She nodded. "Trap."

"But there may be an opportunity there," Dominic said. "Perhaps we can snatch Luis before they can close it."

"He wants Elena," Galen said. "And I don't want that trap closing on her."

"Wait, maybe Dominic is right." She rubbed her temple. "I can't seem to think. It makes sense that he wouldn't show up himself or in force when he knows that you called the DEA on him before. He said there would be a gunman with his sights on Luis."

"There's no way he expects you to go in, look at poor, poor Luis, and then leave. The shooter will try to take you out, or there will be another wild card in the deck."

"I know that." She moistened her lips. "But I may never have a better chance."

Galen's lips twisted. "And clear the way?"

"He's her brother," Dominic said quietly. "He's weak, not bad, and he deserves better than to be treated this way by Chavez."

"Dammit, she doesn't need your encouragement, Dominic."

"You never knew him," Dominic said. "I did. And I loved him. No, I do love him." He smiled at Elena. "Don't feel ashamed of still loving Luis. Forgiveness is a good thing."

"Oh, for God's sake." Galen threw up his hands. "Why am I wasting my breath? You're going to do it, aren't you?"

"I've got to try," she whispered.

"It's a big risk."

"Then I'll have to find a way to make it less."

He stared at her in exasperation for a moment and then turned away. "Okay, we go in. I'll call Manero and have him scope out the situation at the hotel."

"No, I go in alone. Dominic will help me, and I

need someone I trust to watch Barry. I don't like the idea of being away from him. It's not that I don't trust your men here, but I—"

"But no one can take care of your son like you do. I suppose I should be flattered you consider me a trustworthy baby-sitter." Galen shook his head. "I'm going in with you. Dominic will take care of Barry. If you like, we can bring Barry with us as far as an airport outside Orlando and leave him and Dominic on the helicopter while we go into town. At the first sign of danger, Dominic can split with the kid."

She thought about it. She didn't like the idea of bringing Barry with them, but the alternative of leaving him hundreds of miles away was totally unacceptable. "Okay, I suppose that would be safe enough."

"Safer than we'll be." He turned and left the room.

She couldn't blame him for being exasperated. The situation could come unraveled in a heartbeat, and her reasons for going after Luis were purely emotional.

"It's the right thing to do, Elena," Dominic said.

"Contrary to what the knights of Camelot claimed, right doesn't always beat might." She met Dominic's gaze. "I said I'd try, Dominic. But if I find that I'm endangering my son or there's a strong possibility he may lose his mother over this, I'll back out. Barry is innocent, and that weights the scale in his favor."

He nodded slowly. "I understand. Innocence is a bright and shining thing. But someone has to save the lost ones too."

"That's why I'm going." She stood up. "And now I've got to get a plan together. Two days isn't a hell of a lot of time."

Would she come?

Chavez stared thoughtfully out over the rail at the skyscrapers of Miami Beach.

The chances of Elena trading her son for that weakling of a brother weren't high enough for him to bank on. Yet she might be lured into trying to free him if the circumstances were set up correctly. It was the kind of action that would appeal to a woman of her nature. It was a long shot, but he didn't have many options at this point. He hadn't been able to turn up any clues to Elena and Galen's possible whereabouts.

"We go to Orlando?" Gomez asked behind him.

Chavez nodded. "Two days." The setup might not yield his son, but it could rid the boy of his most ardent protector. He'd prefer her to be taken prisoner, but that might not happen. It was more likely they'd have to put the bitch down, and that wasn't all bad. Galen might be more willing to deal for the boy with her out of the picture. "How is Luis?"

"Out."

"Wake him up. We have to get him ready." He paused, thinking. The situation had to be handled carefully. "And I want the bruises to be very visible, Gomez. I want her sweet, gentle heart to bleed for him."

"Manero faxed me a diagram of the hotel and surrounding area." Galen spread the sheet on the kitchen table. "Here's the bridge over the koi pond where Luis is supposed to be waiting. The hotel is six stories, but the garden can only be viewed from about a third of the windows on the south side of the building." He drew a circle around the windows facing the garden. "So this is sniper country."

"Maybe." Judd tapped the hotel across the street. "How much of the garden can be seen from here?"

"That's the Mirado Hotel. Their angle is skewed. Only four rooms have a view." Galen circled those rooms. "There aren't any other nearby hotels with access. Of course, that doesn't mean anyone leaving couldn't be picked off by someone in a car driving by."

"Then you take care of it," Judd said. "You're good at extractions. Extract us." He pointed at the windows of the Kissimmee Hotel. "I'll clear the ground here and scout out the hotel across the street. Who meets with Luis?"

"I do," Elena said. "And we need a car waiting outside that garden gate. I'm not going to waste time talking to him. I'll just get him out."

"You don't even know if he'll be able to walk," Galen said.

"I'll get him out." Elena's lips firmed. "Just have the car waiting."

Galen nodded. "I'll do a sweep through the garden before you go in, just to make sure there aren't any surprises."

"No, you have your job. I have mine." She turned away. "I'll check it out myself."

"Suit yourself." Galen turned to Judd. "How much time do you need?"

"I'll go in tonight and scout around. Chavez may stage a last-minute arrival for his shooter at the Kissimmee Hotel, so I'll position myself across the street at the Mirado and keep watch while Elena meets with Luis."

"Good idea."

"Just don't forget me when you pull everyone out." He smiled sardonically. "It would seriously offend me."

"Then don't waste time when you see Elena and Luis heading for the gate. Be out front waiting." He folded the sheet of paper and put it in his pocket. "I've arranged for a pilot and helicopter to pick us up and take us to Orlando. Josie McFee. I've used her before. She's good, trustworthy, and tough as nails. She'll land at a private field on the outskirts of Orlando."

"Isn't that pretty close?" Elena frowned. "I don't want Barry or Dominic to be put in danger."

"The airport's safe. If we think we're being followed, we won't go back there. Okay?"

It wasn't okay. The entire plan was risky, but at

least Barry's part in it seemed fairly secure. She slowly nodded. "I guess it is."

"Good." He moved toward the door. "Then if you'll excuse me, I'll see what I can do to pull a rabbit out of a hat to get us out of Orlando with our skins intact."

"How are you going to do that?"

"Search me. That's Disney World territory. Maybe I'll put Donald Duck into the mix."

"Good luck," Judd murmured ironically.

"Well?" Elena stared Judd in the eye as Galen left. "Aren't you going to say anything to me? Isn't this what you warned me not to do? I'm putting Galen's life on the line."

He shook his head. "He's doing that himself. You couldn't stop him if you wanted to."

"I do want to stop him."

"Then back out. This is a lose-lose proposition. What are we going to do with your brother if we do get him away from Chavez?"

She didn't know. It was a complication she didn't need, but that didn't matter. "I have to do this, Judd."

He shook his head. "Emotion is a bummer. It really gets in the way of clear thinking."

"And of course you never let it bother you."

"It bothers me, but I've trained myself not to allow it to interfere. It makes a man hesitate, and that can be fatal." He smiled. "You wouldn't want me to hesitate if I see that sniper aiming at you."

"No."

"Then don't talk to me about emotion. I'll see you in Orlando."

She followed him out onto the front porch and watched as he got into the jeep.

"Stop fretting, Elena."

She turned to see Dominic coming up the path from the lake.

"Where have you been?"

"Just sitting and thinking. Nothing like looking at God's wonders to soothe the soul. You should try it." He dropped down on the porch steps. "Your soul needs some soothing."

She sat down beside him. "Yes."

"You always were a worrier. Even as a little girl, you fretted over every little detail. Luis was different. He lived for the moment. But he was good for you. He made you remember that you were still a child."

"Is that who you were thinking about down by the lake?"

"How could I think of anyone else? Are we going to be able to save him?"

"I hope so. Galen and Judd are smart and experienced. They'll make a difference."

"I pray everything will go well."

She leaned her head against his arm. How many times had they sat like this on the front steps at Tomaco? Comfort flowed through her in a blessedly familiar stream. "Then I know it will. You have friends in high places."

He chuckled. "Let's hope they see things my way." He kissed the top of her head. "Now, you go for a walk yourself. Look at the lake and the sky, and when you come back you'll feel better."

"If you say so." She stood up and started down the steps. "I'll give it a try. I wouldn't want to offend your high-placed friends."

Chapter Twelve

POOR CHILD.

Dominic stared after Elena as she walked down the path. So much torment, so much hurt and . . . regret. She believed that everyone was answerable for their own lives, but it had always tortured her that she wasn't able to save Luis from his own actions. She had told Dominic once that if she'd made just one more try it might have been the one that worked. She had always been the responsible one, the carrier of burdens. But she had not been able to carry Luis's.

Neither had Dominic. Nor had he been able to teach Luis to shoulder his own. Perhaps when they freed him, both Elena and Dominic would have another chance to save his soul as well as his body.

"Where is she going?" Galen asked from the doorway.

"Just for a walk. I thought she needed it."

"I wish that was all she needed."

"You're concerned about her."

"You're damn right." Galen's voice vibrated with feeling. "What's wrong with that? Someone has to care whether she lives or dies. She barges in and tries to save a bastard who—Sorry, I know you care about him too. I'll shut up."

"Don't shut up." He smiled. "Sit down beside me and we'll talk."

"Look way down there," Josie McFee shouted over the sound of the rotors to Barry in the seat behind her. "That's Disney World. Home of Mickey Mouse."

Barry eagerly pressed his face to the window. "I see a castle and a—" He turned to Elena. "Is that where we're going?"

"Not this trip. We have business here, and we thought you might enjoy the helicopter ride." Elena glanced at Galen in the copilot's seat. "How far?"

"Another five minutes," Josie McFee answered for him. "It's a little far out, but Galen said it's private. There's a car waiting at the hangar." She smiled at Barry again. "I hear you're going to wait with me in the copter. Maybe we could do a little sightseeing."

"Mama?"

She shook her head. "We need Josie to wait for us."

"Ten minutes and we'll be back at the airport," Josie said. "You can't even drive to Kissimmee in that time."

"It's not a bad idea," Dominic said.

She supposed it would be all right for Dominic

and Barry to leave the airport for such a short time. It would keep Barry from becoming bored and fidgety. It was just weird to think of pleasure excursions in connection with their mission here. But it was no more weird than being forced to bring a child on that same mission. "Ten minutes."

"Right," Josie said. "Trust me. I have grandchildren of my own. I'll give him a bang-up tour."

She did trust the woman. It was strange that she would feel so at ease with a woman she had just met, but Josie McFee inspired confidence. She was a woman in her fifties with graying hair, a plump build, and an animated manner. "I'm sure you will. Just don't drop down too close to that castle."

"No danger," Galen said. "This entire city is controlled by Disney, including the airspace. They're very sensitive to anything that would disrupt the family fun."

"We're going down." Josie banked the helicopter. "We'll be on the ground in a couple minutes."

It seemed less than that when the helicopter settled on the tarmac.

"There's the car. I'll go check it out. Wait here." Galen jumped out of the aircraft and ducked beneath the whirring rotors to run toward the hangar.

"Want to sit up front with Josie?" Dominic asked Barry. "You can see better."

Barry's face lit up. "Could I?"

"Sure," Josie said. "Come ahead."

Dominic was already out of the copter and lifting Barry into the copilot's seat. "There you go." He fastened the seat belt. "Now, you pay attention to everything Josie does and maybe you'll learn how to fly this bug."

Barry's gaze was eagerly wandering over the controls. "Wow. It looks like a spaceship."

"Not quite." He caressingly touched Barry's hair and then stepped back. "I think I dropped a slip of paper when I got out. Will you see if it's on the floor, Elena?"

He was right; there was a square piece of paper on the floor. She bent to retrieve it.

"Have a good trip." He slammed the door and waved at Josie.

Elena stared at him in disbelief. "Dominic!"

The helicopter was lifting, turning, and leaving Dominic standing below.

"Land, dammit."

"I can't hear you," Josie shouted over her shoulder. "And I don't think you want my copilot to hear. You have a note to read."

Elena took one final, enraged glance at Dominic walking toward the car where Galen waited. It was a damn conspiracy.

The note.

She unfolded the piece of paper.

Elena,

> *My job, I think. It's not only because you and Luis and Barry would never have been put into this position if I hadn't trusted Luis. I've always believed he could be saved if I just went that extra mile for him.*

This is the extra mile.

I'm no hero. Galen has promised to check out the garden and make it as safe for me as possible. I'll only take Luis to the car and give my support to ward off his fear. He's always been a frightened boy, and as you've taught your son, fear is a terrible thing. Don't blame anyone but me for this. I convinced Galen, and Galen convinced Josie.

Now I have to convince you that even if you force poor Josie to land, the action will be over by the time you find a way to get to the hotel. In addition, you'll have to leave Barry unprotected and probably frighten him witless.

Convinced?

I hope with all my heart you are. Because you have to bite the bullet and let someone else shoulder this burden. Your job is to take care of our boy.

All my love,
Dominic

Tears stung her eyes as her hand crumpled the note. "Damn you. Damn you, Dominic."

Josie glanced over her shoulder. "Sorry. I obey orders, and Galen's the boss."

But Galen hadn't been the boss in this case. After years of staying in the background, Dominic had stepped forward and was running the show.

God, she was scared.

"What the hell?" As he opened the door, Judd stared quizzically at the police uniform Galen was wearing. "You'll pardon me for telling you that uniform doesn't suit you. It requires a certain air to carry it off."

"People seldom question police officers." Galen entered the room and dumped the large box he was carrying on the bed before striding over to the window. "You checked out the rooms in this hotel?"

"I'm not even going to bother to answer that question." He followed Galen to the window. "The sniper was in the third room to the right, fifth floor of the Kissimmee across the street. Pat Reilly, former IRA, pretty good."

"Not good enough?"

"All passion, no intellect. His demise won't inconvenience us. I left a DO NOT DISTURB sign on the door of his room." He gestured to another room on the sixth floor. "That one has me a little worried. No one was in the room last night and I checked it again two hours ago, but the drapes are drawn now. It's not impossible that someone could pick the lock and take up residence."

"A second shooter."

"We'll see. No time to go over there now. I'll have to handle it from here." He handed Galen his binoculars. "Two men just delivered Luis Kyler to the bench beside the koi pond. He's not a pretty sight."

Galen focused the binoculars on the man on the bench. Luis Kyler might once have been a handsome young man, but he was now so painfully thin that his neat gray suit hung on him. His face was bruised and swollen, and he was sitting on the edge of the bench as if too nervous or too hurt to lean back. "He can walk?"

Judd nodded. "He was getting some support, but he's mobile."

"Then that's all we need. His guards left?"

"Out the back gate."

"I'll do a walk-through just to make sure. Then I'll let Dominic go after Luis." He handed Judd the binoculars. "It should all be over within fifteen minutes."

"If we're lucky." Judd picked up his rifle from the bed and went back to the window. "And if you don't foul up getting us out of here. I'd bet that street out there is crawling with Chavez's men."

Galen opened the door. "No bet."

"What's in that box on the bed?"

"Your disguise."

"Disguise? That box is kind of big for a police uniform." He crossed back to the bed, opened the box, and looked inside. He started to laugh. "My God, you've got to be kidding."

"Ready?" Galen asked Dominic. "You can change your mind. I'll go in and get him."

Dominic shook his head. "He wouldn't trust you. Besides, you're the getaway man." He smiled. "That sounds like one of those old gangster movies."

"The garden is clean and Judd is on watch, but that doesn't mean something unexpected might not happen."

"You forget I spent years with the guerrillas. I know that nothing is safe."

"This had better be pretty damn safe," Galen said grimly. "Or Elena will go for my jugular."

"Stop worrying and go do your job." Dominic opened the garden gate. "And let me do mine."

Dominic was inside the garden.

Judd's gaze focused the telescopic sight of his rifle as Dominic moved down the path toward the koi pond.

He was moving quickly, almost eagerly, as he saw Luis Kyler.

Judd suddenly caught sight of something out of the corner of his eye. He swung the rifle to the window on the sixth floor of the hotel.

Had the curtain moved?

Dear God, the boy looked terrible, Dominic thought as he drew closer to the bench. "Luis."

Luis's eyes widened. "What are you doing here?"

"I've come to take you away."

Luis struggled to his feet. "You're not supposed to be here." His voice was shrill. "Elena is supposed to be the one. It has to be Elena."

"We're going to get you away from here. You'll see Elena soon." He stepped closer. "Come with me, Luis."

"Go away, Dominic. Tell Elena to come." His eyes were glittering feverishly. "It has to be Elena."

"You're hurt. You're not feeling well. Listen carefully. Elena is waiting for you. You have to come with me."

"I can't go. I have to do what they say. They won't give me anything unless I do what they say." His voice was shaking. "They haven't given me anything in two days. I have to have it."

"Coke?"

"Heroin."

Dominic felt sick. "We'll get you off it." He took Luis's arm. "Come on."

Luis pulled away from him. "That's what I'm afraid of. I can't take it. I'm . . . hurting. Send Elena."

"Why?"

He pulled a pistol from his jacket pocket. "I have to shoot her. I have to shoot Elena."

Dominic stiffened. "You don't mean that."

"They said I had to do it. They said they'd give me my injection if I did it. I have to do it. . . ."

"She's your sister. She loves you."

Luis looked at him in wonder. "Doesn't matter. Why should it matter? I have to do it."

Dominic was filled with horror. "Give me the gun, Luis. This isn't you speaking. Give me the gun."

"You always interfered. You should have made her come. It has to be her."

He reached for the gun. "Don't let Chavez and his drugs do this to you. Let me help you."

Luis's lips twisted. "You should have made her come. You've ruined everything."

His finger pressed the trigger.

Pain ripped through Dominic's chest. Dear heaven,

he was shot, he realized. He stared at Luis in disbelief.

"Don't look at me like that. It's your fault," Luis said shrilly. He pressed the trigger again and again. "You should have made her come. . . ."

Three shots.

Dammit. Galen jumped out of the truck and ran into the garden.

Another shot.

Dominic was on the ground and Luis was standing over him.

One more shot and Luis crumpled to the ground. Where had it come from? No time to check. He had to get Dominic out of here.

He fell to his knees beside him. "Come on, Dominic. Let me help you up. We've got to—"

Shit. Shit. Shit.

Judd waddled slowly out of the hotel.

The street was humming with activity. Four police cars were parked outside the hotel, and guests were streaming out and being ushered down the block.

Galen was standing beside a truck parked at the curb. Emblazoned in green letters on the side of the white truck was ORLANDO BOMB DISPOSAL.

"Get in." Galen opened the door to the back of the truck. "We have to get out of here before the real bomb squad arrives."

"I'm going to get you for this." Judd scowled at

him through his protective visor. "I look like someone from outer space."

"Someone had to be the bomb tech."

"And you nominated me." He threw his gun case in the truck. "Hell, I don't think I can even climb into this truck. You called in a bomb threat?"

"It was the only thing I could think of to make sure that the police cleared everyone from this area. It wasn't easy. I had to construct an entire scenario that would convince them to send a disposal unit. I thought the truck would protect Luis and Dominic." Galen helped him into the back of the truck. "You can get rid of the suit as soon as we get out of town."

"I hope so. It's hot as hell."

"Was there another gunman?"

"Yes, the window on the sixth floor. I took care of it." He paused. "Is Dominic dead?"

"Yes, he's dead." Galen slammed the truck door.

Galen parked the truck beside the hangar and stared blindly at the helicopter.

Move, damn you. Tell her. Get it over with.

He heard the truck door open behind him and Judd get out. A moment later Judd was standing beside the driver's window. "You stay here. I'll send her to you." He turned and sprinted toward the helicopter.

Yes, separate her from Barry. If he hadn't been so bummed, he would have thought of the boy himself.

Elena was coming toward him. She was walking

slowly, warily, as if afraid of stepping on a land mine. She knew something was wrong. But, Jesus, she didn't know how wrong.

She stopped and looked at him. Maybe she did know. He had to say the words anyway.

He reached over and opened the truck door for her. "Get in. You won't want Barry to see you."

She couldn't cry. She mustn't cry. If she did, she might never stop.

"Both of them?" Elena asked dully. "Luis and Dominic . . ."

"It all went bad."

"Why?"

"There was a second shooter."

"But you expected there might be. I should have been there. You shouldn't have let Dominic go. I would have been more cautious. I might have been able to turn it around."

"Okay, you're right. I made a mistake."

"For God's sake, stop being so noble." Judd was again standing outside the window. "I'm glad I decided to come back. Tell her the truth."

"The truth?" Elena repeated.

"Chavez threw in a monkey wrench neither you nor Dominic expected. He gave Luis a gun and evidently ordered him to take you out. He killed Dominic instead."

"Luis . . ." Horror on top of horror. "Luis couldn't have done it."

"I was watching the entire time," Judd said. "He did it."

"And then the shooter took out Luis?" Her lips twisted with pain. "I suppose Chavez wasn't pleased at the substitution."

"Blast you, she didn't have to know," Galen told Judd.

"No, but I always opt for clarity. It's better that she realize it wasn't something you could have anticipated. Oh, and I've told Barry that Dominic had to stay over on business." Judd turned and walked back toward the helicopter.

"What happened to the shooter?"

"Judd took care of him. He thought there might be someone in that room." Galen glanced away from her. "I don't want to rush you, but we should get out of here. We weren't followed, but we need to get as far away as we can."

"Yes, of course." She had to get out of the truck and go back to the helicopter. She mustn't think of Dominic or Luis. She must do what was necessary and grieve later. She could do this. She had been a soldier. She had lost other people in the past.

But not Dominic, her best friend, her teacher . . .

The pain was too intense. She had to move now or collapse. She opened the door and jumped out of the truck. "Let's go."

Chapter Thirteen

IT WAS DARK WHEN THEY ARRIVED BACK AT THE COTtage.

"I'll take the kid and put him to bed." Judd picked up Barry and took him into the cottage.

That was kind of him, Elena thought wearily. He had kept Barry occupied and oblivious to anyone but himself during the trip back from Orlando. What a strange man. Strange and violent and yet somewhere in him there must be a soft streak. "I'm glad he kept Barry busy. I didn't know how I would cope, what to say to him."

"Don't say anything until it's the right time." He helped her out of the car. "You'll know when it feels right."

"Will I?" She wasn't sure of anything. "I don't want him to hurt like this. He's so little. He doesn't understand."

"None of us understands death. It sucks." Galen

led her toward the cottage. "I'm calling Logan as soon as I get you settled and asking him to take care of arrangements for Dominic and your brother. The authorities probably won't release the bodies for a while."

"I know. It doesn't matter. I guess we should give Dominic a Catholic burial, but I don't think he'd really care what happened to his body. He knew his soul wouldn't be there anymore." She paused. "Luis? I don't know. I can't think of him right now. Dominic would call him a lost soul and forgive him. But I don't believe I can. Not yet. Maybe never."

"Neither can I." He opened the front door. "Let's get you to bed."

"I can get myself to bed."

"I know you can. I'll just feel better helping you."

She was too numb to argue as he led her to her room and helped her out of her clothes and into bed. He got a washcloth and wiped her face and hands before sitting in a chair beside the bed. "Want to talk?"

She shook her head. "There's nothing to talk about. It's done. They're dead."

He was silent for a moment. "Do you blame me?"

"No, it was Dominic's call. He did what he wanted to do, what he felt he had to do. You just went along with him."

"That's not quite true. I jumped at the chance he offered me. I was looking for any way I could find to keep you out of that garden."

"Like you did that night when I went after Chavez at the ranch?"

He nodded. "I . . . found something in you. It had never happened to me before. I didn't want to lose it."

"It was wrong of you to shut me out."

"I'll never do it again. I promise you."

She looked away from him. "Please. Go away."

"Let me stay. I won't talk anymore."

"Please," she whispered. "I'm going to cry now. I . . . can't keep it back. I want to remember Dominic and do my grieving for him. It's a private thing."

He stood up and gazed down at her. "I want to be with you."

She shook her head. "You can't share my sorrow. You didn't love him like I did. I have to say my good-bye."

He leaned forward and kissed her forehead. "I'll look in on you later." He turned out the lamp.

The tears were already running down her cheeks as he left the room.

Think of Dominic. Think of the good times. Think of the gifts he'd given her, the laughter, the care, the understanding. Crush down the agony, think of Dominic, and say good-bye. . . .

Galen found Judd on the porch. "The boy asleep?"

"Out like a light. How is she doing?"

"Hurting, of course. After all, she lost a brother and her best friend."

Judd nodded.

"After you jumped in the bomb truck, you asked

whether Dominic was dead. Why didn't you ask about Luis?"

Judd smiled.

Galen gazed out at the lake. "I would have thought you'd be able to get that sniper before he shot Luis. You must not be as good as I thought you were."

"We all make mistakes."

"If it was a mistake."

"What are you getting at?"

"Of course the sniper could have had orders to kill Luis if he fouled up or if there was a chance of us saving him." He paused. "On the other hand, what if he didn't?"

"The eternal 'what if,' " Judd murmured.

"What if you did get off a shot at that sniper before he had a chance to fire his weapon? What if you swung the rifle back and took out Luis yourself?"

"Now, why would I do that?"

"You tell me."

Judd tilted his head. "Hmm. You want me to play your little game? Okay. Why would I want to take out Luis? Let's see . . . He was a drug addict who had betrayed Elena. Whether we saved him or not, he would be a weak link who would constantly endanger her and us. He would probably be a torment to her for the rest of her life. We would never be able to trust him if Chavez beckoned. Clear cold logic would dictate that he should be eliminated. Is that enough reason?" He smiled faintly. "Not that I'm admitting anything, you understand."

"I understand."

"Then I'll see you in the morning." Judd started to pass him and go into the house, then stopped and looked back over his shoulder. "Oh, one more reason. I *liked* Dominic Sanders, and the son of a bitch who killed him didn't deserve to live."

Barry's expression was serious as he drew back the arrow of his bow.

"Attaboy," Judd murmured. "Now focus on the target."

Elena stopped on the porch and watched the two of them aiming at a target pinned to a pine tree.

Barry let loose the arrow and then whooped as it hit the cardboard. "I hit it this time!"

"Yes, you did." Judd gave him another arrow. "Now let's see if you can get closer to the bull's-eye."

"Your son's got a good eye," Galen said behind her.

"Where did he get the bow and arrow? I had to leave his in Tomaco."

"Judd made it for him. They've been bonding big time for the last few days."

"I can see that. I'm grateful to him. I've not been much use to Barry lately."

"You deserved some healing time."

And they had let her have that time. No demands. Little conversation. Just peace. "Barry's my responsibility. I can take over now."

"It's not hurting either Judd or me to baby-sit. We like the kid."

"You haven't heard from Chavez?"

He shook his head. "He didn't come out of this too well. I'd guess he's licking his wounds."

"We didn't come out too well either." Her lips twisted. "I'm sure he'll come sliding out of his cave soon and twist the knife."

"Then try to enjoy the hiatus."

She couldn't enjoy anything at the moment. It was an effort to hold on to her composure and keep from shattering into a thousand pieces. But she was much better than she had been yesterday, she told herself. Healing took time. Tomorrow she would be better still. "Has Barry said anything about Dominic?"

He shook his head. "Not yet. Children accept changes better than adults, and Judd has been keeping him busy."

"He loved Dominic. He'll ask about him."

"Don't borrow trouble. Why don't you go for a walk and relax?"

That was what Dominic had suggested on that last night, and she'd done as he asked. While she was gazing at the lake and letting nature soothe her, he'd been making his plans. Dominic loved everything about this earth, and he'd taught her to love it too. She would go down there and breathe the pine-scented air and look at the sky and the lake.

And, maybe, she would feel him there.

Dawn was pearling the sky.

Elena stood at the window of her bedroom and looked out at the lake. She had slept only intermittently during the night, but she knew it was no use going back to bed. When she slept, she dreamed of Dominic—and Luis.

It had seemed as if her life was on hold for the past few days, but that was bound to change. Chavez would call and it would all start again. He'd never stop searching, planning. Maybe he was on his way here now.

Don't think about it. She shouldn't take on any more burdens until she could handle what she had now.

She turned away from the window. It was all very well to tell herself not to think of what Chavez was planning. It was harder to block him out.

But Barry could help her. She would go and sit by his bed and watch him sleep. She would let all the wonder of him flow over her and she would be calmer. Not at peace, but more able to cope with her memories of Dominic and that phone call from Chavez lurking on the horizon.

She slipped on her robe and moved silently from the room to the one across the hall. She carefully opened the door and stood in the doorway.

Barry was huddled beneath his blankets, and she sat down in the rocking chair beside the bed. Children slept so deeply. . . .

She stiffened. But she should be able to hear him breathing.

She leaned forward and pulled back the covers.

Pillows. Not Barry. Pillows!

"No!"

She turned and ran toward the door. "Barry!"

"What the hell's wrong?" Galen met her in the hall. "Is he sick?"

"He's not there. He's gone. I've got to find him."

"He's not in his room?"

"I told you he wasn't. Chavez has taken him."

"Hold it. You're not thinking."

"Of course I'm not thinking," she said fiercely. "I'm scared to death. Barry's gone."

"What if he just went down to the lake?"

"He knows he's not to go near the water alone."

"Kids aren't always predictable. And why wouldn't Chavez come in and kill the rest of us if he'd found out where we are?" Galen went past her into Barry's room and flipped on the light. "The window is still locked. If someone took him, they had to come through the house."

"We should have heard him."

"Maybe not." He crossed to the bed. "It depends on how good—" He picked up a sheet of paper from the nightstand. "Shit."

"What is it?" She ran over to him. "What does it say?"

He handed it to her.

> *Sorry, Galen. I have to have the money. It's the key to unlock the box I'm in. I'll call you.*
> *Judd*

She couldn't believe it. She suddenly remembered watching Judd smiling at Barry as her son drew back the bow he had made him. He couldn't have done this. It didn't make sense.

She had to believe it. Her son was gone.

The note dropped from her hand. "I'm going to kill him."

"Stand in line." Galen moved toward the door. "I'm going to get some clothes on and see if Hughes or any of his guards saw them leave. If I get any leads, I'll come back for you, Elena."

"The hell you will." She was already heading for her room. "Give me two minutes. I'm coming with you."

None of the guards had seen any sign of Judd or Barry.

"I'm going to kill him," she repeated through set teeth as they walked back to the cottage. "And if he hurts Barry, I'm going to crucify him."

"I don't think he'll hurt him."

"But you don't know. I never dreamed he'd take him. How can I be sure what else he'll do? The bastard is an assassin."

"You saw something in him that made you trust him before this happened."

"And he betrayed me. Just like Luis betrayed me." She turned on him. "And you brought him into our lives."

"That's true," he said quietly.

"You should never have—" She swallowed. "Why am I blaming you? Barry is my responsibility. I didn't have to trust Judd. I should have seen through him."

"I'd rather you blamed me than yourself." He started up the porch steps. "Come on, let's get some coffee."

She stared at him incredulously. "Sit around and drink coffee?"

"No, sit around and wait for Judd to call."

"I can't sit here any longer." Elena got up and went to the window. "What if he doesn't call?"

"He'll call."

"How do you know? He won't try to bargain with us. He'll go straight to Chavez."

"He said he'd call."

"Well, he hasn't. It's almost dark. Barry's been gone all day."

"He'll probably try to dig in and get settled first. It only seems like a long time to us."

"It seems like forever." Her hand was shaking as she lifted it to rub her temple. "What if Barry's scared? What if he's hurt?"

"It wouldn't be to Judd's advantage to hurt Barry. He's a commodity now."

"Commodity? He's not a commodity. He's a human being, a little boy." She swallowed to ease the tightness of her throat. "And he's alone with that damn killer."

"Listen to me. Judd isn't going to hurt him. If he wants money, Barry has to be alive and well. That's the only—"

The house phone rang. She hurried across the room and picked up the receiver. "Hello."

"Hello, Elena," Judd said. "I called on the house phone so that you and Galen could both pick up on the extensions."

"You bastard. Where's my son?"

"He's safe."

Galen disappeared into the living room and she heard him pick up the receiver. "What the hell are you doing, Judd?"

"Surviving. I told you that I was going to have to take my fate into my own hands. Logan's taking too long. I could be dead before he's able to get the heat off me."

"And surviving is kidnapping Barry?"

"Surviving is getting millions of dollars from Chavez to bribe all the people I need to bribe. That kind of money can make a lot of people forget I ever existed."

"Sweet. And trading a kid for the money is really great."

"Beggars can't be choosers. I never claimed to be an angel."

"I want my son back," Elena said. "If I don't get him, I'll track you down and slit your throat."

"Always the gentle lady," Judd said. "I don't blame you. I didn't call to make excuses. I wanted you to know that Barry has nothing to fear from me. I like the kid. He's not scared and he's having a fairly good time."

"You're lying."

"No, he thinks he's on an adventure and that you know all about it."

"What?"

"I lied to him. I talked him into coming with me. He didn't think it was that odd, considering you'd made a lot of hasty exits lately. I told him we were pretending to be Indians. He thought it was fun sneaking out in the middle of the night. He grabbed his bow and arrows and crept down that hall like a second-story man."

"You lied to him?"

"Would you rather I'd chloroformed him and taken him by force? This is much better for him."

"You were planning this when you made that bow and arrows for him. My God, and I was grateful to you."

"Bring him back, Judd," Galen said.

"Sorry. I want to stay alive."

"You're going to sell him to Chavez?"

"Chavez won't hurt him. It's Elena he wants to kill."

"You can't do that," Elena said.

"Look at it my way. I'm on borrowed time. If I don't do it, they'll catch up with me and kill me. If I do it, the kid will be upset, but he won't die. You may even have a chance to get him away from Chavez after I pick up my money."

"It will make it a thousand times harder," Galen said.

"You always liked a challenge," Judd said. "Elena, I'm going into the next room so you can talk to Barry. I'll be listening on the extension, and if you ask him any questions I'll take the phone from him. I don't want to do that. I want to keep him calm and happy. Let him think that you know all about our little adventure and that you couldn't be more pleased about it."

"Go to hell."

"You're upset. Think about it. I don't want Barry scared and neither do you. It's up to you to save him from that."

Elena was so angry that she couldn't speak for a moment. "How do you think he's going to feel when you turn him over to Chavez? He'll be terrified."

"I know. I don't like it. So let's put it off for as long as possible. Will you talk to Barry?"

There was no other choice. But she would try to get as much as she could from Judd. "I'll talk to him. But not only today. I want you to call me every day and let me talk to him. I want to know he's safe."

"And try to find out from him where we are?" He suddenly chuckled. "Good idea. Okay, but it won't do you any good. We'll be moving around." She heard a door open. "Hey, scout, want to talk to your mama?"

Barry was laughing as he came on the line. "Mama, you should be here. I saw lions and tigers. And there were monkeys and funny men in skirts."

"I'm glad you're having a good time, baby."

"But when are you coming?"

"I'm a little busy right now. Are you okay?"

"Sure. Judd and I are going to go to a carnival tomorrow night. He said there are Ferris wheels and crack-the-whip and booths where you can win prizes. He's going to buy me cotton candy."

"That's nice. Don't eat too much." Dammit, she was starting to cry. "I love you, Barry."

"Mama?"

"Galen's on the line," she said hurriedly. "He wants to talk to you. Galen?"

"I'm here, Elena."

"Good-bye, Barry. I'll talk to you tomorrow." She hung up and closed her eyes. Damn Judd. Damn him to hell.

"Barry sounds okay," Galen said as he came back into the room. "Happy as a lark."

"Why shouldn't he? He thinks he's on this grand vacation. Which will end abruptly when Judd sells him to Chavez."

"Judd's a hard nut, but he's fighting for his life."

"Don't you defend him."

"I'm not defending him. I'm trying to explain his thinking. I'm mad as hell at him."

"Then let's go after him." She sank down into a kitchen chair. "If he's making a deal with Chavez, then he'll want to remain in the general area. Barry said he's going to a carnival tomorrow night. How can we find out where there are carnivals playing in the Southeast?"

"Local licensing bureaus? Internet? I'll try both."

"He talked about lions and tigers. Could they be near a wildlife park?"

"If they are, then it will narrow the field down."

"Is there a computer here at the cottage?"

"Yes, it's in our hostess's, Eve's, workroom. Can you use a computer?"

"I know the basics. Even guerrilla warfare depends on technology these days. I'll check out the wildlife parks on the Internet while you call the licensing boards."

He checked his watch. "They'll be closed now. We may have to wait until tomorrow."

"I don't want to wait until—" She was being unreasonable. It was just that she didn't know how long this was going to take. "You'll call them as soon as they open?"

"You know I will."

Yes, she knew he would be on top of everything. "Then I'll go to work on the Internet. Maybe there will be some carnivals listed there too."

"It probably depends on how small they are. We do have twenty-four hours. But you have to realize that we may miss him. Judd said he'd be moving around."

"It will at least give us a starting place. I can't just sit here."

"I know." He paused. "We do have another option if we don't find Judd. We can go and stake out Chavez."

She stiffened. "What?"

"He's on a yacht cruising the Florida coast."

"And how long have you known this?"

"Since just before we went to Orlando."

"And you didn't tell me?" She studied his expression. "You were going after him yourself."

He didn't answer.

"Dammit, I don't *want* you to protect me."

He nodded. "Suppose we skip past history and concentrate on finding Barry. I thought you'd be glad to know we have another possibility."

She was very glad, and her annoyance and indignation paled in comparison. "Don't do it again. Everything has to be open and aboveboard."

"It will be." He reached out a hand in comfort but dropped it before touching her. "But remember, I care about Barry too. I'll do everything I can, as quick as I can."

"Thank you, I know you will," she whispered. "I didn't mean to—"

"It's okay. You've been through a lot in the last few days, and you sure as hell didn't need this." He turned and went back into the living room. "I have to go and talk to the security guys and tell them to be on the alert. I don't think we're in any danger of Judd selling our location to Chavez, since it's Barry who's the cash cow. But it doesn't hurt to take a few precautions. Then I'll get on the phone and call the newspapers and see if they have any listings or advertisements for carnivals."

She was glad he'd left her alone. She needed a moment to get herself together. She was just barely holding on to her composure. Galen was doing everything he could, and she shouldn't have spoken that harshly. It was just that—

Barry.

Oh, God, don't fall apart. Get busy. They had a chance of finding Judd.

Would it be in time?

"Chavez? This is Judd Morgan. You don't know me, but we're going to do some business."

"You're right, I don't know you from Adam, and I don't do business with people I don't know. How did you get my phone number?"

"Sean Galen."

There was a silence. "Let me talk to him."

"That's not possible. We've parted ways, but I took a good-bye present. Five years old, cute little tyke."

Another silence. "You're lying."

"I'm not lying. Do you know what the kid looks like?"

"I've seen pictures of him."

"Then you're going to receive another one by FedEx tomorrow. This one has Barry holding to-day's paper. Get out your magnifying glass and check the date."

"You're offering to sell him to me."

"If the price is right. If not, I'll send him back to Elena. I grew very fond of her in the past few weeks. It will take a good deal of money to soothe my con-science."

"Who are you?"

"You have my name. It's not a false one. I'm sure you'll have checked me out by the time you receive the photo." He paused. "You want other ID? I was the shooter at the Kissimmee Hotel. I took down two of your men besides Luis Kyler."

"Then why did you change sides and take the boy?"

"Because you're a man who knows that loyalties last only as long as there's a profit to be had."

"And what price do you want for my son?"

"We'll discuss that when I call back tomorrow. I want you to know that I have the merchandise and I can deliver."

"It could be a trap."

"Then I'll give you the same advice you gave Elena when you set up Luis. Protect yourself. You want the boy, I want the money." Judd hung up and leaned back in the chair.

That was the first step, and it had gone as he thought it would. Chavez was suspicious, but that would be partially erased when he saw the photograph. After that, it would come down to negotiations. Christ, he hated dealing with that slimeball.

But he had dealt with snakes like Chavez before and for less return.

Elena and Galen didn't get the information they needed until the next evening.

"Three touring carnivals operating in Georgia, one in Alabama and one in North Carolina, none in South Carolina or Florida," Galen said. "And the only one near a wild-game park is the one outside Birmingham, Alabama."

"How far is Birmingham?" Elena asked.

"About two and a half hours' drive."

"Then why don't we fly?"

"By the time we get to the airport, find a flight, and arrange for a rental car in Birmingham, we could be there already."

"Then let's go." She headed for the door. "It's only six o'clock. We might be able to catch—"

"It's a long shot, Elena."

"I don't care. Do you have a better idea?"

He shook his head. "I just don't want you to get your hopes up."

"Hope is all I've got. I'm not going to give it up." She opened the front door. "I'm going to Birmingham."

"And I'm going with you." He followed her out to the porch. "You need to remember that Judd heard everything Barry said to you. He might not even take him to the carnival."

She had already thought of that possibility. "He's trying to keep Barry so happy that he won't have time to question anything Judd says or does. An outing like that is a big thing in a little boy's life. He won't want to disappoint him. I think he'll try to take him, even if it's only for a short time." Her lips twisted bitterly. "I've never had an opportunity to take Barry to a carnival. I'm going to owe that bastard for cheating me of that too."

"Hey, big deal. We'll take him to Disney World when we get him back."

When, not *if?*

"We'll get him back," he said quietly to her unspoken question. "Even if we have to take him away from Chavez."

"If Chavez gets him out of the country, it will—"

Galen's phone rang. "Galen." He handed the phone to Elena. "Chavez."

She slowly raised the phone to her ear. "You bastard."

"Why are you so upset with me? It was your dear brother who killed his old mentor."

"You're the one who put a gun in his hand and gave him enough heroin to make sure he wouldn't care if he killed his sister or a man who had been nothing but a friend to him."

"Luis wasn't supposed to kill Dominic Sanders. I was expecting you to show up at the hotel and I told Luis it was his job to take care of you. Those drug addicts never get anything right."

She was so angry that she had to wait before replying. "You didn't get it right either. Luis is dead, and I have no reason to talk to you again."

"That was unfortunate. But you took out two of my men in exchange. I never expected you to have a marksman on call. He was extremely gifted. Galen?"

"No."

"Then who was it?"

"Why do you want to know? Do you want to put out a contract on him?"

"Just curious. How is my son?"

"He's not your son."

"I have an idea he will be soon. What do they say about possession?"

"And I'm in possession."

"Are you?"

"Yes, dammit." She hung up and looked at Galen.

"I think Judd has already contacted him. He was feeling me out. Christ, Judd's moving fast."

"Then we'd better do the same." He started down the steps. "Come on, let's see if we can find that carnival before it closes down for the night."

Chapter Fourteen

THE CARNIVAL GROUNDS SMELLED OF COTTON candy, popcorn, and the sweat of the crowd milling about the booths. The shrill sound of the calliope grated on Elena's nerves as her gaze searched desperately.

"Where do we start?" Elena murmured. "The Ferris wheel. He mentioned the Ferris wheel."

"As good a place as any." Galen grabbed her elbow and was already pushing her through the throng. "You have his picture to show people?"

She nodded, her gaze anxiously searching the crowd. Where are you, Barry? Where are you, baby? She looked up at the giant wheel, trying to see if he was in one of the boats. She couldn't see the one that had stopped on top. . . .

The wheel started again and the occupants of the top boat came into view.

Two teenage boys.

"Let's go," Galen said. "We'll split up. You start at the shooting booth and I'll scout the opposite direction. We'll meet at the front entrance."

"Right." She was already moving, searching, listening for Barry's voice in the crowd. She passed a catch-the-fish booth, a tent advertising hoochie-coochie dancers, a spinning-cup ride. Where *was* he, dammit?

It took only fifteen minutes to make her way back to the ticket booth at the front entrance.

"Nothing?" Galen asked.

She shook her head dejectedly. "Maybe we were wrong about this being the carnival. Or it could be that—"

"Jesus." Galen's hand closed on her arm. "That's Judd's truck pulling out of the parking lot." Galen was running toward their car. "He must have seen us. He's peeling out."

Elena looked over her shoulder as she jumped into the passenger seat. She caught a fleeting glimpse of a black truck with two occupants. One man, one little boy.

Barry!

Then the truck was gone, traveling at high speed down the road.

"Catch him." Her hands clenched into fists. "We've got to catch him."

"I know." Galen's wheels screeched as he backed out of the parking space. "Fasten your seat belt."

By the time they reached the road, Judd was almost out of sight.

Galen's foot jammed on the accelerator and the car jumped forward.

Faster.

Gas stations, convenience stores.

Faster.

She couldn't see the black truck any longer.

One mile.

Two miles.

Where was that damn truck?

"Where is he?" she whispered.

"We lost him. He must have turned off somewhere." He turned around. "We'll go back and go down some side streets."

They spent the next hour crisscrossing the main road.

No black truck.

No Barry.

Galen finally pulled over to the side of the road. "He got away from us."

"I know that." Her disappointment was so sharp it was almost physical. "We were so close."

"We'll get there again." Galen moved the car back into the flow of traffic. "What now?"

She tried to think. "Motels. They had to be staying at a motel in the general area. Let's find a phone book and go check them."

"A slim chance."

"So was the carnival."

"Good point. I'll pull over at the first convenience store and we'll go through the phone book."

They called thirteen room clerks at various motels

before they struck pay dirt. Ten minutes later they were standing in front of the check-in desk.

"That's Mr. Donovan," the woman said. "Real pleasant gentleman, and his son was a charmer."

"Did you hear him call the boy by name?" Galen asked.

She wrinkled her forehead. "Larry, I think."

"Barry?"

She smiled. "That's it."

"What room is he in?"

"Forty-two. But he checked out earlier this evening."

"Could I see the room and look around?"

She lost some of her friendliness. "Why?"

"I'm hoping to find some clue to where he's going next. I need to find him." He gestured at Elena. "They're in the middle of a very nasty divorce and he's taken their son."

The woman glanced at Elena. "I'm sorry. I could see you were upset."

"Yes, I am. Could we see the room? We'll be only a few minutes."

"I'll have to go along and stay while you're there."

"Fine." Galen turned toward the door. "Let's do it."

The motel room was really a suite with a living room, bedroom, and kitchenette. The maids had obviously not cleaned up. There were newspapers on the coffee table and soda glasses on the sink.

And on the nightstand a piece of paper with a

tiger and flowers scrawled in orange crayon. She picked up the paper and agony shot through her.

I saw lions and tigers. . . .

"Take it easy," Galen said beside her. "There's an envelope underneath it." He picked it up and opened the envelope. "It has my name on it. It seems we were expected." He scanned it and handed it to Elena. "No help."

> Galen,
>
> > Sorry we missed you. Good work, though.
> >   Judd

"We can't do anything more here," Galen said gently. "Let's go back to the cottage. Ready, Elena?"

She nodded jerkily and thrust the note back at him. Then she carefully smoothed Barry's picture and carried it to the door. "I'm ready. You're right, there's nothing more we can do."

I saw lions and tigers, Mama.

"Thirty million," Judd said crisply. "Not a penny less."

"You're crazy," Chavez said. "I won't pay more than ten."

"Yes, you will. Thirty million is a drop in the bucket to you. You can get that on a small shipment of coke to Miami."

"Because I can get it is no sign I will."

"What I'm selling you is priceless. You can't get it anywhere else."

"I won't pay it."

"Did you get the photograph I sent you?"

"Yes."

"The next one I send you will show you a dead boy. Then no more dreams of a father-and-son business. No more child to mold."

"You would kill a child?"

"Did you check my background? A kill is a kill. Do you want the boy or not?"

"Fifteen million."

"I need more than that. As you probably found out, I'm very hot. It will take a lot of cash to cool me down. Thirty."

"I'll think about it."

"I'll give you twenty-four hours. I'll call you tomorrow." He hung up.

"Judd," Barry called from the bathroom.

"Coming." He stood in the doorway and looked at Barry in the tub. "Problem washing behind your ears?"

"No." He floated the rubber crocodile on the water. "I was just lonesome. Are you ever lonesome, Judd?"

"No, I guess I like my own company too much."

"I miss Mama and Dominic."

"Aren't you having a good time?"

He nodded. "But I worry about Mama."

"Sometimes it's best to get used to being without people. Then it doesn't hurt so much."

He shook his head emphatically. "Not Mama.

When she had to go to the city to work, I never got used to it. Maybe we should—"

"Your mama wants you to have this adventure. She'll be disappointed if she thinks you're not happy."

Barry frowned, troubled. "I guess so."

"Then get out of that tub before you turn into a prune." Judd grabbed a bath towel and held it for him. "You need to get to sleep. Tomorrow we're going to a petting zoo. Would you like that?"

Barry's face lit up. "Oh, yes. Will they have llamas? I saw a llama once."

"I have no idea. I guess we'll find out together."

"And I can talk to Mama and tell her about it?"

He draped the towel around him. "Absolutely."

"That's good." He ran out of the bathroom.

Well, there wasn't much else good in this entire scenario, Judd thought wearily. The whole business was making him a little sick. Not that the nastiness of it would cause him to back down.

Thirty million dollars was good. Being free to live his own life was good. He could swallow the filth and do whatever was necessary.

"Come on, time for bed." Galen helped Elena out of the car. "Judd will call tomorrow and maybe we'll get another clue as to where he is."

"Yes." She clutched Barry's drawing as she started up the stairs. "He promised, didn't he?"

"Yes." He led her through the dark house to her bedroom. "And he'll keep his promise." He took the drawing from her clenched hand and set it on the nightstand. He started to unbutton her shirt.

"I can do it."

"Sure." He finished unbuttoning her shirt. "But you've had a knockout punch. Let me."

She didn't care. It didn't matter.

He quickly undressed her and tucked her beneath the blanket. "I'll be right back. I'm going to get you a couple aspirin." He gave her the aspirin and then slipped into bed beside her. "God, you're cold." He cuddled closer to her. "Try to go to sleep."

She closed her eyes. "Lions and tigers . . . Barry has a book about a tiger named Sarina. It was a very playful tiger, and I wondered if the writer shouldn't have given a hint about how dangerous they are. But I thought it was okay because you don't run into tigers every day."

"Very rarely."

"But Barry has run into a tiger, and no matter how playful he seems, the danger is there. There's no telling what Judd could do."

"Nothing's happened yet. I agree Judd is an enigma, but we have to hope for the best."

"The best is for him to give me back my son. He's not going to do that."

"No."

"I'm going to sleep now. It hurts to stay awake. It's so lonely. Dominic is gone, Luis is gone, and now Barry. . . ."

"How many times do I have to tell you? You're not alone. You'll never be alone again. Trust me."

"I'm sorry. I'm whining. I'll be better in the morning. Good night."

"Don't close me out. Let me come in. I'll warm you."

He was warming her, but not enough to melt the ice. "Good night," she said again.

He gave an exasperated sigh and his arms tightened around her. "Okay, but I'm here for you. Know that."

She nodded. In some remote part of her mind she knew that as truth and it brought her comfort. She had to get over this deadly malaise. It made it difficult for her to function. It was an enemy. "I'll be better. I have to be better. I have to get Barry. . . ."

"You'll be tough as nails after you get some sleep." He pressed his lips to her temple. "I promise you."

Chavez called at four in the morning.

"He wants to talk to you," Galen said. "You're not in any shape. Let me handle him."

She shook her head and took the phone. "We have nothing to talk about, Chavez."

"I disagree. We have a good deal to discuss. You didn't tell me that you no longer have my son."

"I do have Barry."

"I've had talks with a man who says that he has custody and is willing to give him to me for a price."

"He's lying. You'd be a fool to deal with him."

"I never act the fool. He sent me a picture of Barry and demanded thirty million dollars."

She didn't respond.

"That's a lot of money. Naturally, I told him that I wouldn't pay it. Do you know what he said? He told me the next picture he sent me would be of a dead boy."

She inhaled sharply as pain knifed through her.

"Oh, that got you. I hoped it would. So, you see, it's up to me whether the boy lives or dies. I'm really tempted to let Morgan kill him just to see you suffer."

"Morgan won't kill him."

"Wishful thinking. He's capable of anything. He's killed countless times. I researched him thoroughly, and his background is very nasty indeed."

"He won't . . . do it."

"Oh, he will, if I don't pay the money. Should I do it? Is it worth it to me? You'll have to wonder, won't you?"

"You want my son. It will be worth it to you."

"Your voice is shaking. I feel quite stimulated by this conversation. It's almost as satisfactory as having you here with me. If I do decide to ransom my son, I'll be in total control of his life or death. If I decide that you've spoiled any potential he might have, then I'll get rid of him."

"To hurt me."

"Oh, yes, that's my prime goal."

"I don't believe you. You're bluffing. It would be stupid of you to kill him. That would be a defeat for you."

"But you have to have the tiniest doubt. In the meantime, I'll leave you to wonder whether I'll really pay Morgan. Maybe I'll have him send that next picture to you." He hung up.

"I told you I should talk to him. What is it?" Galen asked as he took the phone from her lifeless hand.

"Thirty million dollars or Judd threatened to kill Barry."

Galen swore. "Chavez could be lying."

"I don't think so. He was getting too much satisfaction out of hurting me."

"Is he going to pay?"

"He wouldn't tell me."

"He'll pay."

"I . . . think so." She compressed her lips to keep them from trembling. "I have to think so."

"Even if he doesn't, Judd could be bluffing."

"Judd never impressed me as a man who bluffs." She got out of bed. "We have to find him."

"He'll call today. Where are you going? We can't do anything right now."

"I can't stay in this bed. I have to do something, anything."

He studied her for a moment and then slowly nodded. "You're right. You have to do something." He got out of the bed and headed for the bathroom. "Get dressed. I'll meet you downstairs in five minutes."

"Where are we going?"

"Outside. It's not the barn, but it will have to do."

———

"No holds barred." Galen threw his shirt beneath a tree. "Come and get me."

"I don't want to fight you."

"You won't hurt me. I'm probably as good as you are."

"What is this? Some kind of therapy? This is useless."

He made a lightning step forward and swept her legs from under her. She crumpled to the ground.

He ran toward her and she automatically rolled over, grabbed his ankle, and twisted it. She jumped to her feet and gave him a roundhouse kick to the abdomen as he got up.

He grunted before grabbing her foot and yanking it, bringing her down.

She felt a surge of anger mixed with sheer adrenaline as she dodged to the side and attacked again.

It was not like sparring with Judd. Galen was better, quicker, and he seemed not to feel the punishment she was inflicting.

"Is that all you can do? Maybe you'd better pretend I'm Judd. It might give you more incentive. Or maybe Chavez."

"I don't need an incentive." She ducked and attacked again.

Fifteen minutes passed, and she was breathless and no longer sure whom she was fighting. Judd. Chavez. Galen. They were all whirling before her as she attacked and attacked and attacked again.

"Okay. Okay." Galen was breathless as he finally backed away from her. "I give up. I don't need any more damage."

She stood there, her breasts rising and falling with every breath. "You're . . . done?"

"*We're* done." He wiped his sweaty face on his shirt. "Let's hit the shower. I have some bruises I need to take care of."

"I hurt you?"

"No more than I expected. I imagine you'll find a few bruises too." He held the screen door open for her. "If you don't, I'll feel more of a failure than I do now."

The haze of adrenaline was gradually ebbing and she was able to think again. "You didn't want to beat me. You were acting as a punching bag."

"The hell I was." He winced as he flexed his arm. "That was purely a side effect. Come on. Shower."

She didn't move. "Why?"

"Because I stink?"

"Why did you do it?"

"What else can you do at four in the morning? Don't answer that. I'm trying not to think of the alternatives."

"So you decided to knock me around."

"That's right. I needed to release my inner hostility."

"Bullshit."

He smiled. "How do you feel?"

She thought about it. "Strong. Very strong."

"Not defenseless?"

"No way."

"Then I'll postpone the shower and make some coffee while we decide what you want for breakfast." He moved toward the kitchen. "Or maybe not. Caffeine may rouse the tiger in you again."

I saw lions and tigers. . . .

The memory brought pain but not the terrible feeling of helplessness.

"You have an unusual way of handling depression, Galen. You see a woman who is down and out and try to pound her into the ground."

"Whatever works. Tender loving care wasn't doing the job." He flipped on the kitchen lights. "You can function now. Lord, can you function."

Yes, she could function. She could feel the blood flowing through her veins, and her mind was alert. Galen had given her release and confidence. God, what enormous gifts in this time of need.

She tore her gaze away from him. "You weren't so bad yourself." She went to the cabinet and took down two cups. "Okay, now we have to decide whether to stake out Chavez or continue to go after Judd."

"I'll pay it, Morgan," Chavez said. "But I want a little something extra."

"You're getting what you pay for. Nothing else."

"Thirty million is an exorbitant fee for one little

boy. I think I deserve more. It won't be anything you're not accustomed to doing."

"And what is that?"

"I want Elena Kyler. Alive preferably, but I'll accept her dead if it proves impossible."

Judd was silent a moment. "Why should I give you anything?"

"I'm reluctant to give you this much money. I can stretch our negotiations out for a long time, and you want them over. You're probably tap dancing to keep ahead of Galen and Elena right now. All you have to do is give me Elena and it's a done deal."

"I'll think about it."

"I'll add another five million dollars to the pot if you bring her to me alive. I'll also put pressure on a few senators I have in my pocket to take the heat off you."

"It's an interesting proposition."

"And one you won't get from me again. It will be easy for you. I don't even know why you're hesitating."

"I'll let you know." He hung up the phone.

It will be easy for you.

It was natural for Chavez to believe that betrayal and murder would be simple for him. It had been his life for too many years. How difficult would it be to slip back into the habits of the past?

Chavez was right. Judd needed to be done with these negotiations. Galen and Elena had almost caught him last night at the carnival. He was lucky that

Barry had not seen them. He needed the money. He needed to be rid of the kid.

So what to do?

Chavez thought he knew what his decision would be. Was he right?

Betrayal and murder . . .

Chapter Fifteen

"WHAT ARE WE WAITING FOR? JUDD'S NOT GOING TO call." Elena stood at the window gazing blindly out at the lake. "I think we should go to Miami to get Chavez."

"Let's give it just a little more time."

"He said he'd call yesterday and he didn't do it." Her hand clutched the curtain so tightly that her knuckles turned white. "He's made his deal with Chavez and he's going to turn over Barry. We have to stop him."

"Wait until noon and then we'll take off. We may be in a better position here to intercept him. He or Barry may drop—"

"No." She turned and headed for the front door. "He can call us on the road. I'm too frightened to—"

The house phone rang.

She jumped for it. "Hello."

"Is Galen on the line?" Judd asked.

"He will be in a minute. Let me talk to Barry."

"After we finish. He's fine."

"How do I know that? You promised Chavez you'd send him a picture of a dead boy."

"He told you that? He'll evidently do anything to hurt you."

"Was it a lie?"

He didn't answer immediately. "No."

"You son of a bitch."

"At times," Judd said. "But it's not kind of you to say so when I'm calling to give you an opportunity."

"What kind of opportunity?" Galen had picked up the extension.

"To get her son back."

Elena stiffened. "What the hell are you talking about?"

"I've made a deal with Chavez. I get my money. He gets Barry. But the terms of delivery are in my court."

"Go on."

"I've told Chavez that he has to do the delivery himself. He brings the money, I turn over Barry. No escort or I don't deal."

"And you think he'll abide by it?"

"Probably not. I'll do a little scouting ahead of time to make sure I'm safe."

"And where do we come in?"

"I'll tell you where and when. You come after I've got my money and take Barry away from him. Simple."

"Too simple," Galen said. "It smells like a trap."

"Or a bad conscience trying to do the right thing," Judd said. "You take your choice."

"Trap," Elena said.

"I'll call you tonight with the time and place. Barry will be there. I'm sure he'll hope to see you." He called, "Barry, your mother wants to talk to you."

"Galen, it's a trap, isn't it?" She hung up after talking to Barry and walked into the kitchen. "That tricky bastard."

"Probably." He hung up the extension. "But it's also an opportunity, just as Judd said. I don't doubt Barry will be there. It's the only bait that would work."

"And Chavez will have his men there."

"Almost certainly. It's very risky." He smiled faintly. "But it's not going to stop you from going, is it?"

Even the slimmest chance to get Barry back? "Hell, no."

"Then we wait for Judd to tell us where and when."

Judd called at nine-forty that evening.

"Tomorrow night. In the glade at the top of Blackjack Mountain. One A.M."

"If this is the trap I think it is, I'm going to hunt you down and draw and quarter you," Galen said.

"Don't you think I know that? You have to do what you have to do. I can't guarantee the unpredictable, and everything about this delivery is unpredictable."

"Including you."

"Including me." Judd hung up.

"That sounded like a warning," Elena said.

"Who the hell knows?" Galen moved toward the desk in the living room. "We need to take a look at a state map and find Blackjack Mountain. We have some reconnoitering to do before tomorrow night."

She followed him and watched as he took out the map and looked up Blackjack Mountain. "It's about forty-five miles north of the city off Highway 76. I don't see any nearby towns. Evidently Judd wanted his meeting isolated enough not to disturb the neighbors."

She nodded. "We're not going to have much time to familiarize ourselves with the area."

"Time enough. I don't think either of us is going to sleep tonight anyway." He headed for the door. "Let's get on the road."

"Galen."

"What?"

"I just want this very clear. This is my son. We both have to go all out. You're not going to try to close me out or protect me."

He hesitated. "It's going to be hard for me not to do it."

"But you'll do it because you made me a promise."

He grimaced. "And I'll keep it. We go in together and we do the job together. Okay?"

She nodded and followed him to the door. "Just so you understand."

"I told you once I was chock-full of understanding. Since then I've begun to regret that particular talent."

They didn't get back from Blackjack Mountain until after noon the next day. They were both sweaty, dirty, and scratched from brush.

"Get a shower and try to nap," Galen said. "I've got to get a few weapons and some infrared night glasses from Hughes."

"You should sleep too."

"I will." He paused. "We'll draft several of Hughes's security guys to take out Chavez's men near the road and stand by for an alert from us. But if we go up that mountain like a SWAT team, there's a greater chance of Barry being hurt. We don't know what Chavez will do if he's cornered."

"I know that."

"And we can't be sure how many of Chavez's men will be guarding the way up to that glade. We'll have to pick them off one by one on the way to him. We can't afford noise."

She nodded. "Knives and hands."

"Right."

She heard the door close behind him as she headed for her bedroom. A few minutes later she was under the shower and the hot water was washing away the dirt, but not the cold anxiety that had gripped her all night. Christ, she was scared.

They had gone over that mountain until she was familiar enough with it to feel fairly certain she wouldn't blunder into unknown dangers. The dangers she knew about were bad enough.

She got out of the shower and toweled off. It wasn't as if she hadn't done this before, she told herself. She would just do what she had been taught all those years ago. It would be fine.

But it was Barry who was at stake.

Fear stabbed her and she had to push down the panic that followed. She mustn't be frightened. Think of something that would give her strength.

Galen. Some of the fear eased. Yes, Galen would be with her this time. Together they would be able to do it. Together they would be able to save her son.

Take care of our boy.

That was the last line of the letter Dominic had written her.

"I'm trying, Dominic," she whispered. "But everything is going wrong and I'm scared. If you're around somewhere, I could use a little help."

12:05 A.M.
BLACKJACK MOUNTAIN

Where was the bastard? Chavez wondered impatiently as his gaze searched the trees surrounding the glade.

"Chavez, I presume."

Chavez whirled to face the man standing in the shadows of a huge oak tree. "Morgan?"

"Yes."

"You kept me waiting," Chavez said. "Come out where I can see you."

"I'm afraid not. I'd be too good a target. Not that I believe you'd double-cross me. Is the money in that suitcase?"

"Yes, come and get it."

"You come to me."

"Where's my son?"

"He's here behind this tree. He's sound asleep. I slipped him a Mickey and he should be out for a few hours."

Chavez moved slowly forward until he was facing Morgan.

"No unfriendly moves." Morgan was pointing a gun at him. "I hear you're very good at hand-to-hand. Put the case on the ground and open it."

Chavez unlatched the case. "It's in large bills. That's a lot of money to be crammed into a case."

"I've no objection." Morgan shone a penlight on the bills and then picked up several stacks and leafed through them one by one. "It seems to be in order." He latched the suitcase and shone the light on Barry, who was sleeping behind the tree. "Your merchandise."

Chavez glanced at the boy. "Where's Elena?"

"She'll be here in forty minutes or so. I wanted to conclude my primary business first and get out."

"And I'm to trust you that she'll come?"

"She knows the boy is here. Think what she's gone through already to save him from your clutches. She's desperate now."

"You're going to stay right here."

"I beg to disagree. Don't worry, I know if I left you with egg on your face you'd never stop hunting me. I don't have the slightest doubt you'll put a contract out on me anyway, but I understand contracts and can deal with them." He started to back into the forest. "She'll be here."

"Did you believe I'd let you leave this mountain alive?"

"Perish the thought. But I'm going to do it just the same. My former occupation gave me unique experience in escape and evasion. I know you have this mountain crawling with your people. I had to take out one to safeguard my chosen exit trail. I'm sure you won't mind. He was clumsy anyway. . . ."

He was gone.

"Gomez!"

The man ran from the trees on the other side of the glade. "I couldn't get a clear shot. Should I go after him?"

"Yes. No. Elena may be on her way. I don't want her scared off by any search parties crashing through the brush. We'll get him later. Give me your flashlight." He shone the light down on the boy. It was definitely the boy he'd seen in the picture, and he still appeared to be in a deep sleep. "I have my son and I'll soon have the woman." He added, "If she does make it this far, I want you to leave her to me. Don't interfere. Now get back to your position."

"Are you ready?" Galen whispered.

Elena nodded and adjusted her infrared night glasses. "I counted five. There could be more."

"Probably are. They may be on the move. You

take the trail to the left; I'll take the right. We meet at the glade at the top."

"Right. Chavez is bound to have a man or two in the woods around the glade. Will you take them out?"

"And what will you be doing?"

She didn't answer. "Will you take them out?"

He muttered an oath. "Yes, dammit. You can trust me. I'll make sure there aren't any surprises. Satisfied?"

She nodded, her gaze on the top of the mountain. Barry.

"Elena, just meet me there. Don't go in without me. Do you hear me?"

"I heard you. Be careful." She bent low and darted to the left.

Clear the way, her father had told her. Be silent but take them out. Clear the way.

Clear the way to Barry.

Two down.

Galen rolled the body into the bushes and jammed his knife back into its calf sheath.

No noise. No alert.

He paused a moment to get his bearings and the next target. A guard a hundred yards farther up on the trail.

He continued to carefully crawl his way up the side of the trail.

The man's neck broke as she twisted it from behind. Elena let him fall and kept going.

Don't stop.

Move faster.

More of Chavez's men on the trail ahead.

But beyond them was the glade.

Beyond them was Barry.

Clear the way.

Panic surged through Elena when she saw there was no one in the glade.

Not Chavez. Not her son.

"Chavez!"

No answer.

Her gaze searched the trees. "Chavez, I know you're there. Come out and face me."

"I was just making sure you had no company. Where's Galen?"

Elena's gaze flew across the glade to where the voice had come from. She'd discarded her night glasses and could only see by the fitful moonlight. Where was he? "Hopefully wreaking havoc on your men."

"Then he's probably dead by now. I hope you weren't fond of him."

Don't think about his words. He only wanted to shake her, weaken her. "Where's my son?"

"Here." Chavez's voice was farther left, Elena noticed. He must be moving.

She started moving herself. "Where?"

"Why should I tell you? It's no longer important. Your status as his mother is at an end."

"Bullshit."

"I've heard that maternal love makes idiots of women, and you've proved it tonight. I was doubtful you'd walk into Morgan's trap."

"I walked in and I'm walking out. I'm taking my son with me. You've moved five yards to the left. You're trying to get behind me. Do you really want to attack me from the rear? Are you afraid to look me in the eyes?"

"Don't be ridiculous. Do you think I believe that lie about you just pretending I'd beaten you? I beat you then. I'll beat you now."

"You know in your heart I was telling the truth. It must be a terrible blow to your pride. Are you afraid you'll fail again if you face me?"

"I won't be taunted into doing something stupid, Elena."

"Will you remember this later and regret it, Chavez? Oh, I know you probably wanted me helpless and unable to defend myself, but that would just prove how ineffectual you are."

"You didn't find me ineffectual when I was driving between your legs."

Don't let him shake you. Memories were also a weapon.

"The only way you could beat me was to tie me down. What kind of victory is that?"

Silence. "You bitch. Knife?"

She drew a deep, relieved breath. "Knife, hands, feet. Throw your other weapons out into the clearing. I'll do the same."

"The knife at last. Not that I didn't enjoy our

less lethal bouts. Do you remember lying on the mat and—"

"Throw out your weapons."

"You first."

"And chance getting shot by one of your men in the forest?"

"You have to take your chances. Maybe I told them to leave you to me. Maybe I didn't. You're so sure I want to redeem myself. Are you certain enough to throw out your guns?"

She had hoped to place him in a position of weakness. She wasn't sure if she'd shoot him when he stepped out into the clearing, but it was definitely a possibility. Hand-to-hand was always a risk, and she had to think of Barry. Now she had no choice. If there was another man in the forest, she had to trust that Galen would take him down. She felt a sudden surge of confidence. Yes, he wouldn't fail her. She could trust Galen.

She threw her rifle and pistol out into the glade. "Now you."

Would he do it?

He stepped out of the forest into the moonlight and threw a rifle and handgun down. "Come, Elena." His tone was mocking. "Show me how you beat me all those years ago."

Elena and Chavez circled each other, knives drawn.

Elena sprang forward. Chavez ducked aside and his knife darted out and raked her. She spun away before he could follow through.

"First blood, Elena," he murmured. "You should have expected that."

She whirled and gave him a roundhouse kick to the stomach. "I did."

He grunted in pain and sank to his knees.

She knew better than to close in on him. She had seen him fake weakness too many times and then take advantage of an unguarded moment.

He lunged to one side and regained his feet. "Good move. Now let's see you counter." He made a series of lightning-quick karate moves she was barely able to counter. God, he was fast. Too fast. The attacks had brought him close enough to her that he got in a punch to the chin.

Darkness.

Hot pain in her arm as his knife lunged forward.

She staggered back.

Clear your head.

She had only seconds before he would be on top of her.

Buy time.

She kicked and connected with his groin.

She was vaguely aware of his grunt of pain as she fought off faintness.

Chavez didn't fall, but she was in no shape to follow through.

Dammit, she had to follow through. Now. Ignore the dizziness. She would never have a better chance.

She did a sidekick to his throat and he fell to the ground. She stepped forward to stomp on the side of his head, but he grabbed her ankle.

She was down.

She rolled over and straddled him, her knee pinning his knife hand while her own knife hovered over his throat.

"Very good," he whispered. "But you can't do it, Elena. You'll never be able to do it."

"The hell I won't."

"No, you won't. Do you know why? Because I've told my man if he sees me down, he's to slit your son's throat."

"You're lying."

"Can't you see the blood spurting? I can—" He spat in her face.

She instinctively flinched and his pinned arm broke free. His knife thrust toward her.

She was able to escape it by inches as she rolled over and away from him.

"I almost had you. You could have killed me then, but that convenient maternal instinct raised its head again." He was on his feet and coming toward her. His foot lashed out, connecting with her wrist, and her knife fell to the ground. She scissored his ankles between her legs and brought him down again.

He recovered and was on top of her, his knife coming toward her chest. She quickly brought her arm up to block it.

A bullet skimmed his cheek.

He stiffened. "What the—"

Elena rolled, grabbing his wrist and pressing the nerve at the same time. The knife fell from his numbed hand, and she scrambled sideways and took possession of it.

Chavez tackled her. She twisted under his body and lunged upward with the knife.

He froze on top of her. "Elena?"

She pushed him off her and sat up.

Blood was gushing from the wound in his chest and he was looking down at it in disbelief.

"I told you I'd do it." Jesus, she was shaking. "Where's my son?"

He shook his head.

"Damn you, where is he?"

"Dead."

Panic soared through her and her hand darted out and clutched his throat. "Stop lying. Where is he?"

"Elena . . ." His eyes closed and he slumped sideways.

Barry couldn't be dead. Even with his last breath Chavez had to be lying to hurt her.

"You're bleeding." Galen was kneeling beside her. "Where are you hurt?"

Did a man lie when he was dying?

"Elena, where are you hurt?"

"Dammit, I'm not hurt. It's nothing." She leaped to her feet. "He said Barry was here but that he was dead. He had to be lying. I have to find him. He had to be—"

"He was lying." Judd stepped out from the trees. "Barry is behind that oak tree. I gave him a Mickey, but he should be coming around in a little while. I'd get him off this mountain before he does. There's quite a bit of carnage he shouldn't see."

"That tree?" Elena was already running toward it.

God, make it be true. Make him be safe.

There he was. But he was so still. . . .

She fell to her knees and gathered him close.

He was breathing. Sleeping, as Judd had said.

She rocked him back and forth in an agony of joy.

He's going to be all right. Do you hear me, Dominic? Our boy is safe.

"He's not hurt?" Galen asked Judd.

"Hell, no. He may wake up with the tiniest headache, but I'm pretty good with sedatives. He shouldn't have any aftereffects."

"He'd better not. If Elena doesn't cut your throat, I will."

"And both of you are very talented in that area. After I finished my business with Chavez, I climbed that poplar tree near the glade and watched you operate."

"Why?"

He shrugged. "I had to keep an eye on the kid to make sure Chavez didn't do anything unexpected, and I thought I might as well be entertained. There's nothing I liked better than seeing those slimeballs meet their maker."

Galen's gaze narrowed on his face. "And helping a couple of them along yourself? I ran into two bodies on the way up that I wasn't responsible for. I thought maybe Elena . . . but she wasn't supposed to be anywhere near that trail."

"I got a little bored waiting."

"Then why didn't you do something constructive and take out Chavez?"

"That was Elena's job. She needed to do it."

Galen started to curse.

"We look at things differently. You're protective. I'm on the outside looking in."

"You came in from the outside and kidnapped Barry, damn you."

"I needed the money," Judd said simply. "I was sorry I had to use him, but I was feeling the pressure."

"You not only used him, you used me. I brought Elena and Barry to the ranch and I trusted you."

"I never told you that you could trust me. You didn't want to believe that I'm capable of doing things you'd never dream of doing. But you might consider that the boy will have no bad memories of this episode. He's had an adventure that he'll remember for some time."

"And Elena's been through hell."

Judd nodded soberly. "And I knew exactly what I was doing to her when I took Barry. I'm not asking forgiveness. I know that's not possible."

"You're damn right it's not."

"Then I'll be on my way. I just wanted to make sure she didn't have to search for Barry." He turned away. "Good-bye, Galen. Good luck."

"And where are you going?"

"Washington. I have some intricate bribing to do."

"You're an idiot. They'll catch you and hang you out to dry."

"What do you care?" He smiled faintly as he strolled toward the trees. "I'm not your problem anymore."

He shouldn't care. He wouldn't care. What Judd had done was beyond the pale. Son of a bitch.

As he reached the edge of the glade, Judd took off his black windbreaker and dropped it on the ground. "Tell Elena to put on my jacket. She's covered in Chavez's blood and she wouldn't want to scare the kid."

He disappeared into the trees.

Galen gazed after him in anger and frustration . . . and regret.

Damn him.

"Let me take him." Galen reached out and took Barry from her arms. "How is he?"

"Sleeping. But he stirred a moment ago."

"Good. I called Hughes to bring the men up and secure our path as we go down the mountain. He should be here any minute."

She looked around the glade. "Where's Judd?"

"He left. He was probably afraid to face a mother's wrath."

"He should be," she said grimly. "I may still go after him and murder the bastard."

"He wouldn't blame you." He handed her the jacket he'd draped over his arm. "He left you this. He said you mustn't scare Barry."

"I'll do what I—" She glanced down at her bloodstained clothes. "Shit." She grabbed the jacket and put it on. "Let's get out of here. I don't know if your shot alerted any rangers or campers, but I don't want to find out."

"I didn't fire that shot. I was very busy disposing of Gomez. He was better than I expected."

"Judd?"

"More than likely. He was perched up in a tree like a bloody angel of death."

She looked back at Chavez. "It was a close moment. I was countering his move, but I might not have been fast enough. He distracted Chavez."

"But didn't take him out. He said you needed to do that."

So many deaths. Dominic, Luis, Forbes . . . Chavez had poisoned her life for years and threatened her child. Yes, she had needed to do it herself. But she resented the fact that Judd had recognized that about her. "I don't want any favors from him."

"You'll have to accept that one. It's probably the only reason I didn't strangle him."

She shook her head. "You like him. In spite of everything, you still like him. You grabbed at the excuse."

He grimaced ruefully. "Maybe."

"I can't forgive him. He took my child."

"No one expects you to." His arms tightened around the little boy. "There's Hughes coming into the glade. Let's go. I think Barry's starting to wake up."

It wasn't until they were only a few miles from the cottage that Barry roused in her arms. "Mama?"

"Yes, baby. You okay?"

"Sleepy." He yawned. "I missed you."

"I missed you too."

He looked at Galen. "Hi, Galen. I saw so many things. So many wonderful things . . ."

"That's good, Barry."

"Where's Judd?"

"He had to go away on business. He told me to say good-bye."

"Oh." Barry's face fell with disappointment. "When will he come back?"

"I don't know. We're going to do some traveling ourselves."

Elena looked at him. "We are?"

"It's a surprise for your mother too." Galen gazed meaningfully at Elena. "There may be some stormy weather around here. We need to absent ourselves until the disturbance settles down."

Elena nodded slowly. They didn't know what kind of repercussions might result from the killing of Chavez and his men. There was little loyalty among the drug hierarchy, but it would be smart to take precautions.

"I think we all need a beach, and I know a place in the Bahamas that will fit the bill," Galen said.

"I like it at the cottage." Barry frowned. "And I'm kind of tired of traveling around."

"I bet you are." Elena hugged him. "But the cottage doesn't belong to us. We can't stay there forever."

"Will Dominic go with us?"

She was silent a moment. How much longer before she had to tell him that he would never have his

Dominic again? Not now. Not until he was more secure. "No, Dominic won't be going with us."

"Why not? He told me he'd take me to the shore sometime. He said he really had fun at the beach in Miami."

"He has something else to do now." Elena blinked back the tears. "But he'd want you to enjoy yourself. He likes to see you happy."

Barry nodded. "Maybe he'll come later. He told me once that he'd always be with us."

She felt Galen grasp her arm for an instant, then release it, and comfort flowed through her at that silent support.

"It's true. He'll never really go away." She cleared her throat. "You'll like the beach. Did you know that you can build castles in the sand?"

Epilogue

THE SUN WAS HOT ON HER BACK, AND ELENA TURNED over and drew farther beneath the huge beach umbrella.

"You're going to burn." Galen dropped down on the blanket beside her. He threw a towel over her legs. "You shouldn't go out at this time of day."

"I like the heat and I hardly ever burn. It's one advantage of having olive skin." She turned on her side to look at him. "Where's Barry? The last time I saw him, the two of you were riding that poor mule down the beach."

"Nothing poor about the blasted animal. He stopped walking and made me pull him back to the hotel." He nodded at a group of children several yards away. "Barry's over there with the children's director."

"Barry's seen more of you than I have during the last two months. Where have you been?"

"Here and there. I thought you needed to just lie

in the sun and be alone with the kid. You were pretty stressed when we left Georgia."

That was an understatement. She had been coiled tight as a wire and was filled with sorrow, regret, and a weariness that was bone deep. She had been almost numb for the first week and then, gradually, she had begun to heal. "*Stressed* isn't the word."

"You look better now." He stared out at the ocean. "I called Logan today, and he said we're clear to go back to the U.S. The DEA isn't going out of its way to investigate the killing of Chavez or his men. They're just glad to be rid of them. Manero says there's no word of any push against us from the drug community. They're too busy dividing up Chavez's territory."

"So it's over?"

"Looks like it. We'll go back to the States and get you settled with proper papers. That's what you want, right?"

"That's what I want."

"Good." He got to his feet. "Then I'll set it up. We can probably leave in a few days."

She watched him walk back to the hotel. The sun was shining on his close-cut dark hair, and he was moving with his usual restless energy. He was clearly on a mission.

Out to tie up loose ends and place a big satin bow on a job well done.

Not bloody likely, Galen.

———

She drew a deep breath as she paused before the door of Galen's room.

Just do it.

She opened the door. The room was in darkness. "Galen."

"Out here on the balcony. Problems?"

"Oh, yes." She crossed the room and went out to join him. "Big time."

"Barry?"

"No. Everything doesn't have to concern Barry."

"Could have fooled me."

"Because you're blind. I love my son, but that doesn't mean he has to be the only one in my life. If you hadn't been so damn considerate, you could have taken me back into your bed at least a month ago. Instead, you made me wait." She took a step closer. "You made me feel uncertain, and I don't like that."

He smiled faintly. "And what are you going to do?"

"I'm going to tell you I love you and I think you love me. I'll give you some time to think about it, but it's only fair to let you know that I believe in marriage."

"And when did you decide you had all this boundless affection for me?"

"I think it was right before I threw out my weapons when I was about to fight Chavez."

He blinked. "What?"

"I knew there might be a sniper in the trees, but I threw them out anyway because I trusted that you'd be there for me."

He threw back his head and laughed. "My God, that's got to be the most original declaration I've ever heard."

"Stop laughing." She tried to steady her voice. "It meant something to me. It's not easy for me to lean on someone else, to trust. You told me I wasn't alone, that I didn't have to be alone. Well, I'm going to take you up on it." She paused. "So make up your mind about it."

"And if I don't?"

"Then I'll make it up for you." She stepped closer and laid her head on his chest. She could hear the sound of his heartbeat beneath her ear. "I'll follow you all around the world until you get tired of seeing me and Barry behind you. You won't be able to look at another woman because I'll scare her off."

"You'll clear the way to me?"

"Anywhere. Anytime."

"I guess I don't have any choice, then. Since I'm such a peaceful man, I wouldn't want to see violence inflicted on an innocent—ouch. You kicked me."

"I'll do worse than that if you're not—"

"Shh. No threats. Do you know what it took for me to wait until you came to me?" He cupped her face in his hands and looked down into her eyes.

She inhaled sharply at what she saw there. "Then it served you right. There's nothing wrong with being a little aggressive."

"There is where you're concerned. You've threatened both my person and my manhood in the past."

"That was different."

"Everything that's between us is different. That's why it had to be right or not at all."

"And is it right now?"

His face was coming nearer and his voice was only a breath of sound. "You tell me. . . ."

Turn the page for a preview of

Fatal Tide

The next electrifying novel
of suspense from
IRIS JOHANSEN

Coming from Bantam Books
in September 2003!

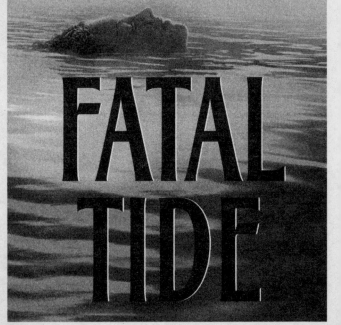

FATAL TIDE

IRIS JOHANSEN

TAKES YOU TO THE EDGE OF SUSPENSE

Fatal Tide

on sale September 2003

Chapter One

NORTHERN IRAQ
January 6, 1991

Cool water, smooth as glass as Kelby swam through it. Jesus, he was thirsty. He knew all he had to do was open his lips and the water would flow down his throat, but he wanted to see beyond the arched doorway first. It was huge and ornately carved, beckoning him forward....

Then he was through the arch and the city was spread before him.

Giant white columns built to stand forever. Streets laid out in perfect order. Glory and symmetry everywhere...

"Kelby."

He was being shaken. Nicholas. He came instantly alert. "Time?" he whispered.

Nicholas nodded. "They should be coming back for you again in five minutes. I just wanted to make sure we're on the same page. I've decided we scratch the plan and I take them out by myself."

"Screw you."

"You'll blow it for both of us. You haven't had anything to eat or drink in three days, and you looked like a truck ran over you when they brought you back to the cell."

"Shut up. It hurts my throat to argue." He leaned back against the stone wall and closed his eyes. "We go as we planned. I give the word. Just tell me when they start down the hall. I'll be ready."

Go back to the sea. There's strength there. No thirst that couldn't be satisfied. He could move without pain through the buoyant water.

White columns shimmering...

"They're coming," Nicholas murmured.

Kelby opened his eyes only a slit as the door was unlocked. The same two guards. Hassan had an Uzi cradled in his arm. Kelby was so hazy he couldn't remember the other guard's name. But he could remember the toe of his boot as he kicked in his rib. Yes, he could remember that.

Ali, that was the bastard's name.

"Get up, Kelby." Hassan was standing over him. "Is the American dog ready for his beating?"

Kelby groaned.

"Get him, Ali. He's too weak to stand up and face us again."

Ali was smiling as he came to stand beside Hassan. "He'll break this time. We'll be able to drag him into Baghdad and show the whole world what cowards the Americans are."

He reached down to grab Kelby's shirt.

"*Now.*" Kelby's foot lashed upward and connected with Ali's nuts. Then he rolled sideways, knocking the Arab's legs from beneath him.

He heard Hassan mutter a curse as Kelby leapt to his feet. He got in back of Ali before he could get off his knees, and his arm snaked around Ali's neck.

He broke it with one twist.

He whirled to see Nicholas smashing the Uzi into Hassan's head. Blood spurted. Nicholas hit him again.

"Out." Kelby grabbed Ali's pistol and knife and ran to the door. "Don't waste time on him."

"He wasted a lot of time on you. I wanted to make sure he'd gone to Allah." But he was running after Kelby down the hall.

In the front office another guard jumped to his feet and reached for his gun. Kelby cut his throat before he could lift it.

Then they were outside the hut and running toward the hills.

Shots behind them.

Keep running.

Nicholas looked over his shoulder. "Are you okay?"

"Fine. Go on, dammit."

Sharp pain in his side.

Don't stop.

The adrenaline was draining away and weakness was dragging at every limb.

Go away from it. Concentrate. You're swimming toward the archway. No pain there.

He was running faster, stronger. The hills were just ahead. He could make it.

He was through the archway. White columns gleamed in the distance.

Marinth...

LONTANA'S ISLAND
LESSER ANTILLES
Present Day

Lacy golden fretwork.

Velvet drapery.

Drums.

Someone coming toward her.

It was going to happen again.

Helpless. Helpless. Helpless.

The scream that tore from Melis's throat jarred her awake.

She jerked upright in bed. She was shaking, her T-shirt soaked with sweat.

Kafas.

Or Marinth?

Sometimes she wasn't sure.... It didn't matter.

Only a dream.

She wasn't helpless. She'd never be helpless again. She was strong now.

Except when she had the dreams. They robbed her of power and she was forced to remember. But she had the dreams less often now. It had been over a month since the last one. Still, she might feel better if she had someone to talk to. Maybe she should call Carolyn and—

No, deal with it. She knew what to do after the dreams to rid herself of these trembling fits and get back to blessed normalcy. She tore off her nightshirt as she left the bedroom and headed toward the lanai.

A moment later she was diving off the lanai into the sea.

It was the middle of night, but the water was only cool, not cold, and felt like liquid silk on her body. Clean and caressing and soothing...

No threat. No submission. Nothing but the night and the sea. God, it was good to be alone.

But she wasn't alone.

Something sleek and cool brushed against her leg.

"Susie?" It had to be Susie. The female dolphin was much more physically affectionate than Pete. The male touched her only rarely, and it was something special when he did.

But Pete was beside her in the water. She saw him out of the corner of her eye as she stroked toward the nets that barricaded the inlet. "Hi, Pete. How are you doing?"

He gave a subdued series of clicks and then dove beneath the surface. A moment later Susie and Pete came to the surface together and swam ahead of her toward the nets. It was strange how they always knew when she was upset. Ordinarily their behavior was playful, almost giddily exuberant. It was only when they sensed she was disturbed that they became this docile. She was supposed to be the one teaching the dolphins, but she was learning from them every day she spent in their company. They enriched her life and she was grateful that—

Something was wrong.

Susie and Pete were both squeaking and clicking frantically as they approached the net. A shark on the other side?

She tensed.

The net was down.

What the hell... No one could unfasten the net unless they knew where it was connected. "I'll take care of it. Go back home, guys."

The dolphins ignored her, swimming around her protectively while she examined the net. No cuts, no tears in the strong wire. It took her only a few minutes to fasten the net again. She set off back to the cottage, her strokes strong, purposeful—and wary.

It didn't have to be a problem. It could be Phil back from his latest journey. Her foster father had been gone for nearly seven months this time, with only an occasional phone call or postcard to tell her if he was alive or dead.

But it could be trouble. Phil had been forced to go on the run almost two years ago and the threat was only partially eliminated. There could still be people out there who wanted to get their hands on him. Phil wasn't the most discreet person in the world, and his judgment wasn't as keen as his intellect. He was a dreamer who took more chances than—

"Melis!"

She became still, paddling in place, her gaze on the lanai a short distance away. She could see a man's silhouette outlined against the lights of the living room. It wasn't Phil's small, wiry frame. This man was big, muscular, and vaguely familiar.

"Melis, I didn't mean to scare you. It's me, Cal."

She relaxed. Cal Dugan, Phil's first mate. No threat here. She had known and liked Cal since she was sixteen. He must have moored his boat at the pier on the other side of the house, where she couldn't see it. She swam toward the lanai. "Why didn't you call me? And why the devil didn't you put the net back up? If a shark had gotten to Pete or Susie, I'd have strangled you."

"I was going to go back and do it," he said defensively. "Nah, I was going to persuade you to do it. I'd have to know Braille to be able to hook it up in the dark."

"That's not good enough. It only takes a minute to pose a threat to the dolphins. You're just lucky it didn't happen."

"How do you know a shark didn't get in?"

"Pete would have told me."

"Oh, yeah. Pete." He dropped a bath towel on the lanai and turned his back. "Tell me when I can turn around. I guess you haven't taken to wearing a swimsuit?"

"Why should I? There's no one to see me but Pete and Susie." She hoisted herself onto the tiles and wrapped the large towel around her. "And uninvited guests."

"Don't be rude. Phil invited me."

"Turn around. When's he coming? Tomorrow?"

He turned around. "Not likely."

"He's not in Tobago?"

"He was setting sail for Athens when he sent me here."

"What?"

"He told me to hop on a plane out of Genoa and come and give you this." He handed her a large manila envelope. "And to wait here for him."

"Wait for him? He'll need you there. He can't do without you, Cal."

"That's what I told him." He shrugged. "He told me to come to you."

She glanced down at the envelope. "I can't see out here. Let's go inside where there's light." She tightened the towel around her. "Make yourself some coffee while I take a look at this."

He flinched. "Will you tell those dolphins I'm not going to hurt you and to stop screeching?"

She'd barely been aware they were still beside the lanai. "Go away, guys. It's okay."

Pete and Susie disappeared beneath the water.

"I'll be damned," Cal said. "They do understand you."

"Yes." Her tone was abstracted as she went into the cottage. "Genoa? What's Phil been up to?"

"Search me. A few months ago he dropped me and the rest of the crew off in Las Palmas and told us we were on vacation for three months. He hired some temporary help to sail the *Last Home* and took off."

"Where?"

He shrugged. "He wouldn't say. Big secret. It wasn't like Phil at all. It was like that time he went off with you. But this was different. He was on edge and he wouldn't say anything when he came back and picked us up." He grimaced. "It's not as if we haven't been with him for the last fifteen years. We have shared a hell of a lot together. I was there when he brought up the Spanish galleon, and Terry and Gary signed on a year later. It kind of . . . hurt."

"You know when he becomes focused on something he can't see anything else." But she had seldom known him to close out his crew. They were as close to family as Phil would permit near him. Closer than he would let her come.

But that was probably her fault. She found it difficult to be openly affectionate with Phil. She had always been the protector in a relationship that had sometimes been both volatile and stormy. She was often impatient and frustrated with his almost childlike single-mindedness. But they were a team, they fulfilled each other's needs, and she did like him.

"Melis."

She glanced at Cal to find him gazing awkwardly at her. "Would you mind putting on some clothes? You're one gorgeous woman, and even though I may be old enough to be your father, it doesn't mean I don't have the usual responses."

Of course he did. It didn't matter that he'd known her from the time she was a teenager. Men were men. Even the best of them were dominated by sex. It had taken her a long time to accept that truth without anger. "I'll be right back." She headed for the bedroom. "Make that coffee."

She didn't bother to shower before she put on her usual shorts and T-shirt. Then she sat down on the bed and reached for the envelope. It might be nothing, totally impersonal, but she didn't want to open it in front of Cal.

The envelope contained two documents. She took out the first one and opened it.

She stiffened. "What the hell..."

HYATT HOTEL
ATHENS, GREECE

"Stop arguing. I'm coming to get you." Melis's hand tightened on the phone. "Where are you, Phil?"

"At a tavern on the waterfront. The Delphi Hotel," Philip Lontana said. "But I'm not going to involve you in this, Melis. Go home."

"I will. We're both going to go home. And I'm already involved. Did you think I was just going to sit around doing nothing after I got that notification that you'd deeded the island and the *Last Home* over to me? That's the closest to a last will and testament I've ever seen. What the hell's happening?"

"I had to turn responsible sometime."

Not Phil. He was as close to Peter Pan as a man in his sixties could be. "What are you afraid of?"

"I'm not afraid. I just wanted to take care of you.

I know we've had our ups and downs, but you've always stood by me when I needed you. You've pulled me out of scrapes and kept those bloodsuckers from—"

"I'll pull you out of this scrape too, if you'll tell me what's happening."

"Nothing's happening. The ocean is unforgiving. You can never tell when I'll make a mistake and never—"

"Phil."

"I've written it all down. It's on the *Last Home*."

"Good. Then you can read it to me when we're on our way back to the island."

"That may not be possible." He paused. "I've been trying to get in touch with Jed Kelby. He's not been answering my calls."

"Bastard."

"Maybe. But a brilliant bastard. I've heard he's a genius."

"And where did you hear it? His publicity agent?"

"Don't be bitter. You've got to give the devil his due."

"No, I don't. I don't like rich men who think they can make toys of everything in the whole damn world."

"You don't like rich men. Period," Phil said. "But I need you to contact him. I don't know if I'll be able to reach him."

"Of course you will. Though I don't know why you think you have to do it. You've never called in help before."

"I need him. He's got the same passion I have and

the drive to make it happen." He paused. "Promise me you'll get him for me, Melis. It's the most important thing I've ever asked of you."

"You don't have to—"

"Promise me."

He wasn't going to give up. "I promise. Satisfied?"

"No, I hated to ask you. And I hate being in this spot. If I hadn't been so stubborn, I wouldn't have had to—" He drew a deep breath. "But that's water under the bridge. I can't look back now. There's too much to look forward to."

"Then why make out your last will and testament, dammit?"

"Because they didn't get a chance to do it."

"What?"

"We should learn from their mistakes." He paused. "Go home. Who's taking care of Pete and Susie?"

"Cal."

"I'm surprised you're letting him do it. You care more about those dolphins than anyone on two legs."

"Evidently I don't, if I'm here. Cal will take good care of Pete and Susie. I put the fear of God in him before I left."

He chuckled. "Or the fear of Melis. But you know how important they are. Go back to them. If you don't hear from me in two weeks, go get Kelby. Good-bye, Melis."

"Don't you dare hang up. What do you want Kelby to do? Is this about that damn sonic device?"

"You know it's never really been about that."

"Then what is it about?"

"I knew it would upset you. Ever since you were a child, you've always had a thing about the *Last Home*."

"Your ship?"

"No, the other *Last Home*. Marinth." He hung up.

She stood there, frozen, for a long moment before she slowly closed her phone.

Marinth.

My God.

THE *TRINA*
VENICE, ITALY

"What the hell is Marinth?"

Jed Kelby stiffened in his chair. "What?"

"Marinth." John Wilson looked up from the pile of letters he'd been scanning for Kelby. "That's all that's written in this letter. Just the one word. Must be some kind of prank or advertising gimmick."

"Give it to me." Kelby slowly reached across the desk and took the letter and envelope.

"Something wrong, Jed?" Wilson stopped sorting the letters he'd just brought on board.

"Maybe." Kelby glanced at the name on the return address of the envelope. Philip Lontana, and the date stamp was over two weeks old. "Why the hell didn't I get this sooner?"

"You might have, if you'd stay in one place more

than a day or two," Wilson said dryly. "I haven't even heard from you in two weeks. I can't be held responsible for keeping you current if you don't cooperate. I do my best, but you're not the easiest man to—"

"Okay, okay." He leaned back and stared down at the letter. "Philip Lontana. I haven't heard anything about him for a few years. I thought maybe he'd quit the business."

"I've never heard of him."

"Why should you? He's not a stockbroker or banker, so he wouldn't be of interest to you."

"That's right. I'm only interested in keeping you filthy rich and out of the clutches of the IRS." Wilson set several documents in front of Kelby. "Sign these in triplicate." He watched disapprovingly as Kelby signed the contracts. "You should have read those. How do you know I didn't screw you?"

"You're morally incapable of it. If you were going to do it, you'd have taken me to the cleaner ten years ago when you were tottering on the verge of bankruptcy."

"True. But you pulled me out of that hole. So that's not really a test."

"I let you flounder for a while to see what you'd do before I stepped in."

Wilson tilted his head. "I never realized that I was on trial."

"Sorry." His gaze was still on the letter. "It's the nature of the beast. I've not been able to trust many people in my life, Wilson."

God knows that was the truth, Wilson thought.

Heir to one of America's largest fortunes, Kelby and his trust fund had been fought over by his mother and grandmother from the time his father died. Court case had followed court case until he'd reached his twenty-first birthday. Then he'd taken control with a cool ruthlessness and intelligence, jettisoned all contact with his mother and grandmother, and set up experts to manage his finances. He'd finished his education and then taken off to become the wanderer he was today. He'd been a SEAL during the Gulf War, later purchased the yacht *Trina* and started a series of underwater explorations that had brought him a fame he didn't appreciate and money he didn't need. Still, he seemed to thrive on the life. For the past eight years he'd lived hard and fast and dealt with some pretty unsavory characters. No, Wilson couldn't blame him for being both wary and cynical. It didn't bother him. He was cynical himself, and over the years he'd learned to genuinely like the bastard.

"Has Lontana tried to contact me before?" Kelby asked.

Wilson sorted through the rest of the mail. "That's the only letter." He flipped open his daybook. "One call on the twenty-third of June. Wanted you to return his call. Another on June twenty-fifth. Same message. My secretary asked what his business pertained to but he wouldn't tell her. It didn't seem urgent enough to try to track you down. Is it?"

"Possibly." He stood up and walked across the cabin to the window. "He certainly knew how to get my attention."

"Who is he?"

"A Brazilian oceanographer. He got a lot of press when he discovered that Spanish galleon fifteen years or so ago. His mother was American and his father Brazilian, and he's something of a throwback to another age. I heard he thought he was some kind of grand adventurer and sailed around looking for lost cities and sunken galleons. He discovered only one galleon, but there's no doubt he's very sharp."

"You've never met him?"

"No, I wasn't really interested. We wouldn't have much in common. I'm definitely a product of this age. We're not on the same wavelength."

Wilson wasn't so sure. Kelby was no dreamer, but he possessed the aggressive, bold recklessness that typified the buccaneers of this or any other century. "So what does Lontana want with you?" His gaze narrowed on Kelby. "And what do you want with Lontana?"

"I'm not sure what he wants from me." He stood looking out at the sea, thinking. "But I know what I want from him. The question is, can he give it to me?"

"That's cryptic."

"Is it?" He suddenly turned to face Wilson. "Then, by God, we'd better get everything clear and aboveboard, hadn't we?"

Shock rippled through Wilson as he saw the recklessness and excitement in Kelby's expression. The aggressive energy he was emitting was almost tangible. "Then I take it you want me to contact Lontana."

"Oh, yes. In fact, we're going to go see him."

"*We're?* I have to get back to New York."

Kelby shook his head. "I may need you."

"You know I don't know anything about all this oceanography stuff, Jed. And, dammit, I don't want to know. I have degrees in law and accounting. I wouldn't be of any use to you."

"You never can tell. I may need all the help I can get. A little more sea air will do you good." He glanced down at the envelope again, and Wilson was once more aware of the undercurrent of excitement that was electrifying Kelby. "But maybe we should give Lontana a little advance warning that he shouldn't dangle a carrot unless he expects me to gobble it with one swallow. Give me his telephone number."

She was being followed.

It wasn't paranoia, dammit. She could *feel* it.

Melis glanced over her shoulder. It was an exercise in futility. She wouldn't have known who she was looking for on the crowded dock behind her. It could be anyone. A thief, a sailor eager for a lay... or someone who was hoping she'd lead him to Phil. Anything was possible.

Now that Marinth was involved.

Lose him.

She darted down the next street, ran one short block, ducked into an alcove, and waited. Making sure you weren't being paranoid was always the first rule. The second was to know your enemy.

A gray-haired man in khakis and a short-sleeved plaid shirt came around the corner and stopped. He looked like any casual tourist who frequented Athens this time of year. Except that his annoyed attitude didn't match his appearance. He was definitely irritated as his gaze searched the people streaming down the street.

She was not paranoid. And now she would remember this man, whoever he was.

She darted out of the alcove and took off running. She turned left, cut into an alley, and then turned right at the next street.

She glanced behind her in time to see a glimpse of a plaid shirt. He was no longer trying to blend in with the crowd. He was moving fast and with purpose.

Five minutes later she stopped, breathing hard.

She had lost him. Maybe.

Christ, Phil, what have you gotten us into?

About the Author

IRIS JOHANSEN has more than twenty million copies of her books in print and is the bestselling author of *Fatal Tide, No One to Trust, Dead Aim, Final Target, Body of Lies, The Search, The Killing Game, The Face of Deception, And Then You Die, Long After Midnight,* and *The Ugly Duckling.* She lives near Atlanta, Georgia.

IRIS JOHANSEN

LION'S BRIDE	_____56990-2	$7.50/$10.99
DARK RIDER	_____29947-6	$7.50/$10.99
MIDNIGHT WARRIOR	_____29946-8	$7.50/$10.99
THE BELOVED SCOUNDREL	_____29945-X	$7.50/$10.99
THE TIGER PRINCE	_____29968-9	$7.50/$10.99
THE MAGNIFICENT ROGUE	_____29944-1	$7.50/$10.99
THE GOLDEN BARBARIAN	_____29604-3	$7.50/$10.99
LAST BRIDGE HOME	_____29871-2	$6.50/$9.99
THE UGLY DUCKLING	_____56991-0	$7.50/$10.99
LONG AFTER MIDNIGHT	_____57181-8	$7.50/$10.99
AND THEN YOU DIE	_____57998-3	$7.50/$10.99
THE FACE OF DECEPTION	_____57802-2	$7.50/$10.99
THE KILLING GAME	_____58155-4	$7.50/$10.99
THE SEARCH	_____58212-7	$7.50/$10.99
FINAL TARGET	_____58213-5	$7.50/$10.99
BODY OF LIES	_____58214-3	$7.50/$10.99
NO ONE TO TRUST	_____58437-5	$7.50/$10.99

 THE WIND DANCER TRILOGY

THE WIND DANCER	_____28855-5	$7.50/$10.99
STORM WINDS	_____29032-0	$7.50/$10.99
REAP THE WIND	_____58612-2	$7.50/$10.99

Ask for these titles wherever books are sold,
or visit us online at *www.bantamdell.com* for ordering information.

FN 37 9/03